# Christmas Angels

## Patra Ann Taylor

"For he shall give his angels
charge over thee, to keep
thee in all thy ways."


Psalm 91:11 (KJV)

<h1 style="text-align:center">Prologue</h1>

In 1933, the menacing tentacles of the Great Depression had entwined themselves into every aspect of American life. My hometown of Jeffries, a railroad hub in north-central Indiana, was no exception. That year, when some 15 million Americans were unemployed and half of the country's banks had failed, all hope for better days had disappeared, leaving in its wake the despair that accompanies unrelenting poverty.

In the weeks leading up to Christmas, despair had indeed heaped itself onto my family. Yet Christmas unfolded as a time of love, joy, and gratitude, creating indelible memories that warmed many family Christmases thereafter.

All these decades later, my memories flow easily even as my hand struggles to keep up with my thoughts. I always settled into these glorious memories whenever I heard carols played on a piano, or smelled the aroma of cookies baking waft from an oven, or felt fresh falling snowflakes kiss my cheeks. Now I work to capture those memories on paper, so generations to come might find hope in the depth of their own despair, to expect miracles in the darkest of times.

So many seasons of my life have passed since nine-year-old me crept onto the porch of a stranger. One minor act of kindness brought a wonderful new friend into my life, an incredible woman despite the tough hand life had dealt her. Oh, how I marveled at her grace, her beauty, her talents. I remembered her dancing eyes as they looked into my soul, sparking my desire to reach for my best self, just as she had done despite the odds stacked against her.

For my older sister, Gem, that Christmas brought the sweet taste of a first kiss, more glorious and romantic than she'd ever imagined it. Fred, the first boy she ever loved, became the *only* man she'd ever love. He orbited her world for decades, touching her life with his sweetness now and again. Each goodbye left her breathless and numb for months or years at a time. Her only consolation was that she knew he'd find her again. On that Christmas, when perfect first love bloomed from a perfect first kiss, Gem was Fred's one and only, and he was hers.

My youngest sister, Thea, had no memories of her own of that Christmas, so Gem and I wove hers from our own, painting her the mental pictures of the many miracles that unfolded before us, and her special place in them. Through the years, my sisters and I re-told the story of that Christmas hundreds of times, adding our adult insights and fresh details that revealed themselves throughout our lives.

Bits of memories flicker in the twilight as I gaze from my window onto the quiet boulevard in Jeffries, where I await the dawning of another Christmas Day. Our family's story of that glorious holiday in 1931 defined so many aspects of our lives. As darkness falls, the multitude of stars across the night sky rival the number of heaven's angels, I await the glorious Coming.

Gem passed away a decade ago. Thea died too young. Now the story of our Christmas of 1933 is mine alone to tell. I share it with you here.

With love,

Anna Ghere

# Chapter 1

Holding the skirt of my favorite blue dress high above my knees, I ran the last block of Walnut Street with my coat billowing behind me. The coal smoke belching from the chimneys smelled of winter. As I turned onto Jackson Street, I ran headlong into a stiff October wind that chilled me to the bone before rattling its way through the last of the lifeless leaves clinging to the sugar maples that lined the street at perfect intervals.

There's nothing colder than the ashes of love. Those words slipped across my mind at the most unexpected moments. Where did I first hear them? Not in a feature film I watched with my sister Gem at the Clinton Theater. Not from a book my cousin Charlie read to me while curled up in our window seat. I resolved the words came to me in a dream some weeks ago, drifting up the cold air return to pierce my sleep, but for a moment. I wondered if those ashes were colder than an Indiana autumn wind. Tugging my coat around my body, I kept running.

I felt the ground pitch and shake beneath me as the 4:20 entered the Wanatah Depot. Out of breath, I gulped the cold air into my lungs. "Popo, I'm coming," I whispered.

My patent leather shoes, now a season too tight, clattered along the sidewalk as I picked up speed, leaving a whirl of dead leaves in my wake. On Friday afternoons, I took my place on the platform alongside the station master to await my father's arrival from another long week selling feed and seed to farmers across the state.

Today, I'd gotten a late start, losing track of time watching Mother prepare my sister Thea's birthday supper of stewed chicken and dumplings with all the fixings, plus chocolate cake with a thick layer of frosting for dessert. Mother had called her special supper "a real celebration." It had been a hard year for her. It was good to see an aura of contentment return to her face as she moved gracefully about her kitchen chores toward our perfect family meal.

While Mother prepared for the celebration, my brothers, sisters, and cousin gathered around the big Zenith radio in the green room listening to the National Barn Dance on WLS out of Chicago while taking turns playing checkers on the floor. After beating my cousin Charlie, I'd ignored his demands for a rematch, choosing instead to climb atop a stool in the kitchen to watch Mother drop the thick dumplings, one at a time, into the simmering stew pot. I could almost taste the egg sac, rough in my mouth. On this special day I was sure everyone would get a small bite of the delicacy, but Mother always saved the chicken liver and gizzard for Popo, who would make a lip-smacking production out of eating them while praising Mother's cooking as the rest of his family chuckled at his antics. Anticipating Thea's birthday supper, heightened by the sweet smell of chocolate cake wafting from Mother's oven, distracted me from my Friday afternoon vigil-by-the-clock.

"Aren't you meeting Popo at the Wanatah Depot this afternoon?" Mother had asked me, as she pulled her round cake pans from the oven, careful to set them carefully on the counter to prevent the layers from falling. "You'd better get moving if you're going to make it on time."

"Did you hear it?"

Mother had nodded. Two long whistle blows followed by a short toot and another long blow signaled the train was approaching its last street crossing before the depot.

As I jumped down from the stool and raced for the front door, Mother followed me. "Be sure to wear your winter coat, young lady. It's cold outside today. I don't want you catching your death."

This year's mild Indiana autumn had finally bowed to a Canadian front, amping up its frigid fury each time it licked across Lake Michigan. Despite the cold, I focused on being on the depot's platform for my father's grand exit from the passenger car.

"Remember," Mother had called from the doorway as I ran across the yard, still struggling to get an arm into one of my coat sleeves. "I'm serving supper promptly at six o'clock, so remind your father not to linger. And button that coat!"

***

I watched the passenger train pull into the station as I ran across the tracks toward the platform that ran along the northbound rails. As one foot landed between the rails, I caught my other heel on the other rail, which caused me to slip across the slick worn steel and fall onto my hands and knees in the gravel along the track.

I sat up, tears of frustration flowing down my face, and picked off the stones clinging to my hands. One minute I was crying, the next I felt my father's arms lift me from the gravel and pull me to him.

"Is my girl okay?" Popo held me close, stroking my hair.

"I missed you on the platform," I now sobbed, allowing my emotions to wash over me.

"You didn't miss me, Angel. I'm right here."

Burying my face in my father's warm neck, he soothed me a moment, then carried me to the platform and sat me on one of the wooden benches that lined the outside wall of the depot. Taking his white handkerchief from the inside pocket of his long coat, he knelt in front of me and dabbed at the slight wound on my knee, brushing away the last stones clinging to my skin.

Popo held the hem of my dress in his hand. "Look here, Angel, I don't think you tore your dress. I'm glad because it's my favorite. It matches your eyes."

Folding his handkerchief in half, he wiped my wet cheeks. "Now your tears won't freeze." I offered him a weak smile, knowing that was what he wanted to see. "We'll have your mother put something on that knee when we get home. I'm sure she can fix you up, good as new."

I nodded, a sense of joy flooding over me at the undivided attention of the father I so adored. Popo brushed my bobbed blond hair from my face and smoothed it down in back.

"What's this?" Popo held up a crisp brown maple leaf he'd pulled from my hair, then opening his hand, he let a gust of wind lift the leaf from his fingers and carry it down the train platform.

I sniffled, unable to hold back another smile. Popo smiled back before sitting down on the bench next to me, his hand covering mine. We sat in silence, as was often our way, and watched as the conductor assisted several passengers aboard, readying the train to continue its journey north to Chicago. We sat as the train shook and rattled past us, watching until it was out of sight. Then we sat a while longer.

Finally, Popo stood and smoothed his coat. "Someone's going to be disappointed if we don't stop by."

"Miss Roxy! She's probably wondering what happened to us. We should go. Mother said supper is at six. We don't want to be late."

"Nor would we want to walk past the Blue and White Café without stopping to say hello to everyone."

My father summoned the porter, who retrieved his leather satchel from inside the depot where he'd left it earlier. "Do you have a present for Thea?" I eyed Popo's familiar satchel, hoping he'd let me in on his secret.

"You'll have to wait and see, little Miss Nosey." Popo held out his satchel where I could see the bulge of the gift tucked inside.

Then he straightened his worn felt fedora and held out his hand to me. "Let's go see Roxy. I could use a cup of hot coffee right about now."

With that, the two of us departed the train depot hand-in-hand. We walked up Jackson Street toward the center of town, the wind at our backs.

***

The supper rush had already begun when Popo and I arrived at the Blue and White Café. Many of the town's men, especially widowers, appreciated the hot home-cooking offered by the café's proprietor, Roxy Lockwood. Railroaders working either the east/west-bound Nickel Plate line or the north/south-bound Wanatah line found Roxy's food and hospitality especially satisfying. On late afternoons like this one, the oily odor of the railroaders' overalls succumbed to the pleasing aroma of vegetable soup, pot roast, and Roxy's special spicy mincemeat pie, which she offered on her menu as soon as the weather cooled. It was one of the first signs of autumn in our small town of Jeffries.

As soon as we walked in, Roxy called out from behind the counter and offered a quick wave. "Where have you been?" Without waiting for Popo's response, she pointed. "There's a table toward the back. I'll be right with you."

Popo nodded a thank you, then guided me down the narrow aisle between the row of high stools at the counter and the single line of tables along the wall. Nestled between the Clinton Theater and the National Bank building a half block off the public square, the inside of the Blue and White Café always reminded me of a cave. Sunlight poured in through the plate glass door and window at the front of this busy eating establishment, but beyond the second or third stool at the counter, the room fell into perpetual shadow, lighted only by a sparse row of bare bulbs along the ceiling. On weekend nights, Roxy often opened her basement room to capture the overflow of departing patrons from the Clinton Theater, who stop in for a cup of coffee and a slice of her delicious pie before calling it a night.

My father walked toward our designated table, greeting his many friends and acquaintances.

"Good to see you."

"How's the family?"

"Have you heard if Joe Pence recovered from that fall he took the other day?"

Popo always commanded the spotlight when he entered the diner.

I sat down on the chair Popo pulled out for me and sighed, wishing we'd arrived in time to find a couple of empty stools along the counter. I preferred sitting there where I could better see the comings and goings and take the occasional spin on the stool when Popo was otherwise engaged with one of the café's patrons. Too short to touch the tarnished brass foot rail that ran the length of the lunch counter, I'd content myself by dangling my feet while Popo absorbed the local news.

I decided it didn't matter that we were sitting at a table where I couldn't see over the patrons' heads. We had Thea's birthday celebration to get to, so I knew we wouldn't stay long.

"What will it be?" I heard Roxy's gravelly voice behind me. "How about a hot cider or a cup of cocoa?"

"I think my daughter prefers a bottle of pop, even on the coldest days of winter. Am I right, Angel?"

The thought of those cold ashes crossed my mind again. "Cocoa, please. It's chilly outside today."

Popo chuckled. "Unpredictable as are all my girls. I'll have coffee, please."

"No pie?" Roxy looked astonished. "I saved a piece of Dutch apple just for you."

"Roxy, now don't you tempt me with pie today. It's little Thea's third birthday, so if I know what's good for me, I'll save room for the feast Maggie is preparing. I'll have to pass on the pie, just this once." Turning, he asked me, "Is pie on the evening's menu?"

"Cake."

"Well, of course. Birthday cake. Chocolate, I hope."

I nodded.

"Any news from Indianapolis, Mr. Ghere?" Roxy listened intently, her curly hair spilling out around her face from the loose bun she'd fashioned that morning. With her arms folded over her white apron soiled with the day's specials, Roxy listened to Popo's account of the week, biting her lip as she took in every detail so she could pass it along to someone else later. Her carnation pink lipstick looked fresh and perfect, accenting rather than softening her thin, weathered face. Popo once told me that Roxy was a beautiful woman in her youth, but too many years of long hours at the Blue and White had taken their toll. I always thought about that whenever Popo spoke to Roxy, his eyes affixed to her animated face. I think he still saw the beautiful young woman of long ago.

"Order up." Roxy turned toward the serving window and nodded. Paul, Roxy's latest husband, worked six days a week alongside his wife.

"I'm coming, hon." Giving the table two quick raps with her knuckles, she added, "It won't be but a minute."

When Miss Roxy was back behind the counter, calling out a string of orders, I asked Popo why Miss Roxy never had children.

"I suppose it just didn't work out for her."

"I think Miss Roxy would have been a wonderful mother."

"Yes, you're right, but she would have brought the child with her when she was working. That child would never have known for sure who its mother was."

God may not have blessed Roxy with children, but He blessed her with a steady stream of husbands, some better than others. "Roxy's been working in her family's diner since she was thirteen," Popo added. "The only time she's ever taken off work was for one of her honeymoons."

"That's funny, Popo. Does Miss Roxy have a lot of money?"

"She has enough. As long as the railroads are running, she'll always have enough."

My family had enough children, I thought. We had enough animals and enough friends, but we didn't have enough money for new shoes or coats or "frivolous things," as Mother called them. I wanted to ask

Popo if we were poor, but I knew the answer. His saying we had enough wouldn't change things.

The chatter of Roxy's customers muffled the clatter of forks hitting plates. Popo said his goodbyes to a couple of gentlemen who were vacating a nearby table. Upon hearing Popo's voice, Old Man Gregory, who had taken a seat three tables away, twisted his chair to face the back where we sat, his pale blue eyes appearing huge through his thick spectacles.

Old Man Gregory called out to my father, his powerful voice cutting through the din. "Augie, my friend? Is that you?"

"Yes, Will, I'm here with my daughter, Anna. Would you care to join us?"

Old Man Gregory put his hands on the table and pushed himself up. He made his way to our table and sat down next to me. "I just now heard your voice, Augie. Are you in later than usual? Was the 4:20 late today?"

"Annie fell and scraped her knee... it slowed us down a bit. It's Thea's birthday, so we can't stay long. Maggie's got some big doings planned."

"Ahh, yes." Old Man Gregory looked at his hands and nodded, as if remembering a time when he went home to his family for special occasions. He was alone now. "You're a lucky man, Augie. Marvelous cook, that Maggie. When I stopped by last week on my debit route, she offered me a slice of her special honey-poached quince pie and a cup of coffee. Best I'd ever eaten, and that's saying something when you consider where I'm sitting right now. That Roxy serves some tasty pie herself, that's for sure."

Popo agreed.

The two men continued their talk, Old Man Gregory telling Popo the latest news in the county, and Popo adding a few tidbits he'd picked up in the state capital. I sipped the cocoa Miss Roxy had delivered and listened patiently to the two men exchange stories.

"Hey, Mr. Ghere," Roxy called from behind the counter a few minutes later. "Maggie just called to remind you she's serving dinner in fifteen minutes. You do not want to miss Thea's birthday supper."

"Sounds a bit like a threat." Old Man Gregory chuckled at Popo's comment. With that, Popo gulped the last of his coffee, stood, and said goodbye to his friend. As he paid our bill, Roxy turned to me.

"Annie, will you and your friends and family be coming to our party after you go begging on Tuesday night? Paul and I are decorating the basement room again. We've got several new games planned and we are serving Coney dogs to everyone who attends."

"Coney dogs?" I think my eyes were the size of saucers.

Roxy smiled. "Yes, we're serving Coney dogs this year. I take it you'll be here?"

"Yes, I'll be here. I'll let everyone know."

How could I resist Coney dogs? Popo told me that on Roxy's third honeymoon (Paul was her fifth husband), the happy couple traveled to New York City. While there, they took the subway to Coney Island, where they came across a small hot dog stand at Surf and Stilwell, where the two enjoyed their first Coney dogs. After Roxy returned to the Blue and White Café, then owned by her parents, she spent days perfecting the seasoning for her own Coney sauce. Then she spent her savings on two steamers, one for the buns and one for the dogs. Her parents told everyone their daughter had lost her ever-loving mind... until their customers started ordering the New York delicacy left and right. Roxy offered her Coney dogs with any combination of mustard, onions, and cheese on top, all for a nickel. She'd served them at the Blue and White ever since.

As I waited, I looked at the candy in the glass case beneath the cash register. Roxy always carried a nice selection of candy. Necco Wafers were Gem's favorite. I once asked my sister which of the eight flavors she like the best. She told me she liked them all the same, but I thought they all tasted like chalk. Charlie, Thea, and I preferred Chuckles—except for the liquorish ones, which we always gave to Gem.

When Popo and I walked out onto the sidewalk, I noticed the marquee on the Clinton Theater was lit up. Someone replaced all the burnt-out lightbulbs that plagued the sign for months. When I pointed it out to Popo, he said two words, "New owners."

The top line on the marquee read, "Welcome" and the second line read, "42nd Street." I wanted to linger a moment to ask Popo about the film, but I knew we had to hurry. Thea's birthday supper would be on the table any minute.

# Chapter 2

Gem stood in the front doorway with Thea in her arms when we arrived home with five minutes to spare before supper. "Popo, Popo!" my youngest sister called out loudly to our father, her arms outstretched. Setting his satchel by the door, he peeled off his coat, adding it to the heap on the rack, and took his baby daughter from Gem's arms, kissing his oldest daughter's forehead in the same effortless motion. After taking off my coat, I peeked into the dining room.

The table was set with the family's fine china. Mother and Aunt LoRetta, Popo's sister, moved back and forth from kitchen to dining room, placing bowls and platters of food on the table.

My family often did without, as did most families we knew. Special occasions seemed to ease the Depression's iron grip on us, if only for a short while. Mother had a knack of knowing how and when to stretch what little we had so we could enjoy the occasional "Feast Fit for a King," as Aunt Lo had dubbed our special times together. I watched as the two women worked in harmony on the meal's ultimate presentation.

Handing Thea back to Gem, Popo excused himself to wash up. "You, too," Mother instructed. As I soaped up my hands at the kitchen sink, the fresh scrapes in my palms stung. I took a dishcloth and wiped away the dried blood on my knee and left the kitchen, vowing not to mention my wounds to Mother. I didn't want to ruin the celebration.

Everyone took their regular seats around the large oak dining room table. Popo waited patiently at the head of the table while everyone settled in: my brother Gus, my cousin Charlie, me, and Thea to his left, and my twin brothers Cory and Blinn, along with Gem and Aunt Lo to his right. Mother sat at the opposite end of the table from Popo, the place closest to the kitchen.

After Aunt Lo said grace, the birthday festivities began without further ado. When the noise level permitted, Popo relayed the latest news from across the state—who had died, who had gotten married, and, occasionally, who had gone to or been released from jail during the previous week.

Mother's commentary was all about family—Gus's date with Vivien Wentworth, Gem's top grade in history, Belva's latest shenanigans in the barn, and my Aunt Iris's incessant telephone calls to her complaining about whatever was on her mind at that moment. As Mother delivered her latest stories about Popo's brother and his insufferable wife, my father rolled his eyes.

"If the Mississippi River ran between us, she'd still have her nose in whatever was going on over here. Just ignore her, Maggie, or she'll make you believe you're the crazy one."

Popo took a bite of his chicken gizzard and smacked his lips before continuing. "Where is my only brother and his delightful wife this evening?" Sarcasm fit Popo's personality like a glove.

Mother sniffed. "I didn't invite them. After a long week of work, you didn't need the aggravation."

"Am I correct in assuming that you didn't want my brother and his wife eating us out of house and home?"

"You are correct."

"Then what is my beloved sister doing here?" Popo nodded toward Aunt Lo. "She, too, has quite an appetite."

"I'll have you know, dear brother, that I played an important role preparing this supper."

Everyone laughed, including Aunt Lo. When everyone around the table turned their attention back to their dumplings, Aunt Lo made an announcement.

"Speaking of roles, I've been asked to direct the Christmas pageant at Holy Cross Church again this year. The Widower Pastor Burke thought I did such an excellent job last year that he insisted I take on the job again. Last year's production was the talk of the town for weeks—maybe months!—afterwards. Everyone who came into the library talked about it."

Charlie and I often go to the library after school with our friend, Bernard Thompson, but we hadn't heard anyone talk about the pageant.

I looked at Popo and shrugged, which made him smile broadly and shrug back. Popo and I had the same odd sense of things... that's what Mother always said.

"In the coming weeks, I'll let you children know what parts I'll expect you to play in the pageant." With that, Aunt Lo returned her attention to the last dumpling on her plate.

A collective groan went up around the table, one that excluded Charlie, who was happy to be a part of Aunt Lo's nonsense (that's what Popo called it) again this year.

"Count me out." Leave it to my brother, Cory, to be the first to decline a role in my aunt's little production.

"Tell me, sister dear, are there any eligible bachelors over at Holy Cross these days?" Popo looked at his sister and winked.

"Yes, brother dear, there are several, including the Widower Pastor Burke." With a coy smile on her face, she returned his wink.

As Mother and Aunt Lo cleared the plates from the table, Popo retrieved Thea's present from his satchel. She squealed with delight when he presented her with a doll, a lifelike girl with painted-on wavy blond hair and bright blue eyes. The doll wore a flared green dress with a striped bodice, ankle-high lace stockings, and red shoes that matched the stripes in the bodice. It only took a moment for Thea to become enchanted with her gift.

Mother gasped when she returned to the dining room with the cake and saw the doll. "Augie, you shouldn't have. It must have cost a fortune."

Popo eyed his youngest daughter with her special gift. "It looks just like her, so how could I resist? I also bought several fabric remnants. I thought you could make the doll an entire wardrobe."

Mother nodded as she set the cake down in front of Thea amidst the *oohs* and *ahhs* of anticipation from the others. Then she walked around the table, placing proper dessert plates in front of each of us, with Aunt Lo following with proper dessert forks. Even the snooty Gheres perched atop their high horses on the other side of Prairie Creek would have approved.

Once everything was in place, Mother pulled a Diamond match from her apron pocket and, with a quick flick of her thumbnail, set it aflame. Then she lit the three candles that topped the triple-layer chocolate cake. We all dutifully joined in, singing an off-key version of "Happy Birthday," throughout which Thea poked at her new doll's eyes.

"Now blow out your candles, sweet girl," Mother urged. Thea continued to poke at her doll. "Like this." Mother demonstrated to Thea how to do it. "Blow out your candles."

I took an impatient breath as I watched the wax from the candles roll down the small candlesticks into the thick layer of frosting. "Thea, blow out your candles." Mother insisted. "Everyone is waiting."

One candle flickered out. "Now," Mother rapped the table next to the cake with her palm. "Blow out your candles, young lady!" With that, she pulled the doll from Thea's hands, which caused my sister to cry out.

"Mother, stop!" I blurted out in complete frustration. "She can't hear you!" With her eyes glued to my face, Mother handed the doll back to Thea, which immediately calmed my sister.

"Anna, what did you just say?" Mother asked, finally breaking the uncomfortable silence.

I looked around the table, hoping for support from my siblings and cousin. Gem's eyes were wide, and Blinn and Cory seemed frozen in place. Popo leaned forward, his mouth agape. Aunt Lo's right hand covered her mouth, her left open at the base of her neck. The look in her eyes told me that a piece of a giant puzzle had suddenly fallen into place in her mind.

I took a deep breath and spoke quietly, my voice now as controlled as Mother's. "Thea can't hear you. She's deaf."

There, I'd said it. I'd pointed out the pink elephant in the room that had somehow eluded all the adults for months. Mother's hand gripped the back of her chair, a support to hold her upright.

"Gem, is this true?"

My sister nodded once, then looked down at her plate. Mother looked around the table, receiving somber nods from Gus and the twins.

"I see. And none of you thought to tell me this?" My brother, Gus, finally came to my rescue. "We thought you knew."

With that, Charlie was on his feet, racing to his little cousin's side. "Thea isn't completely deaf. Watch."

Charlie leaned down and spoke loudly into Thea's right ear, reciting words from her favorite book by heart. "'Next day was gloriously fine, and the sun shorn on all the great dock leaves. The mother duck with her whole family went down to the moat. Splash! into the water she sprang.'"

Thea giggled, still poking at her doll's eyes. I saw the moment Aunt Lo's hand fall from her neck, her face beaming with pride at Charlie's recitation. Charlie was Mother's sister's son and Aunt Lo was Popo's sister. Despite their lack of a shared bloodline, Charlie and Aunt Lo were kindred spirits, two completely different people bound through eternity by their love of the written word.

"'Quack, quack, she said, and one duckling plumped in after the other. The water dashed over their heads, but they came up again and floated beautifully. Their legs went of themselves, and they were all there. Even the big ugly gray one swam about with them.'"

Charlie blew gently into Thea's ear, then kissed her cheek. "What do the ducks say, Thea?" he asked, speaking loudly into her ear.

"Quack, quack."

"Yes, Thea, that's what the ducks say." Charlie's eyes filled with tears.

I saw a single tear rolled down Mother's cheek. Was it grief or disappointment? Or both?

"Mother, I..."

"Not now, Anna." Mother turned to my aunt and said, "LoRetta, would you do the honors of cutting and serving Thea's birthday cake?" Then turning to me, Mother issued her orders. "When everyone is finished, I want you and your sister to clean up the kitchen."

Her command had been icy, and for the second time today I felt chilled to the bone. As usual, Mother had refused to dignify her anger by yelling at me. I would have preferred to bear her anger just to get it behind me. Instead, her utter disappointment hung in the room like a dark cloud.

"I have a headache coming on. I'm going to bed." Then Mother leaned down and blew out the remaining two candles on Thea's birthday cake and left the room.

***

Charlie and I were the first to realize Thea had lost much of her hearing. That day was hard to forget. It was the first lovely spring Sunday after the long, dreadful winter in which my sister and I had suffered the red scourge (that's what Aunt Lo always called it). Mother had asked Charlie and me to look after Thea in the green room while she made pies for supper.

Long and narrow, the green room extended along the west side of our house. Originally built as a porch, my parents had converted it into a room for Father Blinn when he became ill and had to move into town from his farm to be closer to Doc Becker. According to Mother, Father Blinn had insisted that the wall facing the creek have several windows. "No dreary sick rooms for me!" he'd declared. Since he was paying for it, almost the entire west wall had windows, regardless of how much coal it took to warm the room during the winter. The toilet under the stairs was installed about the same time.

My mother's hands had been full during those eighteen months Father Blinn lived with his daughter and her growing family—Popo, Gus, the twins, and baby Gem. I'd been told Mother Blinn preferred the quietude of the farm, which by that time was being run by Aunt Rachel and Uncle Madison... she rarely visited her ailing husband.

In early spring, the windows captured every sunbeam and directed it into the cheerful room. I pointed out the window. "Look, Charlie. The leaves are sprouting."

With Thea still in his arms, my cousin moved next to me. We both loved gazing at the narrow patch of woods that lined the edge of Prairie Creek. We could still see Aunt Lo's painting shed behind MaMaw Ghere's house, but once all the walnut, American elm, and sugar maple trees turned green, it would hide the shed from us for another season.

"Look there... on the ground." Charlie pointed out the window. "It's a robin."

Seeing the first robin meant we'd made it through the winter. Before too many more days passed, the trees would be host to a variety of birds: cardinals, blue jays, sparrows, goldfinches, and woodpeckers raising their own families.

After a few moments of wonder, Charlie sat Thea on the floor in a sunbeam, took up his perch in the window seat, and began chattering about the new book he'd gotten from the library on Friday called "Little House in the Big Woods" by Laura Ingalls Wilder.

While Thea played, I joined Charlie in the window seat, hoping to get a look at the book's pictures.

As Charlie read, I heard Mother call out to me from the dining room. "Anna, please come here."

When I returned to the green room a moment later, I was carrying Mother's large silver bowl. It was in the dining room when she went there to place potholders on the table where she cooled her pies. She'd asked me to set the bowl on a table in front of one of the windows in the green room. As I entered the room, Charlie looked up from his book.

"Listen to this."

Before he could continue, I caught my foot on the edge of the rug and fell with a hud, the airborne bowl landed a split second later right behind where Thea played on the floor.

Charlie jumped up and rushed to my side. After he'd pulled me up from the floor, he'd looked into my eyes to see if I knew what he knew. Thea hadn't responded. She hadn't jumped, hadn't gasped, hadn't turned her head to see what had caused the loud noise behind her.

Mother called from the kitchen. "Is everything all right in there?" Even Mother had heard the crash.

"Everything's fine!" Charlie picked up the bowl and placed it on the table where it belonged. Then he knelt behind Thea and clapped his hands near one ear, then the other. Thea continued to play with her toys. Realizing the gravity of the situation, my cousin pulled me by the arm to the window seat where we sat for the better part of half an hour, our eyes glued on Thea.

Finally, Charlie asked me, "Should we tell Aunt Maggie?"

"I don't know. Winter was so hard on her." I thought about how sick Thea had been and the red rash that had covered Mother's hands and neck. I thought about how she'd been alone, for the most part, taking care of Thea and me.

"I don't know," I finally muttered. "I'll tell Gem. She'll know what to do."

The children's grapevine came alive with the news of Thea's hearing loss, racing from one of my siblings to the next, each concerned with what another major blow might do to our mother. Over time, Charlie had quietly figured out that Thea responded when he spoke directly into her right ear. He'd sit with his little cousin tucked under his arm, reading her favorite books and teaching her to say words. He taught Gem and me how to help Thea learn. Even my big brothers took their turns. It had all seemed perfectly reasonable at the time.

At least now, Mother and Popo knew the truth.

# Chapter 3

Silence ruled the day following my revelation about Thea's deafness. It was as if no one wanted to make a sound, perhaps in deference to my baby sister and the struggles she would face over her lifetime. The only one in the Ghere household who seemed happy was Thea, who carried on with her usual curious play and childish demands for attention that were indulged by Gem and me. Fear seemed to flit between me and my older sister like a moth seeking the light of hope where there was none, a relentless pest of which we could not rid ourselves.

Now and again, I'd open our door to listen for any signs of life behind my parents' bedroom door across the hallway. I heard nothing... no arguing, no wailing, and no pleas to God Almighty for intervention on behalf of my sister. That was one way my mother differed from the mothers of my friends. Certainly, my friend Pauline's mother requested a favor or two from God on behalf of her daughter from time to time; Barbara Jean's mother nattered away with anybody who would listen, including our Heavenly Father, regarding the needs of her daughters; and Emerson Keller's mother often called out right in public, "Good Lord, please help that boy." Aunt Lo also made that plea on behalf of poor Emerson on particularly troubling days, though watching Emerson continue to lumber about oblivious to the realities of the world did little to strengthen one's faith.

The fact was, I never heard Mother speak aloud to God. Not a word of thanks, nor a request for help in any circumstance life handed her. Neither did I detect any objection (or resentment) when others blessed the food set upon her table or prayed for help or comfort for those she loved. She always remained respectful, but silent.

Occasionally, Mother talked about our family's Huguenot background. It was her way of slipping in the trace of French royalty in our bloodline into the conversation, though she never spoke of the Huguenot people, the hard-working Calvinists with whom she had so much in common. Despite our poor circumstances during the Depression, Mother reminded us that our royal blood demanded that we always conduct ourselves with dignity inside and outside the walls of our home. "Act like a lady today." Those were often her parting words to Gem and me as we headed out the door for school.

Late that morning, Charlie joined my sisters and me in our bedroom. He told us that Blinn and Cory had slipped out of the house early to tend to Belva, our goat, and Old Barney, our family's horse named for the famous race car driver Barney Oldfield. Since Aunt Rachel and Uncle Madison brought Belva in from her farm, Old Barney and Belva had become fast friends, sharing the stall in the small barn at the back of our lot. The children in the neighborhood loved Belva, but Mother viewed adding the mischievous goat to our already large family as "just another mouth to feed."

First thing every day, the twins fed Mother's chickens after collecting the eggs and cleaning the coop. My brothers also saw to the needs of Old Barney and Belva. Once they'd completed their chores that morning, Blinn and Cory stayed outside with the animals, while Gem, Charlie and I endured the silence inside.

Charlie said that after stoking the fire in the furnace, Gus left the house just before eight o'clock to report to the A&P where he worked Saturday mornings and some weekday afternoons, delivering groceries to people around town for a nickel tip.

After working at the market, Gus would put his day's earnings into a small canvas bag he kept in his bureau drawer. Sometimes when our brothers weren't around, Gem and I would sneak into their bedroom, pull out Gus's bag of coins, and take turns rolling it back and forth in our hands, imagining how much money it held and what it felt like to be rich. We'd often fiddled with the twine that held it closed, but we never dared open it to count the money. How much Gus had saved wasn't ours to know.

Tired of staying in our rooms, Gem, Thea, Charlie, and I went down to the kitchen just after noon. Gem fixed each of us a plate of leftovers from Thea's birthday dinner. After eating, we quietly retired to the green room, wrapped in blankets against the perpetual chill that infiltrated the former porch this time of year. Thea fell asleep on the window seat, while Gem and I played checkers on the floor. Charlie sat next to us with his latest book; he often read passages aloud to us whenever he ran across those that he found interesting, but not today. Even though we were out of hearing range of Popo and Mother, Charlie read to himself.

As Gem set the board for another game, my eye caught movement outside one window that overlooks the narrow stretch of woods and Prairie Creek beyond. I got up and looked out.

"Popo." The word escaped me as a faint breeze.

Gem and Charlie joined me as I watched my father through the bare trees standing on the creek bank. Barefooted and wearing only his undershirt and trousers, he seemed numb to the wind stirring the leaves at his feet. Then his head fell into his hands. Did I hear him sobbing?

I turned and ran for the door, desperate to be at his side, but Gem caught me by the arm and stopped me. She shook her head. I looked at Charlie for support.

"Popo needs me," I insisted.

"Leave your father be." Charlie's word sounded harsh, out of character. "He has a headful of problems he's trying to work out. He needs time alone to think."

"Let's take Thea upstairs. It's too cold in here for her." Gem gathered Thea and her doll in her arms and led the way up the stairs. I reluctantly followed.

We spent most of the afternoon in our room. Charlie and I played checkers, or read, or played with Thea while Gem sat on the floor and wrote page after page in her diary. As we went through the motions of passing the time, I couldn't help but wonder how stillness had overtaken our house and my role in the abrupt transformation. I tried to talk to Gem about it—Gem knows everything—but she ignored my questions.

Charlie finally stood up and paced back and forth in the small room for a few moments before announcing his intentions. "I'm going to go see what Bernard is doing. If anyone needs me, I'll be across the street."

I curled up next to Thea and napped for the rest of the afternoon.

***

I awoke with a start. Gem and Thea were gone. When I heard Gus's heavy foot on the stairs, I got up and followed him to his room. Standing in the boys' bedroom doorway, I watched as he opened his bureau drawer, remove his canvas sack, and drop his coins inside, one at a time. One, two, three, four, five, I counted.

"Did the Widow Winslow give you a nickel today?"

"How do you know if I delivered to the Widow Winslow today?"

I smiled at my oldest brother. "Well, did she?"

"Nope."

"Why do you carry her groceries clear over to Clinton Street if she doesn't tip you?"

"Annie, she's old and deserving of a kindness. She doesn't have much money or anyone to look out for her. I don't want her nickel. It would do me no good thinking about that when I was trying to get to sleep tonight."

"You could have bought a piece of pie at the Blue and White Café with that nickel."

"Mother's pie is better."

"You could have bought Necco Wafers from Miss Roxy's candy counter."

"No, thank you. They taste like chalk."

I chuckled. He was right.

Then I asked what had been on my mind for a while. "What are you saving your money for, Gus?"

"For the big adventure I plan to go on someday." His smile lit up his eyes.

"When are you going? Can I go with you?"

"Little sisters don't go on big adventures with their brother. Don't worry, Annie, I'm not going soon."

Good, because I couldn't image life without Gus around. I walked into my brothers' bedroom and sat down on Blinn's bed.

"Something on your mind, little sister?" Gus asked.

"Do you think Mother and Popo will ever stop being angry with me, Gus?"

Gus sat down next to me. "Annie, they're not angry with you. They're angry with each other, which isn't anything new. And I think they're angry with themselves."

"But I kept a secret from them."

"They didn't see what was right in front of their own eyes. When Charlie and you figured out that Thea couldn't hear much, I think you just put words to what the rest of us already knew. I talked to Aunt Lo about it, and she said the same thing. Thea's hearing loss is no-body's fault. It just happened. Now stop worrying and go downstairs. I brought a stew bone home from the market, and Gem's making soup. Go help her."

I nodded. "Thanks, Gus." With that, I got up and ran downstairs.

***

The next morning, I heard Gus go down to the basement to stoke the furnace. During the night, Thea had crawled up between Gem and me and burrowed under our blankets. At some point, Gem had pulled Thea's blanket from her bed and added it to the ones covering us. Not wanting to disturb my little sister, I didn't move until I felt the heat from the furnace warming our room.

When I sat up, Gem was standing in the doorway wrapped in the robe Mother had made her last Christmas. "I'm making breakfast." I could tell my sister's patience with our feuding parents and the silence in our house had worn thin. "I need your help."

It was Sunday morning and the soup we'd eaten the night before had worn off. Gem and I bounded down the stairs and began rooting around for whatever we could find. I found the eggs the twins had collected from the chickens the last two mornings in a basket on the back porch, two dozen in all. In a drawer, I discovered most of a loaf of bread Mother had baked on Friday.

"Go to the cellar and get a jar of stewed tomatoes and a jar of apple-sauce," Gem ordered. "Then go find Gus, Blinn, Cory, and Charlie and tell them breakfast will be ready shortly, so they need to get washed up. But first, go upstairs and tell Mother and Popo I'm making breakfast if they want to join us."

I nodded, though it felt like Gem had ordered me into the lion's den. After taking a gulp of air for courage, I climbed the steps slowly, avoiding the two squeaky ones just before the landing. When I got to the top, I saw the door to my parents' room was slightly ajar. When I pushed it open, my father was there, fully dressed, his old satchel open on the bed.

"Popo, Gem is making breakfast. Do you want to come down and eat with us?"

Popo turned to look at me, a slight smile crossing his lips. "Thank you, Angel. I could use a little breakfast. I don't suppose there's any coffee?"

"Gem can make some." I looked around my parents' bedroom. "Where's Mother?"

"She's in the bathroom. I'll let her know about breakfast."

As I turned to go downstairs, I paused. "Popo, I am so sorry." I was sorry... about Thea's hearing loss and that I hadn't told Mother or Popo sooner. I'd ruined Thea's birthday celebration by keeping a secret from them.

As tears spilled from my eyes, Popo knelt and gently brushed the tears from my cheeks. Then he continued, a note of bitterness slipping into his voice. "Your mother... well... she should have known Thea couldn't hear without her nine-year-old daughter having to tell her. It's your mother's responsibility to... "

"No, Popo, no! Ever since her fever broke, Thea hasn't been the same; she's been thin and frail. Mother has worked so hard to make her well again. The angels came for her, but Mother ordered them away. Thea is alive because of Mother. We're both alive because of Mother. You don't know all she did to save us because you weren't here."

Popo's eyes widened at the sound of those incriminating words. You. Weren't. Here. A shadow of anger crossed his face, but quickly fell away. "Please go see to that coffee, Annie. I'll be down shortly."

A few minutes later, the family gathered around the kitchen table: Gus, Blinn, Cory, Charlie, Gem, Thea, Popo and me. Mother's kitchen without Mother seemed odd, though it didn't stop us from feasting on scrambled eggs, toast with butter and homemade jam, and stewed tomatoes and applesauce. As the chatter reached its level of normalcy, the fear that had been flitting about the house for most of two days seemed to have taken its leave.

As we were finishing our breakfast and arguing about who was going to clean up the dishes, Mother appeared in the doorway, cheeks sallow, eyes rimmed in red. I knew then that the fear that had been tormenting us since Friday had found a home in Mother's soul. We all felt it. The secret had opened a chasm between our parents, and I knew the price we would pay for our silence would be more silence, but now between Mother and Popo.

# Chapter 4

In the winter of 1932, the authorities quarantined our house soon after I came home from school one afternoon feeling poorly. After examining me, Doc Becker made the dreaded pronouncement that every family in our town feared: scarlet fever. "The only consolation, Maggie, is that scarlet fever is rare in adults and children younger than three." My two-year-old sister Thea came down with the dreaded disease a couple of days later.

Lying in bed those first few days of my fever, I remembered dreaming about the sign I saw posted on the front door of Emerson Keller's house. The sign was red with bold black letters at the top that read:

## QUARANTINE SCARLET FEVER

*All persons are forbidden to enter or leave these premises without the permission of the* HEALTH OFFICER *under* PENALTY OF THE LAW. *This notice is posted in compliance with the* SANITARY CODE

OF INDIANA *and must not be removed without permission of the* HEALTH OFFICER.

The HEALTH OFFICER had nailed a sign just like it to our front door.

In my fevered state, the fact Emerson survived his bout of scarlet fever somehow comforted me. Emerson was one of Gem's classmates, a big, dumb kid who couldn't afford to lose so much as a day of school, let alone the six weeks that usually came with a quarantine. Despite his long absence from school, Emerson passed the fifth grade that year. Gem insisted that Emerson's advancement had little to do with his marks, and everything to do with the fact that he had outgrown the classroom.

Popo and the boys weren't home when the quarantine sign went up on our door. My father wanted no part of six weeks of confinement, so he promptly turned my brothers and cousin over to his sister LoRetta and went about his business.

Aunt Lo lived in the house on the other side of Prairie Creek with her brother Karl and his wife Iris. MaMaw Ghere, my widowed grandmother, lived there, too. "The aristocrats" ...that's what Popo called his family... "lived right next door, but a world away." Except for Aunt Lo, who roamed freely between the family's aristocracy and the *hoi polloi.*

***

Mother always said Uncle Karl and Popo were cut from different cloth. Uncle Karl was lanky, and a bit on the homely side. He possessed a stern countenance exaggerated by the balding patch at the front of his skull and his emotionless steel-gray eyes that only lit up at the sight of a piece of Mother's sugar-cream pie.

Popo told us at supper one evening that a fart had never passed from the backsides of either Karl or Iris, and that was why they both looked so turgid all the time. Aunt Lo insisted that wasn't true, that she'd frequently overheard her brother through the cold air return let loose during his reluctant trips to the basement to shovel coal.

"It always surprises me that so much hot air can travel so vociferously through the cold air return." Aunt Lo's straight-faced delivery made the children laugh, despite Mother's obvious disapproval, dubbing it "inappropriate table conversation." When Popo conceded that Karl was, in fact, an old gasbag, Mother's failure to scold Popo for being inappropriate showed she shared the same opinion of her brother-in-law.

My father, Augustus Ghere, was a short, stocky man. Square-jawed and handsome... that's how Mother's friend, Alma Mae Butler, described him one day to the clerk at the A&P. (The clerk promptly called Mother to relay every word of the conversation between her and Alma Mae.) A piece of Popo's thick wavy brown hair had a habit of breaking free from the liberal amounts of pomade he applied to it each morning and tumbling onto his forehead where it came to rest casually over his lively sky-blue eyes.

A complete contradiction to both her brothers, Aunt LoRetta referred to herself as "the rose between those two particular thorns." Possessing neither the classic movie star looks of her older brother nor the old-before-his-time demeanor of her younger brother, my aunt fashioned an identity all her own. No one ever referred to her as Augie and Karl's sister, even though less than three years separated the three siblings in age. After Karl was born, the Ghere children were never seen in public outside their tight family unit until Augie started school.

Individually, Aunt Lo's features were perfect... her soft gray eyes, the gentle slope of her up-turned nose, her rosy full lips... but her face's ultimate composition somehow failed in its ultimate execution. Neither beautiful nor ugly, Aunt Lo was the epitome of elegance.

LoRetta Ghere traversed through life in anything but low gear. Some days she'd make her grand entrance into our green room "swaying and sashaying," as Popo called it, to whatever lively ditty blared from our Zenith radio, her arms moving in rhythm with her narrow hips.

Oh, how she loved to goad my brothers.

"Come dance with me, Cory."

He'd wrinkled his nose. "I thought the church didn't approve of dancing."

"You must be referring to the Baptists over on Washington Street. They don't know what they're missing. Now come over here and dance with your favorite aunt."

That's when Cory would make a run for the door.

Aunt Lo's overall appearance was nothing less than perfection. The Depression be damned, (her words, not mine) she made weekly visits to Huffer's Beauty School to have her coiffured hair tended to by none other than Mrs. Cuba Spaulding herself. None of Mrs. Spaulding's beauty school students ever touched my aunt's hair, but years later I learned that they frequently stood in awe watching their mentor's artistry come to life as she curled and wound Aunt Lo's locks tightly to her head and secured them with hidden bobby pins. There her hair stayed until my aunt's next appointment.

The best description of my aunt's wardrobe? Meticulous. The best description of her sewing skills? Supervisory.

Aunt Lo's only talent in creating her distinctive wardrobe lay in her picking skills. First in line at the perpetual rummage sale held every

Saturday morning in the otherwise vacant storefront two doors down from the Blue and White Café, Aunt Lo had a knack for spotting the unblemished areas of an otherwise worn garment. Old Man Gregory always seemed to have the goods on her latest pickings, which he offered Popo during our late Friday afternoon visits to the Blue and White Café. This gave me a good idea of what went on Saturday mornings. All the stories were similar.

"How much do you want for this old thing?" my aunt would ask the volunteer clerk.

"Now, Miss Ghere, you know every penny goes to charity."

"How about fifty cents for this sack-full?"

"But there's more than a dollar's worth of usable goods in there."

"I'll give you sixty cents, not a penny more."

"Fine."

Everyone knew who got the better end of that deal.

When Aunt Lo got her weekly finds home, she and MaMaw Ghere would go to town with their stitch rippers, reducing the sack-full to various piles of pieces she'd use in a new dress, or a skirt for herself or one of her nieces, or patches for trouser knees and coat elbows that came in handy for her rambunctious nephews.

Then she'd show up bright and early at our house on a Saturday morning with a piece of fabric and her favorite old pattern and begin wiping down our kitchen table. "Gem, dear, would you be so kind as to help your old aunt lay out this pattern? I'm so afraid I won't get it cut exactly on the bias."

Before long, I was running upstairs retrieving the straight pins, scissors, and chalk while my sister and Mother smoothed the fabric over the table as my aunt doled out instructions.

"This remnant for the bodice and sleeves, this one for the skirt, and I've a scrap or two we can piece together for the belt and collar."

"Are you sure about all that, LoRetta?"

"Yes, Maggie. I'm sure."

"What about buttons?"

"Dear, you just leave the buttons to me."

While Mother and Gem got to work, my aunt mostly drank tea.

***

During our household's quarantine, the prim and proper Uncle Karl and Aunt Iris were none too keen on having a pack of unruly teenage boys running about, eating them out of house and home and otherwise disrupting their long succession of perfectly boring days. "We're doomed," Aunt Iris pronounced after losing the war of words with my determined Aunt Lo.

Despite the couple's vociferous objections, Aunt Lo rose to the occasion, taking charge of the rambunctious foursome. She arranged for my three brothers to report to the loading dock at the Ghere-Douglass Company after school every weekday and on Saturday mornings. Under Uncle Karl's watchful eye, the three helped load and unload the wagons and trucks, and otherwise kept the loading dock "spic and span," as Aunt Lo described their work in the daily letters she left for us on our front porch. In return for their labors, each received a dime a day. "An extravagant wage for half day's work," protested Uncle Karl. Gus later said that Uncle Karl had gotten the better end of that particular stick.

When school let out for the day, my cousin Charlie reported to the Clinton County Library, where Aunt Lo worked as the head librarian. Because the county was broke, she was not only the head librarian; she was currently the only librarian. She put Charlie to work shelving books, cleaning floors, washing windows, and taking care of any other chores that needed to be done.

For his efforts, Aunt Lo paid Charlie a quarter each week out of her own pocket, truly an extravagant sum for a ten-year-old. When Charlie called Gem on Sundays, he said he couldn't stop dreaming about the Dewey Decimal System. "What a nightmare." While Charlie complained about how hard he worked to meet Aunt Lo's high expectations, he continued to go to the library to help her even after the quarantine lifted, and the quarters stopped.

Those six long weeks of quarantine included six long Sunday mornings in a church pew for the boys. Aunt Lo began those mornings at the crack of dawn by wrangling all four boys out of their nice warm beds to bathe. Mimicking Aunt Lo to a T, Blinn told Gem and me later that she would stand in the doorway of their cramped sleeping quarters and, with a hand on her hip, proclaim, "Gentlemen, you cannot enter the house of the Lord with dirt under your fingernails. Now get up and get on with it." Cory dubbed her many proclamations, "The Gospel according to Aunt Lo."

My aunt also insisted they dress in their Sunday best, but the quarantine left the boys locked out of our house with only the clothing on their backs. Gem gathered up a couple changes of clothes for each, placed them in a canvas sack and set it outside on the back porch for them to pick up. (We later learned she should have gotten permission from the HEALTH OFFICER, who remained none the wiser to Gem's infraction.) After Aunt Lo rooted through everything Gem left, she declared it all unsatisfactory for the LORD, and purchased her version of their Sunday best at the next rummage sale.

On Sunday mornings, with the four boys uncomfortable in their unfamiliar clothing, Gus hitched-up Old Barney to our carriage and carried Aunt Lo, MaMaw Ghere, and the boys to Holy Cross Church over on Wabash Street. Aunt Lo often boasted that the church was a beautiful example of Greek Revival architecture, one of our town's founding structures. My brothers came to appreciate the church's historic details. Gazing about the beautiful sanctuary helped keep them awake when the Widower Pastor Burke's mush-mouthed, muddled delivery of the Word did everything it could to lull them back to sleep.

My memories of those early days of my illness remain foggy. I know I was in the bed with little Thea beside me. Mother had moved Gem into the boys' room to sleep until the house returned to normal. I remember waking up when Mother placed a cool rag on my forehead or sat next to me rubbing calamine lotion on the red scaly rash that covered my neck, chest, and arms. My clearest memory was of Mother singing to us. Her amazing memory captured the latest hits by the Hoosier Hot Shots, whose music often dominated our old Zenith radio. Those Hoosier Hot Shots were something else.

On the worst nights, I remember waking up to Mother pacing the floor at the foot of the bed, limp Thea in her arms, my mother pleading with her youngest daughter to live until daybreak. Other times, she would sit by our bedside, her hands resting on the feather mattress next to me as she struggled to stay upright. On one of those days, I noticed the red rash covering the top of Mother's hands. Gem told me that adults didn't get scarlet fever, but the look on my mother's face as she attempted to comfort me told me otherwise. With all the strength I had, I place my hand on one of Mother's. My voice soft and strained from dryness, I revealed my greatest fear.

"Don't leave me."

"I won't leave you, Anna. I promise. Don't you leave me."

"I won't." As the fever dragged me under, the words "I promise" never escaped my lips.

On the day my fever broke, Mother was sitting beside me on the bed, holding my hand. When I opened my eyes, she was smiling. From then on, I started getting my strength back. I devoured the chicken noodle soup and egg sandwiches Gem had brought me. It wasn't long after I started eating again that I began asking about Charlie, my brothers, and Aunt Lo, and if she'd heard anything from my friends, Pauline and Helen, or any of the other children at my school. Gem told me one of my classmates, Earlynn Musgrove, died of scarlet fever. I was sorry to hear that. I was sorry I hadn't been nicer to her.

"Gem, has anyone in your class died of scarlet fever?"

"No, I won't hear of it," she insisted with a stomp of her foot. I looked at her bright face and didn't know if she was teasing me, or if she meant what she'd said.

"Do you pray for the children in your class?"

Gem tapped her diary on her lap and considered her answer. "I guess you could call it that. Emerson came out of it none the wiser but at least he's still kicking."

Even as Gem chattered on about all I'd missed, I was afraid to ask her about Popo, for fear she'd tell me the truth. Hearing about Earlynn was enough truth to deal with for a while.

***

One bitter cold morning, Mother summoned Doc Becker, who arrived on foot and pronounced the glorious news: Thea's fever had broken, and the toddler was finally out of the woods.

Within minutes of the quarantine sign being removed from our door by the HEALTH OFFICER, the boys wriggled out of the clutches of Aunt Lo and raced home, bringing with them their noise and energy and a large sack of dirty clothes, including their Sunday best. Though Mother looked worn out, I knew she was happy to be surrounded by her family again.

Through our entire scarlet fever ordeal, Popo was nowhere to be found. He did not know what happened during those arduous weeks when the very lives of his two youngest daughters fell squarely on Mother's shoulders alone. Nor did he know about all the days she never slept, rarely ate, barely left our sides. He had no clue about how the red rash had erupted on the back of Mother's hands, and later how it crept up her neck. Gem and Mother shared many secrets.

Mother never asked me to keep her sickness a secret, but I never breathed a word of it to anyone.

A couple of weeks after Gem and I started back to school to face the mound of homework required to get us caught up, Popo returned home. The strain between my parents was palpable in those weeks and months after the scourge that scarred my family forever.

I ignored it.

# Chapter 5

As Sunday morning slipped quietly into afternoon, not a single unnecessary word escaped from either of our parent's lips. Growing restless, I persuaded Gem to put away her diary—she couldn't possibly have anything left to write—and help me finish my costume for the Lockwood's upcoming party at the Blue and White Café.

"Charlie, will you read to Thea?" My cousin was lying across his bed on his stomach, Arthur Ransome's new book, "Peter Duck," open in front of him. "Gem and I have work to do on my costume to get ready for Tuesday night."

At twelve years of age, Gem could sew almost as well as Mother. Altering the crone's costume she had worn last year to fit me was easy for her. Shortening the skirt, replacing a missing button, and adding a tassel to the pointed black hat wouldn't take her long. Gem thought sewing a tassel on a crone's hat was a dumb idea, but she agreed to do it for me.

As Charlie held out his arms to Thea, he looked up at me.

"I thought her hearing loss was obvious, so I thought Aunt Maggie knew. Maybe we should have told her... or Popo... when we figured it out."

I shrugged. "Maybe."

Charlie wrapped his arms around Thea.

"It was the scarlet fever, wasn't it? That's what caused her deafness." Charlie had a habit of stating the obvious.

I nodded. "That's what Gem said. She thinks Thea's hearing was fine before she got sick."

"You were sick, too, but you can hear just fine."

I shrugged again. I'd thought about that many times during the last few months and still didn't understand why the fever had taken my sister's hearing and not mine. I didn't want to think about it anymore.

Charlie gave me a weak smile. He then cooed into Thea's ear, "Pretty girl, pretty girl." As I left the room to join Gem in Mother's sewing room, I wondered if Thea could hear Charlie at all.

Gem sewed the edge of a scarf she'd created from a remnant of black wool she'd found in Mother's fabric box. The scarf was my idea. The weather was getting colder, so Mother might insist I wear my regular scarf, a bright red one, when I went begging with my friends, and then to the party at the Blue and White Café. I decided the red scarf would look awful with my black dress, but a black scarf wrapped around my neck wouldn't distract from the rest of my spooky costume.

"Try on the dress," Gem insisted as she cut the last stray threads from the scarf.

As I slipped on the full black dress, I groaned. "I think it's too big. It looked better on you."

Gem straightened the dress and buttoned the back. "Remember, you'll have on long johns underneath and there's plenty of room for your coat."

My sister left the sewing room, returning a moment later with a handkerchief. "I don't think Cory will miss this." After waving it around like she was surrendering, she wrapped it around my neck and secured it with a safety pin.

"What's that for?"

"It will keep your neck from itching when I put the wool scarf on you." She wrapped the scarf over it and tied it in a loose knot. "What do you think?" Gem turned me toward the full-length mirror that stood in the corner of Mother's sewing room. I watched my sister in the mirror as she adjusted my costume until it was just right.

"Oh, I almost forgot... " Gem ran out of the room again and returned with a pair of old button-up black leather boots. "These were Mother's boots when she was a child. She got them in Chicago when she was about your age. Sit down. I want you to try them on."

"Did Mother say I could wear these?"

"It was her idea."

I slipped on the boots while Gem rooted around in Mother's sewing boxes. "Here it is." Gem held up the hook. She sat on the floor and used the hook to slip the buttons into the buttonholes. "How do they feel?"

"I'll have to wear extra socks." After considering that for a moment, I added, "But that's fine. These boots aren't too small."

I thought about the patent leather shoes I'd been wearing. They were so tight that I'd been wearing the thinnest worn socks I had just so I could get them on. Sometimes in school I liked to slip off the backs of my heels and wriggle my feet around, so they didn't feel numb.

Gem pulled me to my feet and turned me toward the mirror again as she adjusted the pointed crone's hat on my head, pulling the piece of black elastic she's sewn onto it beneath my chin.

As I stared at myself, I knew I'd have the best costume at the party. "Thank you, Gem. It's perfect." I hugged my sister, feeling her affection.

"All that's left to do is get Cory to go next door and get that old broom Aunt Iris uses to sweep out her back stoop." Gem continued to fuss and tug at my costume. "According to Popo, that's the only work Aunt Iris does."

"Do you think Cory will get it?"

"Aunt Iris has whacked him with that broom enough times that I think he'll be happy to snag it for a worthy cause. Now take that dress off so I can hang it up. If you wrinkle it, I'll have to iron it again before you go begging."

"But what about you? Beggars' Night is on Tuesday, and you don't have a costume."

An air of Greta Garbo about her, Gem stuck her nose in the air. "I'm too old to go begging." Her comment made me think that a bit of the aristocracy from our relatives next door had seeped into Gem's blood. "Mother will insist that Blinn and I walk with you children," the word "children" bore more than a hint of distaste, "but I am not begging at the doors of our neighbors. It's so undignified." She sniffed; her nose turned upward again.

"Is Fred coming with us?"

"Fred? How should I know what Fred Moore is doing on Beggars' Night?"

"If he comes along with us, are you going to kiss him?"

Gem blushed. "Of course not. I'm a lady. Besides, I'm waiting for him to kiss me."

Gem's sea-blue eyes sparkled, her face bright with joy. I'd never seen the ocean, but I somehow knew the description was perfect.

***

Last summer when Gem and I stopped by the Blue and White Café to buy candy—Necco Wafers for Gem's birthday—an old man was sitting at the counter talking to Roxy Lockwood.

Miss Roxy looked up at us and smiled. "Girls, have you met Captain Willet?"

We both shook our heads.

"He was in the Navy during the Great War."

Capt. Willet swiveled his stool around to face us. "It's a pleasure to meet you." He stuck out his hand to Gem. "I must say, young lady, your eyes are the color of the deep blue sea. Has anyone ever told you that?"

"No, sir." My sister was silent for a moment. "Do you live in town, Captain?"

"I'm just passing through. I live in Chicago, but I'm on my way to visit my daughter and her family in Bellevue. She's got five little ones, so I go there as often as I can to help her out. I even help my son-in-law, Eddie, while I'm there. Eddie has a fix-it shop. He's good at fixing things, but his customers aren't so good at paying him." Capt. Willet smiled before muttering, "Oh, how times have changed."

Miss Roxy offered us more information on Capt. Willet as she mopped up the countertop with a rag. "He takes the Wanatah here, then catches the Nickel Plate to Bellevue. He passes the time between his two trains trips entertaining me with his sea stories."

"Our mother has five children, too. Our cousin Charlie lives with us during the school year because the school near his farm in Mulberry isn't much good, and Charlie's real smart. Isn't he, Gem?"

She nodded.

"Sounds like your mother has her hands full, just like my daughter."

Gem bought her Necco Wafers and thanked Miss Roxy before saying goodbye. As Gem pulled the door open, I turned and walked back toward the captain. "Why don't you move to Bellevue?"

"What?"

"Move to Bellevue so you can help your daughter all the time. You could tell your grandchildren all your sea stories."

"Not all of my stories." Captain Willet laughed heartily. Then his smile faded. "Young lady, I don't know if they'd have me."

"You should ask."

"Maybe I will, young lady. Maybe I will."

***

Turning back to the mirror, I took another look at my old crone's costume, then whirled around, the dress's full skirt flaring out as I spun.

"Gem, can I borrow your crinoline on Beggars' Night?" I knew full well what her answer would be. My sister loved fine clothes and since there seemed to be a shortage of them, she took meticulous care of the few she had.

"Absolutely not. Old crones don't wear pretty things. Besides, you'd get it dirty."

There was no point in arguing. "I'm going to go show Popo."

When I left the sewing room, I saw the door to my parents' room was open. I didn't see Popo or Mother, so I ran down the stairs and into the green room where my father often sat in his favorite chair, reading the newspaper.

"Popo, where are you?"

"He's gone." Charlie was standing in the doorway, his eyes revealing his sadness.

"Gone?" Popo always left on Monday morning after having breakfast with his family. He'd often walk with Charlie and me to school on his way to the Wanatah Depot.

Charlie nodded toward the front door. It took a moment to comprehend what had happened. I pushed past my cousin, flung open the front door, and ran down the porch steps to the street. I saw Popo, satchel in hand, walking toward downtown.

"Popo, come back."

My father turned toward me, his hand raised. I didn't know if it meant stop, if it meant goodbye, or both. Popo turned and continued walking... away from me.

I don't know how long I stood there, but at some point, I felt Charlie's hand on my arm. "Come back inside, Annie. It's cold out here."

I climbed the steps to the porch and went inside. Without stopping, I went upstairs, stumbled into my bedroom, and fell face down into my pillow. I sobbed until I fell asleep from exhaustion.

# Chapter 6

On Monday, when Charlie and I returned home from school, Doc Becker was sitting in our parlor talking to Mother, Thea on his lap. Our usual noisy entrance drew Mother's immediate ire.

"Go upstairs. Doc Becker and I are talking. I'll let you know when I need you to set the table for supper."

Doc Becker pushed Thea's doll head out of his face and gave us a little wave. "Nice to see you both."

Charlie went straight to his bedroom, but I lingered by our furnace's cold air return near the center of our upstairs hallway. As I knelt beside it, I heard a voice in my ear. "What are you doing?"

I gasped. "Gem, you scared me half to death," I whispered.

"Again, what are you doing?"

Gem knew perfectly well what I was doing. I'd learned everything I knew about eavesdropping on conversations in our parlor from her.

I put my finger to my lips. She knelt next to me, and the two of us listened to the conversation going on below us.

Doc Becker's voice was soothing, but confident. "The good news, Maggie, is that Thea's health is steadily improving. It's not always obvious when you are with her night and day, but I assure you, she's physically much better than the last time I saw her. She's getting stronger every day. Of course, she could still use another few pounds on her bones, so continue to coax her into eating as much as possible."

Doc Becker paused before continuing. "The bad news... well, Thea has substantial hearing loss, just as you suspected."

"Will any of what she lost ever come back?" Mother already knew the answer to that question.

"I'm afraid not." Doc Becker paused, allowing that to sink in. "She has profound hearing loss in the left ear, maybe only ten percent now, although I have no way of knowing exactly how much. I'm guessing she still has about twenty-five to thirty percent of her hearing in her right ear. That's good because she can still hear you, provided you speak loudly into that ear."

"Charlie already figured that out."

"Charlie's a smart young man."

"I should have realized she had lost much of her hearing sooner. I should have known my baby girl couldn't hear, long before my eleven-year-old nephew and nine-year-old daughter figured it out. I'm the one who's with her day in and day out."

"Stop being so hard on yourself, Maggie. You focused on taking care of your girls when they got sick. Unfortunately, the fever took its toll on little Thea... she was the youngest patient I had who contracted scarlet fever. Think about it... it took a toll on many families. This town suffered a dozen deaths last winter, but believe me, it could have been a lot worse. Your girls made it through the fever alive, so count your blessings."

"Thea's a fighter. She had a rough beginning."

"Yes, she did. Little Thea *is* a fighter, and so is her mother."

Doc Becker allowed a lingering silence to settle over the room before continuing. "Remember, Maggie, once Thea was out of the woods, she still had a tough row to hoe to get her strength back. You would have figured out Thea's hearing loss eventually, but there's not much more you could have done when she was so weak."

"But I..."

Doc Becker wasn't interested in any more of Mother's whining. "Now that Thea's health is improving, it's important for you to teach her all the same things you taught your other children. The only difference is you'll have to speak louder and right into her ear. Maybe try to figure out other ways to communicate with her. There's a lot happening in the world of medicine. Just last month, I read an article about how scientists are using vacuum tubes to make hearing devices smaller."

Mother sighed. I wondered what she was thinking.

"Even though Thea has substantial hearing loss, she will eventually make her own way in this world, with the help of her family, of course. Don't worry, you'll see."

In a loud voice, Doc Becker spoke to my baby sister. "You're going to be just fine, aren't you, little one?" In his normal tone, he continued his conversation with Mother. "For now, I want her to continue getting plenty of rest. Keep feeding her that wonderful food you make, as much and as often as she'll eat it, and have Charlie and your children continue to read to her."

"There's not much chance that will stop. Charlie would read to the goat if he thought she'd listen."

Charlie does read to Belva from time to time, but Mother and Aunt Rachel didn't need to know that.

"Most importantly, Maggie, love this sweet child until the cows come home."

This time, the silence that fell over the parlor was palpable. I could hear Gem breathing in my ear.

"One last thing I want to mention... something for you to consider. The nuns at St. Luke's run a little school for the blind and deaf. The school's in an upstairs room in the rectory. The nuns do incredible work with the children."

After a long hesitation, Mother sighed. "I'll think about it. I promise."

"That's all I can ask. The nuns will also come here and teach you and the rest of the family how to help Thea live a normal life. I'll be happy to introduce you to the Sisters whenever you're ready."

Doc Becker got up to leave. "Are you sure you won't stay for a piece of pie? I'll make a fresh pot of coffee."

"I wish I could, Maggie, but I've got a couple more stops to make before I can get on home to the missus. Can I get a raincheck on that pie and coffee?"

"Yes, of course."

As Mother and Doc Becker said their goodbyes, Gem and I tiptoed into our bedroom.

***

"Who's going begging tonight?"

I felt relief that Mother's voice sounded almost normal. Since ruining Thea's birthday, she had barely spoken to me. I wanted to tell her I wasn't interested in going begging without Popo. I wanted to ask her if he was coming home on the train on Friday, but I didn't want to upset her all over again, especially now that she was speaking to me again.

Gem moved past me as she stacked the supper dishes. "The children are gathering here at six o'clock. Helen and Pauline the Pest, are coming."

Pauline was my best friend if I didn't count Charlie. If all the world's a stage, then Pauline's place on that stage was front and center, with me looking on as her devoted admirer. Helen was my other best friend, if I didn't count Charlie. Studious and demur, Helen was the opposite of Pauline. Mother often said that since Helen got straight As in school, I should follow her example rather than Pauline's. I ignored Mother's advice.

Pauline, Helen, and I had met on our first day of first grade. Pauline enchanted me with her hard-to-forget doe eyes that revealed her enthusiasm for life. Dark, round, and expressive, they were an authentic reflection of her every thought, hiding nothing of that which pirouetted about in her lively mind. When Pauline rolled her eyes at a teacher, the teacher pointed at the door, sending my friend straight to the principal's office. Helen was equally infatuated with Pauline. "You can't very well have a fan club with only one fan," Gem often teased about our devotion to Pauline.

Mother moved a stack of dirty dishes to the sink. "What about the Smith girls? Are they going begging with you tonight?"

"Yes, Barbara Jean and Millie are coming. So is Emerson Keller." Gem liked to tease me about catching scarlet fever from Emerson, which I most certainly did not! Fortunately, Gem had dropped her usual mocking of me because scarlet fever was a taboo topic in our household, at least for the moment.

"I think that new boy, Marshall Manning, is coming. Charlie asked him during school the other day. He's so cute, isn't he, Gem?"

"He's a bad boy. I heard him singing a dirty song down by the creek the other day. Stay away from him."

I giggled. "What song, Gem?"

Before she could answer, Mother interrupted. "Did you ask Albright?"

"Gus did. He saw him on Saturday when he was delivering groceries to the Widow Winslow. Albright said he'd have to ask his mother."

"If he comes, ask Gus to take him home on the way back from the party. I don't want Albright walking all the way to Clinton Street alone after dark."

"Gus is dropping everyone off at their houses after the party."

Mother nodded. "Did you invite Bernard?"

"Bernard invited himself. He always invites himself."

***

Bernard Thompson lived across the street from us. He carried his Bible everywhere he went, including to school in the morning and to his barn in the evening, stashing it on an old workbench when he was shoveling manure. He said he liked to keep it handy, just in case an uncertainty arose in his life that required the soothing ointment only a Bible verse could provide. Those uncertainties arose frequently, so Bernard knew his Bible inside and out.

Whenever a child in the neighborhood found a dead bird, we'd hold a funeral and burial for it with Bernard presiding. I believed an ordinary flock of birds had found its way into heaven because of Bernard's eloquent send-offs. Conducting bird funerals and otherwise praying over whatever might benefit from a good blessing seemed to be the best of Bernard's days.

From a young age, it seemed Bernard's passion for the Bible des-tined him for the pulpit, although the ministry wasn't in his blood, like farming was in mine. His father spent his days selling ice around town from his horse-drawn cart, and, according to Aunt Lo, spent his evenings and most of his nights on a bar stool at the Sleepy Owl Saloon down on the public square.

Bernard's mother spent her days scrubbing floors and doing laun-dry at the Little Palmer House, also on the public square. Named after the Palmer House in Chicago, where its chef invented brownies (served warm with a scoop of homemade vanilla bean ice cream) that headlined the establishment's dessert menu, the Little Palmer House was a poor man's version of that iconic landmark, and our little town's only hotel. While it offered a fraction of the glitz and glamour of its big city namesake, it served the Palmer House's famous brownies.

Again, according to Aunt Lo, Mrs. Thompson may have spent her days working at the Little Palmer House until her hands were raw and her back ached, but she spent her evenings at a table in the back of The Cave (also on the public square) flirting under cover of near darkness with any man who wasn't Mr. Thompson.

Eager to get on with his evening, Mr. Thompson usually left his horse and ice cart sitting out front of their house, providing him a few extra minutes a day on his favorite bar stool. When Bernard arrived home from school, he'd pull the cart to the back of the house, and unhitch and tend to his beloved horse. Once he settled Cooter in for the night, he went inside to wash the breakfast dishes his mother left in the sink and straighten the house, as he preferred things to be orderly.

"It's the Lord's own way, I reckon."

***

"Bernard will probably bring his Bible along." Gem smirked, not even attempting to hide her bewilderment with our friend and his odd ways.

"Yes, I'm certain he will." After a pause, when her attention seemed focused on washing the dishes, Mother looked up at her oldest daughter. "What about Fred Moore? Is he going begging with you tonight?" Mother always slipped the weighty questions into a conversation along with the garden variety ones.

"Fred?" Gem replied as if the name was vaguely familiar. Then, pretending to think about it for a lingering moment, she added, "He's going to walk along with Blinn and me to help look after the *children*."

I rolled my eyes. If Pauline had seen me, my eye-rolling would have impressed her.

"I see." Mother paused before asking her next question. "Is Cory going along, as well? To help look after the *children*?" I loved how Mother wrapped a layer of disgust around the word "children" just as Gem had done.

"Good Lord, no," Gem proclaimed. "You know Cory. He'd just shuffle along like a hobo as he did last year... and the year before... and hold the rest of us up. This year, I think he's going to help Gus with Old Barney and the hay wagon."

"That's good." Mother nodded her head as she dried a plate. "Old Barney gets skittish after dark, but Cory has a way of calming that horse so he'll to do what he doesn't want to do."

"Those two have a lot in common," added Gem. "Shuffling seems to be the top speed for Cory and Old Barney. I think it would embarrass Barney Oldfield if he knew we named a slow horse after him."

That made Mother smile, something I hadn't seen her do since the day of Thea's birthday.

It was tradition that after the children went begging, one father in the neighborhood would take us on a hayride through Bunnell Cemetery, which lay north of town just past Woodside Park. The hayride duties had fallen to Popo five years ago when Mr. Bellows, who lived with his family on the other side of Uncle Karl and Aunt Iris, had asked my father to take over. He said it was because his youngest daughter, Maura, didn't want to go begging—that she thought she was too old—but I overheard Popo talking to Old Man Gregory about it one afternoon when we stopped by the Blue and White Café for a piece of pie. Popo thought Mr. Bellows had lost his shirt in the stock market crash, and then lost his job, to boot. I heard about it again a couple months later when they found him dead in the family's shed just before Christmas. Gem didn't tell me how he died. She said I was too young to know.

For the last several years, when we returned from begging, Old Barney and the wagon were waiting in front of our house, a torch lit to help guide the children into the back. Sitting atop hay bales, we'd ride to the cemetery in silence. As soon as we entered the graveyard through the wrought-iron gates, Popo would begin telling his best stories about the spirits that lingered there. Thinking about his booming voice echoing through the chilly night made me miss him all the more.

Before returning home, the hayride would take a detour to the Blue and White Café for the Lockwood's party, where at least a dozen children from the westside of town would join us from the east side for games and treats. Miss Roxy's promise of Coney dogs for everyone this year was the only reason I was going. That, and my old crone's costume that was sure to win first prize.

Mother dried her hands on her apron and sat down at the table. "Aunt Rachel and Uncle Maddy dropped off the hay wagon this afternoon. They got here about the same time Roxy stopped by to pick up the caramel apples I made for the party."

Charlie appeared in the kitchen doorway. "Aunt Maggie, Cory went over to Bernard's house for a few minutes. Cooter seems lame, so Bernard asked him to look at the horse's hoof before we go out begging."

"Do you want to take food over to Bernard before you go out?" Mother asked. "I have a few leftovers."

"No. He helped Miss Roxy set up tables in her basement this afternoon, so she fed him."

"Charlie, your mother left you a pair of old jeans for your scarecrow costume, and a few other things she thought you'd like. They're up on your bed."

"Did she leave me any newspapers? I want to read the latest editorials by Ernie Pyle." Madison Caldwell, Charlie's father, had an uncle in northern Virginia who sent back issues of the *Washington Daily News* to the farm for Charlie to read.

"I'm sorry, Charlie, but I don't know if she left any newspapers this trip. You'll have to go up to your room to see for yourself. If she left newspapers, be sure to pass them along to Cory when you're finished reading them. He needs them for bedding in the chicken coop."

Charlie always passed his newspapers on to the chickens, right after he read anything of interest, and carefully clipped out any items by his hero and jotted down any words he wanted to look up in the big dictionary at the library. Ernie Pyle was the managing editor of the *Washington Daily News*, but to hear Charlie tell it, the man walked on water.

When Charlie was a toddler, he seemed to gravitate to his father's lap when he was tired and fussy. One day, Madison picked up a newspaper that was on the table and started reading aloud the aviation column written by Ernie Pyle. To Madison and Rachel's surprise, the readings comforted little Charlie. Aunt Rachel told us that at first, she thought it was the soothing sound of his father's voice, but when Madison read anything else from the newspaper, the boy fussed. "We thought he'd grow up to be an aviator," Rachel mused.

Charlie had a different idea. "Someday, I'm going to be a journalist just like Ernie Pyle."

After we put away the supper dishes, Gem helped me get into my costume, layering long johns and my coat to fill out my black crone's dress. Then my sister pinned Cory's hankie around my neck before wrapping the wool scarf over it. I began tugging at it.

"It's too tight. Can't you loosen that safety pin a little?"

"It's pretty cold out this evening." Gem re-tied the scarf in a looser knot. "This will keep you nice and warm."

After Gem placed the tall black hat on my head, securing it under my chin with the elastic strap, she took me by the hand and pulled me into Mother's sewing room. Then she turned me toward the big mirror. "Except for your hair, you look exactly like an old crone. It will be the best costume at the party."

I frowned. "I wish Popo was here to see me. He should be the one to take us on the hayride."

Gem knelt to look right into my eyes. "Charlie is downstairs with your stupid friend, Pauline the Pest. The other children will be here soon. I want you to stop worrying about Popo and go have fun."

I nodded. "I'll try."

A few minutes later, ten children were standing in our parlor with their heads bowed, an approving Aunt Lo looking on as Bernard Thompson prayed that we'd all return home safely with a load of goodies.

As Mother dropped fresh popcorn balls into each of our burlap sacks, she asked if anyone had any new jokes this year. It was also our tradition to tell a joke in exchange for treats.

"My father sent me a few farmer jokes."

"Let's hear one, Charlie."

"Okay. Here goes." Charlie rubbed his hands together, as if he was warming them. "Why did the farmer have to separate the chicken and the turkey?"

"I don't know. Why?"

"He sensed fowl play."

The children giggled.

"Are you going to tell that joke to Aunt Iris if she answers the door?"

"No."

Mother smiled. "Good plan. Now you'd better get moving so you don't miss the party at the Blue and White Café. Remember, you have school tomorrow, so you can't stay out too late."

All the children groaned, including Gem and Fred.

Mother called after us as we headed out to go begging. "Remember, only go to houses that have porch lights on." As the Depression wore on, fewer and fewer families could afford to hand out apples, candies, and other treats on Beggars' Night, but the party at the Blue and White Café made up for it.

"And no tricks!" Mother yelled from the porch as we moved up the street.

# Chapter 7

We began our journey through the neighborhood next door at Aunt Iris and Uncle Karl's house. As usual, Aunt Iris handed out horehound drops, her favorite. Despite their sugar coating, horehound drops tasted like medicine... bad medicine. Aunt Lo always called them bittersweet, adding that Aunt Iris was bitter like horehound but with none of the sweet.

"Why do we even come here?" grumbled Pauline, as we made our retreat from my aunt and uncle's porch. Her eyes widened to the size of silver dollars, then her nose scrunched up and her tongue popped out. I was about to add my own thoughts on the matter when Gem slipped between us.

"Don't be rude." My sister elbowed my friend, then moved past us to rejoin Fred at the head of the pack. Blinn trailed behind to corral any stragglers.

With Gem out of earshot, Pauline finished her thought. "Giving children horehound drops seems pretty rude to me."

"Belva will get her fill of horehound drops tonight," I told my friend.

We continued tramping up South Street for three blocks, climbing the front steps to all the houses with their porch lights on, Charlie and Bernard taking turns delivering jokes for our treats.

"What goes up, but never comes down?"

"Your age."

We crossed the street and came back down the other side, passing a dark Thompson house. Mr. and Mrs. Thompson were out enjoying their evenings at separate beer joints.

Once we reached the end of the block, we paused for a moment under a streetlight that cast an eerie circle of yellow light around our little troupe of costumed joke-tellers. Though the excitement among my friends was palpable, my mind drifted to a memory of Popo telling me about how the *Indianapolis Star* once dubbed our little town the "Gem City." My father said that on a clear night when our prairie town was lit up by dozens of electric streetlights, people could see it from miles around. While nearby Wabash was the first electrically lighted town in the world, he said that sheer happenstance had provided our town its own measure of fame.

Since the Depression set in like an unwanted guest, many of our streetlights had long-since burned out, with no money in the town's budget to replace them. I looked up at the single glowing orb on the lamppost and basked in its soft golden light, knowing that when it flickered out, there was no telling when—or if—it would illuminate my way again.

"It doesn't look like there are many porch lights on down that way." Gem looked one way and then the other before pointing to the right on Harrison Street. "Let's cross over and go back the other way."

As we walked to the other side of the street, the rhythmic padding of our feet drifted upwards and enveloped us in an ambience befitting our mission, gathering strength for its next phase of plundering. Leave it to the harsh cracking voice of one Emerson Keller to shatter our moment of truce with our newly found freedom.

"There it is," he spouted, as he poked me in the ribs with a sharp finger that I felt all the way through my thick layers of clothing. "There's where Ghosty lives." Then he redirected his pointy finger to the corner where a Victorian house sat on a small hill.

Marshall Manning, the latest addition to my class, bent over with laughter.

"She's a ghost, you know. She only comes out at night." Marshall added his two cents to Emerson's tale.

I stamped my foot. "How would you know? You just moved here. You know nothing about her."

Marshall pointed at my boots. "You're funny when you stamp your foot like that."

Infuriated all the more, I stamped my foot again.

Emerson piped up again, defending the new kid. "My pop says she's dead, but just not gone."

"That's ridiculous. She doesn't bother anyone."

"Goody, goody two shoes," taunted Marshall. "Annie's a goody two shoes."

I glared at Pauline, daring her to join in, but she remained stone-faced and silent for a change, her brown eyes searching the street ahead for a distraction behind which to hide her genuine emotions. Helen, of course, stood firmly in all camps. A moment later, Emerson ran up behind me and yelled, "Boo!" I screamed bloody murder, igniting a chain reaction of sheer chaos.

"You thought it was a ghost! You thought it was a ghost!" Emerson yelled as he ran past me. The other children, including my best friend and cousin, joined him in a laugh at my expense. The taunting didn't last long.

"Ghosty, Ghosty, tonight's your night," chanted Emerson, who had taken up a position on the sidewalk directly in front of the big Victorian. "Come out now and give us a fright." The other children immediately joined in.

"Ghosty, Ghosty, tonight's your night. Come out now and give us a fright."

All the beggars but me stood there chanting until Gem stepped in and, with the help of Blinn and Fred, herded the group along toward a lit porch a couple of houses down the next block. As the cluster of excited children moved up the street, Emerson broke away and ran back toward the Victorian. With the accuracy of a pitcher, he flung a raw egg toward the house, hitting Ghosty's big oak door dead-center. I gasped, covering my mouth with my free hand.

"You are such a bad boy," I yelled. "I hope that wasn't one of Mother's eggs."

Emerson laughed heartily, then skipped ahead and faded into the din of the group. I lingered there on the sidewalk in front of the big house looking at the egg oozing down the door, caught up in my thoughts about my father. If he were home, I would run and ask him to help me clean the egg off the door. I knew he would handle everything because Popo had a kindness that drew people to him like moths to a flame. He would talk to Ghosty and explain that a big dumb kid got swept up in the moment. He would ask her to please pardon my friend's naughty behavior and allow us to clean up the mess from her door.

Alone, I stood, wondering what I should do. I saw the other children running off the porch of another house and head further up the street to the next lit one. I took a deep breath. Gathering my courage, I made my way to the front steps of Ghosty's porch. I wished the streetlight would flicker out and give me the cover of darkness. It refused, casting its dim glow onto the front of the house and reflecting off its many windows. As I paused a moment gulping the cold air, my eyes caught sight of the name "Beall" chiseled into the bottom granite step, with the number 354 engraved in the next one up.

"Beall," I thought, searching my memory for a first name.

"Laura Beall... that was it." I remembered hearing the name from Aunt Lo who said she was the heiress to the Wanatah Railroad fortune. Since scrimping and cutting back had become ingrained in our lives (and in the lives of everyone we knew) I couldn't imagine a "fortune" except for the small one hidden in the canvas bag tucked into Gus's bureau drawer.

I remembered Popo and Old Man Gregory discussing the Wanatah Railroad a few months back during one of our stops at the Blue and White Café.

"The Hosier Line"—that's the nickname for the Wanatah because almost all of its tracks are in Indiana—"is still going strong," insisted Old Man Gregory.

"Good management," noted Popo. "And they sure get a lot of my money." With that, the two men shared a nod.

***

Taking a breath, I climbed the steps to the porch and laid down my beggar's sack and hat. I hunkered down and softly made my way to the door. After dropping to my knees, I unpinned Cory's hankie from around my neck and began wiping the raw egg from the door with it.

Confident that I'd gotten most of it off, I folded the egg goo into the hankie as best I could, then raised up to my feet to make my silent escape. As I turned, my foot accidentally bumped against the door.

I froze.

I could barely hear the din of my friends as they moved from house to house, begging for treats further up the block. Suddenly, my attention strayed to the rustle of late autumn leaves in the sugar maples lining Harrison Street as the wind gently called out to winter, coaxing it to begin early this year. In an impetuous act of bravery, I looked back over my shoulder at the big oak door. To my horror, it was open, and the skirt of a full-length black dress filled the doorway.

Slowly, my eyes followed the figure upward, from her black button shoes to her face, so pale in the soft glow of the streetlight that its ghost-like quality fascinated me. She wore her white hair piled atop her head above her perfect heart-shaped face; and donned a pair of round tortoiseshell spectacles with gold earpieces that hooked around her ears. The spectacles seemed out of place on her face. Through the thick lenses, I could see her dancing eyes, the color of Mother's delphiniums, which seemed twice their normal size.

Each spring, when Mother planted her beloved delphiniums, she'd tell Gem and me all about them. "They are the July birth flower," she'd say, a lilt in her voice. "These lush dolphin-shaped flowers symbolize an open heart and ardent attachment. They convey a feeling of lightness and levity." I believed Mother had memorized that perfect description from a book she'd once read.

In that moment, the color of Laura Beall's eyes was the only contradiction in an otherwise expressionless gaze that chilled me to the bone.

I stood there in the presence of this strangely intriguing woman, the toes of my black button-up shoes facing the toes of hers, the flair of my dress touching the flair of hers. As I straightened myself up to make a proper presentation, it occurred to me that my dress was practically a mirror image of hers. I wondered if she'd dressed for Beggars' Night, expecting a horde of children to knock on her door. Or was I looking into a magical looking glass that was reflecting my future back to me?

"I presume you are on my porch for a reason."

I nodded.

"What is your name, child?"

"Annie. Anna Adele Ghere."

"Augustus and Margaret's girl, I presume. I've met your parents."

That surprised me.

"You live just up South Street next to Prairie Creek." She pointed toward my house.

"Yes, ma'am."

"I remember the day your family moved into that house." I watched the woman's eyes looking upward, searching her memories. "Three little boys, as I recall. Little Gus and twin baby boys. Corwin and Blinn, as I recall."

"Family names," I muttered. I'd heard Mother say that a thousand times.

"I knew Nina and Frank when they lived there, and I lived here with my father. They were very kind to me." The woman's countenance softened at her memory of my great aunt and uncle, who had both passed before I was born. "Now their house is filled with children, just as they both dreamed it would be."

"Yes," I answered. "My sister, Gemma Marie—we call her Gem—was born after the twins. Then me and my baby sister, Dorothea. My cousin Charlie lives with us during the school year."

Miss Beall nodded. Having run out of things to say, I stood looking at up her.

"So, Miss Ghere, did you come here begging?"

"No, ma'am. I... well... I was out begging with my friends and a stupid boy threw an egg and hit your door." I opened my hand to reveal the hankie with the egg oozing from it.

"Stay here a moment, please." The woman held up her index finger before going inside. She soon returned with a wet rag she wrapped around Cory's soiled hankie, lifting it from my hand. Then she used a clean edge of her rag to wipe the egg from my fingers. When she finished, she stepped back into the doorway.

"Miss Ghere, I suppose you would like a treat."

I nodded, not wishing to disagree with the woman.

I retrieved my hat from the edge of the porch and secured it to my head with its elastic strap. Then I picked up my sack. Standing before Ghosty, I opened it. That's when she slipped a silver coin from her pocket and flipped it into the midst of the sparse number of goodies I'd received.

"Thank you, Miss Beall."

"Now be on your way, child." With a wave of her hand, she stepped back another step and closed the oak door.

# Chapter 8

I stood for a moment at the edge of Laura Beall's porch, turning a Walking Liberty half-dollar I'd fished out of my sack over and over in my hand. It was the most money I had ever had in my life.

As I made my way toward the certainty of my family and friends, the sound of Gem's voice in the distance caught my attention, drawing me out of my thoughts of the odd woman I had just met.

"Annie, Annie! Where are you?" she called, her voice filled with irritation... maybe even a hint of concern. I stopped walking a few houses away from where the children gathered and stood there until my sister caught sight of me. "There you are." Gem ran up to me. "What is wrong with you? I told you to stay with the group."

After straightening my hat and scarf, she crossed her arms over her chest. "We only have a little time before we have to leave for the cemetery. Let's hurry and catch up with the others so we can go to a few more houses before we go home."

I walked a few feet, then stopped again.

"Annie, what's wrong now?" Gem demanded.

"I want to go home."

"There are several lights on up that way." Gem pointed toward the group of children waiting for us to rejoin them. I saw Fred pacing about as if he was trying to keep his charges corralled.

"I still want to go home."

"Not until you tell me what's wrong."

"Emerson Keller threw an egg at that house." I felt the tears forming in my eyes as I pointed toward the corner.

"Which house?"

"The Beall house." I sniffed, refusing to give into my tears. I'd shed enough bitter tears over the last few days.

"He didn't throw one of Mother's eggs, did he?"

"That's what I wondered."

"After Emerson threw the egg, then what happened?" my sister prompted me.

"I went to her house to clean the egg off her door."

If Blinn had known where you were going, he would have gone with you."

"If I had my broom right now, I'd whacked that Emerson so hard."

Gem laughed. "Fine, but don't let Emerson ruin your night. Beggars' Night only comes once a year. You can whack Emerson later."

I planned on whacking him good.

"I still want to go home."

"I'll take her." Blinn had walked up behind Gem as my sister and I were talking. "You catch up with the others. I'll walk Annie home. We'll see you at the house for the hayride."

With that, Blinn took my free hand. We walked back past the Beall house in silence, crossing the street and heading around the corner toward home.

Already hitched to the wagon, Old Barney stood out in front of our house, ready for our ride to Bunnell Cemetery. Blinn stroked the old horse's muzzle and cooed into his ear, "Good, boy."

I looked around, hoping to see Popo ready to man the wagon's front bench, but he was nowhere to be found.

"Do you want to go inside?" asked Blinn as he straightened Old Barney's harnesses.

"No, I'll wait here for everyone to come back."

Blinn nodded, then lifted me up into the bed of the wagon. I stood there looking down into his handsome face, one that looked much like my father's, with the same hard-to-tame wavy hair, the same chiseled cheekbones, and the same penetrating blue eyes (though my fifteen-year-old brother's eyes didn't seem capable of hiding secrets the way Popo's did.)

"I heard Miss Roxy is serving Coney dogs at the party tonight." It was Blinn's attempt to draw me out of my pensive mood.

"She told me that herself." I offered Blinn a weak smile that seemed to appease him. "Miss Roxy's word is good as gold. Get yourself a seat up front there." Blinn pointed to a hay bale just behind the front bench. "It'll be warmer there once we get on our way to Bunnell."

As Blinn joined my other brothers waiting on the curb, I scrabbled over the hay bales and made my way forward, then sat down to wait and to think. A nudge at my burlap sack that I still gripped in one hand interrupted my thoughts.

"Belva!" I cried. "What are you doing here?"

My cry caught Blinn's attention. His face appeared over the side of the wagon, followed by Cory's. Gus stood behind them, a few inches taller than his younger brothers.

"What's the goat doing in the wagon?" Blinn, the practical one, asked his quixotic twin.

"Belva had a hissy fit when I hitched up Old Barney, so I put her up front on the bench to keep company with her pal. I guess she hopped into the back here when Annie climbed in with her sack of goodies."

I opened my sack and pulled out the horehound hardtack, along with the popcorn ball Mother had given me, and handed them over to our hungry goat, who enjoyed the treats more than I would have.

Holding up my burlap sack, I asked, "Blinn, would you take this upstairs and put it under my bed, please? I don't want to carry it around at the party."

"Are you sure? Miss Roxy might have a few treats to add to it."

"I'm sure."

He took it and headed inside.

As my other two brothers moved away from the wagon, I stretched out on the hay to await the return of my friends and dumb ole Emerson. As I gazed upward, the dim streetlight flickered, then held, flickered again, then held. Except for the occasional swish of Old Barney's tail hitting the front of the wagon, the street in front of my house seemed draped in stillness. My mind wandered back to my encounter with Laura Beall.

In that stillness, I also thought about Thea, about her hearing loss that would change all our lives forever, but especially hers. I thought about Popo, about the solemn look on his face when he'd waved goodbye to me on Sunday. I wondered if he'd come home Friday, as usual.

But mostly, I thought about Ghosty... Laura Beall... the elusive woman who lived in the big Victorian house on the corner. Before this evening, I'd spent little time thinking about her. In fact, I could only recall seeing her a few times, on spring days when Gem and I caught sight of her from the corner. We'd watched as she moved gracefully about her front yard turning the blooms of her potted flowers toward the sun, a lacy bonnet shading her face and a long-sleeved full-length black dress fluttering out behind her, revealing the bottom edge of her white petticoat as she moved. I ran my hand along the skirt of my dress at the memory.

In the moonlight, I thought about Laura Beall's ivory skin and her dancing blue eyes. I thought about her calm voice and graceful movements. I thought about the gentle touch of her hand as she cleaned the egg from mine. More than anything, I thought about the silver half-dollar she'd flipped into my sack. In my grief over Thea and Popo, Laura Beall seemed a flicker of light on a still night. As I looked up at the sky, I did not know what would become of my father or Thea, but I knew I wanted to find out everything I could about the mysterious Laura Beall.

***

For half an hour, I waited with Belva in the back of the hay wagon for the other children to return from begging. Exhausted from the gathering clouds of my thoughts, I fell into a gentle half-sleep on my bed of prickly hay. Suddenly, I felt a nudge on the bottom of my foot.

"You forgot something, little sister."

I opened my eyes to see Gem standing over me, holding my broom. "Cory came through for us. He sneaked next door and grabbed it."

"I checked the back stoop first, but it wasn't there," Cory offered. "So I figured it was in Aunt Lo's painting shed."

"Aunt Lo didn't catch you, did she?" I asked groggily.

"No, Aunt Lo didn't catch me." Cory had already climbed onto the bench seat behind Old Barney, which was almost directly over my head. "But Aunt Iris did. I forgot the shed door squeaks when someone opens it. You know what sharp hearing Aunt Iris has."

Gem and I giggled.

"So, what happened?" Gem asked.

Cory weighed his words. "Aunt Iris yelled, 'Get back here with my broom, Blinn Ghere, or I'll call your mother.' Since she thought I was Blinn, I just kept running."

Gem shook her head. "After fifteen years, she still can't tell the two of you apart. It's not like you look a thing alike."

"Aunt Iris has worn out this broom." I looked at the blackened tree branch with jagged bristles bound to the stick with cord. "This thing must be older than MaMaw. Why is everyone so protective of it?"

"Because it once belonged to an old crone. It was her prized possession." A sinister smile spread across Cory's face.

"Cory, are Aunt Lo's paint boxes still in the shed?"

"Nope. It looks like she already stashed them inside for the winter." Gem and I gave each other a knowing look. We knew exactly where Aunt Lo stashed those paint boxes.

***

Aunt Lo loved to tell the story.

When the first chill of autumn came that summer after Aunt Lo had "misappropriated" her brother's "useful" shed—"ramshackle" was a more accurate description—Aunt Lo gathered her paint boxes and moved them onto their back porch for safekeeping for the winter. Even after several months, Aunt Iris hadn't gotten over the "tragic loss" of the shed to her sister-in-law and had maintained an intimate relationship with her festering grudge since the takeover. When Iris spotted LoRetta's paint boxes on the back porch, she threw a royal hissy fit. "I will not have your smelly paints on my porch," she insisted.

"They don't smell," Aunt Lo had replied calmly.

"You have taken over our shed with those horrible smelly paints, but you will not take up so much as one square inch of this porch for your heathen hobby."

"Fine." Aunt Lo had gathered up her paint boxes and huffed out the back door. A minute later, she had walked in the front door, up the stairs and into Iris's bedroom, where she slipped the paint boxes under her bed.

"I've stored my paint boxes there every winter since," she quipped.

Aunt Lo was a pistil. Everyone said so.

***

"It won't be long before we get underway," Cory called over his shoulder before turning his full attention to our horse.

Gem dropped the broom with a *thunk*, then sat down next to me, settling her back against the headboard. Then she pulled me up against her, an arm draped around my shoulders. We watched as Blinn helped the children, one at a time, into the wagon by the light of the torch. Pauline scrambled over the hay, Helen on her heels, taking seats on the bench to my left. Charlie sat down in the hay next to Gem while Bernard took up a sentry position on the wagon bench directly across from Pauline and behind Cory, who was offering words of encouragement to Old Barney ahead of our journey. Surrounded by so many important characters in the story of my life, my heart ached for that one missing player.

Where are you, Popo?

As Emerson climbed aboard, Pauline leaned down and place her lips near my ear. "You missed it. I caught Emerson peeing in Mrs. Potter's flower bed... a big smelly puddle. I wonder if her prized chrysanthemums will bloom next fall after that downpour."

I looked up at Gem, who smirked before shooting Emerson a menacing scowl. He didn't notice.

"I'll tell you all about it later." Pauline leaned back against the side of the wagon and Helen snuggled up against her. That's when it occurred to me that the temperature had dropped.

"All aboard." Blinn's last call for the hayride. Refusing help from my brother, Marshall Manning somehow hoisted himself into the wagon and rolled into a sitting position in the hay. Everyone laughed, with Marshall laughing the hardest. I noticed pieces of hay sticking out of his coal-black hair and caught sight of his classic profile, back-lit by the golden light of Blinn's torch.

Perfect. It amazed me that this newcomer had so easily found his place in our lives. I thought about Earlynn Musgrove, a girl I had known since first grade. Would she be here with us tonight if she had survived last winter's plague? Probably not.

Blinn lifted Albright Flud into the wagon. Bright and gregarious, Albright was two, years younger than me, but only one grade behind me in school. Pauline noticed one day that his mop of sandy hair matched his freckles.

Albright had been to our house a handful of times. I think rumors of Charlie's stack of newspapers from the *Washington Daily News* lured him to our house the first time, whereas most of our friends showed up hoping to get some of Mother's baked goods. Albright was the only child I knew who shared Charlie's interest in world news. Thereafter, when he happened by, it seemed he enjoyed sitting at our kitchen table talking to the adults about adult things rather than playing with Charlie and me.

Albright certainly baffled Popo. "For the life of me, I can't figure out how a child that young can see through all of life's bullcrap."

"Augie, that language is not appropriate in front of the children."

"Sorry, Maggie." Popo looked over at me and winked. I heard much worse on Friday afternoons at the Blue and White Café.

Before getting underway, Blinn doused the torch, climbed aboard the wagon, and sat down in the hay. Barbara Jean Smith suddenly jumped up from where she was sitting, crawled over several children, and sat down on my brother's lap. Blinn looked at Gem and me and shrugged. Then he raised an arm, pointed forward, and yelled, "All clear, let's roll."

Gus looked back at his load, then shook the reigns gently across Old Barney's back.

"Giddy up, boy."

"Are you okay, Annie?" Gem pulled me closer to her.

"Yep."

"I know you're thinking about Popo and Thea."

"Yep." And Laura Beall, but I didn't say so.

Once the wagon found its rhythm, I settled in to enjoy the ride.

"Why aren't you with Fred?"

"He went on to the Blue and White Café to help the Lockwoods with the final preparations for the party. I wanted to ride to the cemetery with my little sister. Is that okay with you?"

"I thought you didn't want to go to the party. What changed your mind?"

"Coney dogs. And I wouldn't miss seeing you wallop Emerson with Aunt Iris' broom for the world."

We rode along in silence for a while.

"Is anything else bothering you, little sister?"

"No, I'm fine." I thought about the Walking Liberty half-dollar that Laura Beall had given me. I decided I'd tell Gem about that later.

"We're sisters, so if you want to tell me any secrets, I promise to keep them between us." Gem squeezed my shoulder.

"I know. But I don't have any secrets to share." Well, maybe there was something akin to a secret between Mother and me, but I wasn't ever going to tell Gem about that.

"I have a secret. Do you want to hear it?"

I nodded eagerly.

"Do you promise not to tell? Sisters don't tell each other's secrets."

"I know. I promise." Whispering into my ear, she told me the biggest secret I'd ever heard.

"Fred is fourteen."

Holy cow.

# Chapter 9

While on our way to Bunnell Cemetery, I again put thoughts of Laura Beall and the silver half-dollar she'd given me out of my mind. But for the *clack-a-de-clack* of Old Barney's hooves and the churn of the wooden wagon wheels on the pavement, we rode in silence.

Having had her fill of Aunt Iris's horehound drops, Belva quit begging for treats from the children and settled into the loose hay in the middle of the wagon to enjoy the ride. As we left the dim light of town behind, I could see a cascade of stars polka-dotting the sky. All my thoughts about Popo and Thea seemed to drift upward, leaving me gently pitching and swaying with the motion of the wagon, carefree and completely at peace for the first time in days.

Gus's storytelling during our ride through the graveyard wasn't as eloquent as Popo's, but good enough to scare a wagon full of children half to death. I looked at my brother with greater admiration. While Aunt Lo occupied all camps in the hierarchy of my immediate family, Gus commanded the middle ground, that sacred space between my often-feuding parents. Gus was the conduit that bridged the chasms, the glue that bound the opposites. I often pondered how my oldest brother could be so much like both of our parents, the perfect collaboration of their union, easily displaying the resolute temperament of my mother in one moment, and the flamboyant fun-loving nature of my father in the next.

On any day, Gus was the hard-working miser counting his pennies behind closed doors and the happy-go-lucky ne'er-do-well smoking cigarettes behind the barn. But it was on that Beggars' Night I saw my oldest brother clearly for the first time. Out of Popo's shadow, he was his own man, the best of everyone I had ever known. His voice rising out of the quietude, a flourish of his hand for emphasis, Gus took command of the chore left to him by our absentee father.

"Here lies the body of Malcolm M. Marlowe, murdered in his bed on Beggars' Night by a stranger-come-to-town, a mysterious case of mistaken identity, or so the townsfolk thought... at first." I realized I wanted to be like Gus when I grew up.

***

The party in the basement of the Blue and White Café was the best one ever. The Lockwoods had decorated the room with papier-mâché bats hung from the ceiling with string. In one corner Paul Lockwood had built a small graveyard, with black cats made of painted cardboard lurking about the rows of tombstones engraved with inscriptions such as "Ima Goner," "R.I.P. Jack O. Lantern," and "Gil O'Teen—A tisket, a tasket, his head was in a basket," and my favorite, "R.I.P. Seymour Butts."

The Lockwoods topped the tables in the basement room with bowls filled with candy corn and carved pumpkins Miss Roxy would certainly use in tomorrow's pie. After our hayride through the cemetery, we spent the rest of the evening in the basement of the Blue and White Café, bobbing for apples, playing Pin the Tail on the Donkey and pulling taffy until it turned a dingy gray from our unwashed hands. The evening ended with Miss Roxy serving Coney dogs to all the children, as promised, from her deceased mother's fine silver platter. That Roxy Lockwood was a class act.

I won first place, a large caramel apple rolled in pecans, for the best costume. Pauline won second place for her old crone's costume. Her costume wasn't all that good, but she had fashioned a wart from dried glue and affixed it to the side of her nose. No one figured out how she'd given that wart its greenish tinge, and she wasn't telling. I told Mother later that it was Pauline's wart that won second prize, a roll of Necco Wafers, which my best friend promptly handed over to Gem.

***

It was already past nine o'clock when Paul Lockwood announced the end of the party. I grabbed my hat and broom and made my way up the basement steps to wait. Gus appeared first, giving the children he'd hauled over to the party from our side of town instructions as they ascended from the basement.

"Let's load up. Your parents are probably wondering what happened to you, so don't dawdle."

The line trailed through the narrow aisle between the counter and the row of tables. I ignored my friends' pleas to get in the wagon as Gus instructed. Before long, a familiar voice boomed up the stairwell... the person I'd been waiting for was clomping toward me.

"Take that." I walloped Emerson Keller on the back of his legs with my broom.

"Gee, Annie, what was that for?"

"For throwing that egg at Miss Beall's door."

"Oh, you mean Ghosty's door? Ghosty, Ghosty, tonight's your night..." I walloped him again, only this time on the front of his legs.

"Stop that, Annie!" he yelled. I felt the broom slip from my hands. "Annie, what's going on here?"

My brother Gus was next to me, my weapon in his hand.

"Emerson threw an egg that hit Laura Beall's door."

"I hope it wasn't one of Mother's eggs," Gus opined.

"I bet it was."

The anger on Emerson's face melted away, a glimmer of fear taking its place. "Annie owes me an apology," he insisted. Emerson was good at skirting the important things.

"You are absolutely right," agreed Gus. I looked at my brother with the evil eye of an old crone. "There is no excuse for hitting each other. Tomorrow after school, I'll bring Annie around to your house to apologize. I want your parents to be there to witness her making amends."

Emerson's eyes widened to the size of silver dollars.

"In the meantime," Gus continued, "I will make sure none of Mother's eggs are missing to clear your good name. Does that sound good to you?"

"No, I'm good." With that, Emerson pushed through the crowd of children and darted out the door.

With the broom still in his hand, Gus turned to me, a hint of a smile on his lips. "We don't hit other people, not even if they deserve it, little sister." With that, he walked out the front door, urging the children to hurry as he went.

As Charlie, Pauline, Helen, and Bernard gathered round me, I frowned at the thought that I hadn't whacked Emerson enough. "If Gus hadn't taken my broom, I'd whack him again." Pauline was the only one of my friends who laughed.

***

That night after everyone had gone to bed, I tip-toed out of my room and across the hallway to my parent's bedroom. The door was slightly ajar, so I pushed it open a few inches to see if Mother was asleep. She was sitting in her chair by the window, looking up South Street toward town.

Lit only by the dim light from the hallway, Mother's face reminded me of MaMaw Ghere's in the days following the death of PaPaw Ghere. Placid, emotionless, almost indifferent, Aunt Lo had called it the face of mourning. Was Mother mourning? Certainly, she had experienced loss. She had given birth to a beautiful baby girl, who, despite the odds, was perfect in every way.

Now that Thea had lost much of her hearing, did Mother think her daughter was imperfect? Maybe nothing else mattered to Mother now, including Popo's absence?

In the dim light shining from the lamp on Mother's nightstand, I could see her long wavy hair, recently released from the braid she wore wound about her head, cascading over her shoulders and down her back. She held her hairbrush in one hand as she sat motionless, gazing into the night. As I paused in the doorway, deciding if I should enter or return to bed, I saw the light of the waning moonlight dancing across her profile through the wind-blown trees. If I hadn't known better, I'd have thought she was someone I'd never met before, a solitary stranger in a house filled with life, her face completely devoid of emotion.

"Mother, can I tell you something?"

"Anna." Mother turned her head to look at me and said my name again, almost to herself. Her impassive eyes regained their life as she invited me in. "Come talk to me, Anna."

The last time I had kept something from Mother, that secret had hurt her terribly. Now she held out her hand to me, a gesture that immediately put me at ease. I knew I was a welcomed visitor.

With my hand in hers, Mother moved from her window seat onto the bed and pulled me up next to her. As I leaned against her, I noticed a few silver strands of hair woven subtly through her thick, golden hair. Silver and gold, the colors of Christmas.

"What do you want to tell me, Anna?" she asked as she wrapped her arms around me.

Without hesitation, the words poured out of me. I told Mother about how Emerson Keller had thrown an egg that hit Laura Beall's door, and that I'd sneaked up onto her porch to clean it off. I told her that before I'd gotten off her porch, Laura Beall had discovered me there, with the egg wrapped in the hankie I'd taken off my neck.

I told her that Laura Beall had cleaned the egg from my hand, and we had talked, and that she had placed a coin in my beggar's sack. I left out that the coin was a shiny Walking Liberty half-dollar, not because I wanted to keep more secrets from Mother, but because I wanted to have time alone to look at it, to turn it over in my hands, to feel the sway of being able to have my own money and to take care of myself. I also left out the part about whacking Emerson with Aunt Iris' broom, knowing that detail would get back to her soon enough.

"That's quite a story."

"Laura Beall told me that your Uncle Frank and Aunt Nina had been kind to her," I added. "She said she met you and Popo when you first moved into this house." I looked up into Mother's face, then waited. It was her turn to tell me a story.

According to Mother, when Uncle Frank bought this property, he'd purchased two lots, the one on the creek where the house stands, and the one next to it. With the same farmer's blood that flows through her own veins, Mother described how Uncle Frank had planted a large vegetable garden and a small apple orchard with eight trees on the second lot.

"Without realizing it, Uncle Frank's plans for his own family allowed us to keep food in our bellies during these hard times, much of the food grown in our garden."

"And from Aunt Rachel and Uncle Maddy's farm?" I asked. Mother nodded.

"So many people are homeless and go hungry. We should never forget how fortunate we are. I feel grateful every time I think of how my dear Uncle Frank's misfortune became our good fortune."

Mother kissed my head and ran her fingers through a few strands of my hair before continuing. "When Rachel and I were about the ages of you and Gem, we came here with Father Blinn to visit Uncle Frank and Aunt Nina just after they moved in."

Mother paused again as she searched her memories. "Uncle Frank and my father were very close," she continued. "Although my father was a few years older than Frank, he was so proud of his younger brother. As you know, after my grandfather died, Father Blinn stayed in the country to take over the family farm. Uncle Frank was much like your cousin Charlie. He loved words and writing and decided he wanted to write for the newspaper."

Then she told me that when Frank was at Culver Military Academy studying, he met Nina, the daughter of the school's commandant. The two fell in love. After he graduated and took a job in journalism at the *Morning Times* here in town, the couple married. His father, who is my great-grandfather, gave him the money to build this house. It took many months to get the house finished, but finally the day arrived when the happy couple moved in. A few months later, they found out Nina was pregnant. Both wanted a big family to fill their new house. Aunt Nina died in childbirth, and Frank's infant son died three days later. "The tragedies devastated my uncle."

Mother wiped away a tear from her cheek before continuing. "Frank was never the same. After he buried his wife and son in Bunnell Cemetery, he buried himself in his work. He worked long hours, took most of his meals at the Blue and White Café, and only came home to sleep. A few years later, the *Chicago Tribune* offered my uncle the position of editor-in-chief. He seemed relieved to leave town. He never returned, nor did he ever re-marry."

Mother paused a moment in her story, shifting on the bed.

"When Uncle Frank died, Father Blinn inherited this house and suggested that Popo and I move in. After Father Blinn died, he left this house to me and the farm to your Aunt Rachel."

"Will the farm belong to Charlie one day?" I asked.

"Yes, if he wants it, although I expect he'll follow in his great uncle's footsteps. He'll tell anyone who will listen he wants to be a journalist."

"What about Laura Beall? Tell me more about her."

Mother told me that Laura Beall and her father had moved into the big Victorian house on the corner a few months before Uncle Frank and Aunt Nina finished their house. Laura's father owned the Wanatah Railroad.

"We heard that her mother passed away suddenly, so her father moved her here from Chicago."

"Mother, how old is Miss Beall?" That was the question I had on my mind since meeting her.

"I think she's Aunt Rachel's age, about forty."

"But she looks so old. Her hair is white, and she wears thick spectacles."

"Occasionally, Anna, people are born without color in their skin and hair," Mother explained. "They lack pigmentation."

"Pigmentation?" I mimicked Mother's pronunciation of the new word.

"Ask Charlie to look it up for you at the library."

"He might want to put that word in his collection."

Mother smiles and nodded before continuing. "Other problems go along with the lack of coloration. I know she doesn't see well, even with her spectacles."

I pondered everything Mother was telling me. "Do you know anyone else who was born without pigmentation?"

"Just one other person. You know him, too. Old Man Gregory."

I thought about Popo's friend. "I just thought he was old."

"He is that. Did you know that Old Man Gregory is Father Blinn's and Uncle Frank's second cousin?"

"No, I didn't. Why didn't Popo tell me that? We talk to him almost every Friday."

"Maybe he thought you knew."

I sat there in my mother's arms, thinking about all she'd told me, allowing silence to envelop us. After a time, Mother sat up straight and nudged me. "Don't you think it's time to go to bed, young lady? You have school in the morning."

I wriggled out of Mother's arms and stood up beside her bed. I had one last question for my mother, the real reason I'd come to visit her.

"Can I go to Laura Beall's house again? I want to thank her for the coin she gave me."

Mother smiled.

"That's a wonderful idea, Anna. Come straight home from school tomorrow, and I'll have some fresh-baked cookies you can take her. How does that sound?"

I nodded eagerly. It couldn't wait to see the mysterious Laura Beall again.

# Chapter 10

I stood on Laura Beall's front walk, looking up at her beautiful Victorian house. Though I lived less than a block away, I saw it in all its splendid detail for the first time. How could I have missed something so extraordinary that was so close to where I lived? Maybe because my life flowed in the other direction. When I ran off my front porch, I usually turned right toward downtown to school or the library, Pauline's or Helen's houses, the A&P or the Wanatah Depot. My life followed a distinct path carved out for me by other people in my life.

Today I turned left.

Lined with a neat row of boxwood hedge on either side, Laura Beall's front walk invited me forward as I absorbed the details of this curious place. Painted beige with cream-colored trim and a scalloped blue roof, the Beall house reminded me of the dollhouses I'd seen in the Thrasher's Department Store window the Christmas before last. The only other Victorian house in town I knew of was now a boarding house near the Nickel Plate Roundhouse off Morrison Street. Mother had such fond memories of that house growing up, memories she loved to share with Gem and me when she felt nostalgic.


***


The house in Mother's past was once owned by the Goodman family, the established undertakers in town. Mother went to school with Billy Goodman, the town's current undertaker. Mother said that for a man who dealt with death daily, he was always so full of life.

During their high school days, Billy hosted lemonade parties on Friday afternoons during the spring for all the high school students. Billy held the parties on the Victorian's wide wrap-around porch. Everyone came. Even those students who had to rush off to after-school jobs came by to enjoy an hour of socializing on the Goodman's lemonade porch. It had become a town tradition by decree of Mrs. Goodman, Billy's socialite mother.

The first spring when Billy introduced his get-togethers, his mother got wind that one schoolmate wasn't in attendance because of his work obligations. She immediately telephoned the boy's employer and persuaded him to make accommodation for the boy. The employer consented, though both he and Mrs. Goodman would deny to their dying day that their discussion involved any threats by Mrs. Goodman to withhold business. Everyone knew otherwise.

For the elegant spring soirees, lavish bouquets of seasonal flowers arranged to perfection in Mrs. Goodman's best crystal vases helped secure the starched white tablecloths from aberrant northern Indiana breezes.

"Mother doesn't actually arrange the flowers herself," Billy once admitted to his friends, who encircled him on the porch. "She doesn't want to risk a pricked finger. However, she oversees the arrangement to the last flower."

According to Billy, his mother delivered exacting and brisk instructions that often result in her housemaids suffering sore fingers for the rest of the week. When spring passed into summer, the house staff breathed a collective sigh of relief.

Two housemaids attended the tables, keeping the Wedgwood pitchers filled with Mrs. Goodman's own special recipe for fresh-squeezed lemonade, along with a supply of sparkling crystal glasses. (Billy insisted his mother's secret ingredient was extra sugar. "Everything tastes better with more sugar," he quipped.)

Another housemaid served petit fours brought in from a baker in Delphi. The housemaid served the delicacies from a silver tray lined with doilies, walking silently amongst the guests with straight backs and kindly demeanors. Guests loved counting the number of bandaged fingers the three had between them.

Billy was the perfect host, mingling among his honored guests, making certain there were no wallflowers, no one left out. He made it his mission to ensure everyone at the high school knew everyone else. The students bonded for life, thanks to Billy Goodman.

Precisely at six o'clock, Mrs. Goodman opened a set of French doors off the porch and called out sweetly, "Yoo-hoo, Billy, dear. Supper is served," the cue for everyone to say their goodbyes and go home to their own suppers.

My mother said she had often lingered in front of the house to watch the kitchen staff descend on the lemonade porch and clear it of any trace of the party that had ended just moments before. Then she lingered another moment, trying to imagine how it felt to be rich.

***

Not as ornate nor as superfluous as the Goodman's former Victorian, the Beall house was impressive, with detailed gingerbread trim accenting its many peaks. I noticed a stone lintel above the grand oaken door that read, "One note at a time." I also noticed a colorful stained-glass image of a train that filled the transom above the window next to the door. The porch that wrapped around one side of the house had a twin on the second floor.

My favorite aspect of the house was its turret, topped with a pointed roofline that mimicked the crone's hat I'd worn the night before. The porches on both floors followed the curve of the turret before straightening out across the front of the house. Three long windows in the turret faced up Harrison Street toward a frontier I had never consciously explored, except in the fading light of Beggars' Night under the watchful eye of Popo or one of my older siblings.

As I stood looking at the house, a plate of Mother's apple sugar cookies wrapped in waxed paper in one hand, I vowed that before the blistering cold of winter set in, I would walk around this block... and every unfamiliar block I came upon... to take in the details of the town that enveloped my life. I knew Charlie would be up for such an adventure and would put his vast vocabulary to good use to describe what we saw. It surprised me that Charlie hadn't already thought of it.

As I stepped forward, I again noticed the concrete step with "Beall" carved into it. Today I walked up the steps, crossed the porch, and knocked on the door without hesitation. As I waited, I wondered if Miss Beall had housemaids, servants, and a kitchen staff as the Goodman family did.

A few moments later, I heard footsteps, then Laura's voice, faint behind the heavy door, asked, "Who's there?"

"It's Anna Ghere."

The lock turned, the door opened, and I got my first closeup look at Laura Beall in full daylight. I noticed she was wearing the same long-sleeved black dress she'd worn the night before. The dress hugged her thin body, then flared slightly at the waistline, its skirt likely held in perfect form with a full cotton petticoat. It had to be a petticoat. You can hear crinolines coming.

Her delphinium-colored eyes danced behind her spectacles as she looked down at me, her tiny figure somehow filling the doorway. "Miss Ghere, to what do I owe the pleasure of your visit?"

Her tone was flat, emotionless. Off-putting, even. Had I made a mistake coming here again?

"I-I-ah..."

"Miss Ghere, I promise not to bite," she urged. "Why have you come?"

I held out the plate with the cookies on it. "To thank you for your generosity last night," I muttered. "These are cookies my mother baked for you. They're delicious. Mother makes the best cookies in town."

"How thoughtful, child." Miss Beall seemed pleased with my gift.

"Mother sends her regards," I continued. "She asks that you please return the plate. With all the boys in our house, plates are in short supply."

Laura Beall's wry smile lit up my heart.

"It is so kind of you to think of me," she replied. "Your visit today is most fortuitous, as I have something of yours. Won't you please come in?"

As I stepped across the threshold, Laura Beall lifted the plate from my hand, and stepped aside, an outstretched arm directing me forward.

More beautiful than anything I ever imaged, I looked around the house, mesmerized by what I saw. In the reception hall, a crystal chandelier hung overhead. A beautiful wrought iron staircase with polished wooden handrails rose to my left. The only piece of furniture in the room that was larger than the one I shared with my sisters was a solid mahogany hall tree that sat just inside the door. It had a mirror, and an attached upholstered seat, perhaps where Miss Beall or her guests sat to remove their boots. I glimpsed to my right into what appeared to be a music room. A grand piano, much like the one at Holy Cross Church, occupied the center of the room, with two groupings of couches and chairs positioned along two of the walls. One overstuffed chair with an ottoman sat next to the piano.

I also noticed an inviting bay window with a cushioned seat that overlooked the front porch. Several books lay scattered across the seat. I imagined Charlie sitting there, content in his world of words.

"Child, would you care to join me for tea and one of your mother's cookies?" Miss Beall asked as we entered the formal parlor. Without waiting for my answer, she continued, "As I wasn't expecting company, I hope you don't mind me serving you in the kitchen."

"No, Miss," I replied. "The kitchen is fine."

She disappeared into the kitchen, but I stopped in the parlor to take in its unusual tidiness. A sofa covered in red velvet, its wooden legs and frame polished to perfection, faced a corner fireplace. Two upholstered chairs flanked the couch, and a coffee table that held a silver tea service sat in front of it. I saw another room off the parlor, but the door was partially closed. I wondered if I would ever know what was in there.

Laura Beall's kitchen was the most modern I'd ever seen. With bright yellow walls and a checkerboard green and white linoleum floor, the kitchen looked unused, spotless. White cabinets, with solid doors on the bottom cabinets and glass doors on the upper ones, lined two walls.

The sink, with its plumbing hidden behind a set of double doors, was built into a cabinet that had a wide bank of drawers on either side. A set of three windows, each pane covered with a white sheer curtain, dominated the wall over the sink, capturing the late afternoon sun, making it unnecessary to turn on the overhead electric lights.

"Please sit over there." She pointed to a small table that sat in front of a window overlooking the backyard. "Make yourself comfortable while I make the tea."

As I wriggled in my chair, a heard a clock chime four o'clock. I spotted the wooden mantel clock sitting on a shelf above the windows. I wondered who climbed up there every day or two to keep the clock wound. I'd looked around for any sign of a housemaid or cook but saw no evidence of one.

A lacy tablecloth covered the rectangle table where I sat. Two green chairs painted to match the green floor squares sat across from each other. I watched in silence as Miss Beall moved easily around her kitchen. Mother told me the woman couldn't see well, even with her spectacles, but it seemed she moved through her kitchen tasks as gracefully as Mother moved through hers.

After putting the teakettle on the stove, she set the table, placing two china teacups and matching saucers on the table, along with cloth napkins and silver teaspoons. I watched as she opened her refrigerator and pulled out a bottle of cream. To me, her refrigerator was a marvel to behold. From where I sat, I could read the word "Majestic" on a panel atop the refrigerator's two doors.

I remembered the story of the refrigerator in our house. Popo purchased the Frigidaire second-hand (or as Popo referred to it, "almost brand new") soon after he and Mother moved into Uncle Frank's house with their growing family. Popo had it delivered for Mother's birthday. She was delighted to have such a modern appliance until the bill collector began calling to secure Popo's late payments. When Father Blinn become ill and moved into the house to be near his doctor, he paid off the used Frigidaire to save his daughter the constant irritation. Mother kept her old icebox, which she had moved to the back porch, to store whatever she can't get into the Frigidaire.

Miss Beall poured a few ounces of cream into a silver cow creamer and set it with a matching sugar bowl on a small silver tray. She added two small plates to the tray, each with one of Mother's cookies on it, and placed the tray on the table.

She filled a silver tea ball and placed it into an ornate china teapot, carefully pouring boiling water over it, and left it on the counter before sitting down across from me.

"We'll have to give the tea a bit of time to steep. This is my favorite Earl Grey from France. I save it for special occasions such as this. I hope you enjoy it."

A few minutes later, she retrieved the pot and poured tea into our cups. "Oh, before I forget, here is your handkerchief, cleaned and pressed." She pulled it from her apron pocket and laid it beside my plate.

"Thank you, Miss," was all I could think to say.

"One sugar, or two?" she asked me.

"Two, please."

"Two it is." The woman picked up the small silver tongs and dropped two sugar cubes into my cup and one into hers.

We sipped our tea and nibbled our cookies in silence for a few moments.

"I am quite fond of cookies. This one is delicious, just as you said it would be. I have a favorite baker in Delphi who bakes for me, but your mother's cookie may be the best I've ever eaten. Do you know her secret?"

"Apples," I answered. "She's saving her sugar for Thanksgiving, but we have plenty of apples and honey."

"I see," Miss Beall replied.

As another long stretch of silence played out between us, I pushed away all the questions I had about this woman who lived alone in this big house. I was trying to do what Gem taught me to do in uncertain situations: to let things settle.

"Forgive me, child." Laura Beall poured the last of the tea into our cups. "Not having any children, I'm not sure what you'd like to talk about. Maybe you could tell me something about yourself, then I'll tell you something about me. How does that sound?"

I was eager to learn about her, so I agreed.

"I'm nine years old, almost ten. I'm in the fourth grade."

That seemed to get the conversation going.

"Do you enjoy going to school? I never went to school. My parents hired a tutor who came to our home to teach me because I couldn't see well. Mr. Ellis was very strict, but I learned so much from him."

"School is fine, but I learn more from my cousin Charlie. He reads to me and explains all the words I don't know. He's not really teaching me, but I pick up things, anyway."

"Is Charlie the son of your mother's sister, Rachel?"

"Yes, Aunt Rachel and Uncle Maddy live on the family farm out near Mulberry, but Charlie wanted to go to the school here in town. He lives with us during the school year. I don't like it when he goes home for the summer. He's my best friend, besides Pauline and Helen."

Miss Beall smiled. "Do you play with Pauline and Helen after school?" she asked.

"I used to, but not much anymore. Charlie and I like to go to the library after school to help Aunt Lo. Charlie started going to help her shelve books and clean last winter when my baby sister and I came down with scarlet fever. Charlie loves to climb up on a stool in front of the big dictionary stand and write down words that interest him. He collects words. He's going to be a journalist someday, just like Uncle Frank."

"Scarlet fever is a terrible disease. I'm glad to you and your sister recovered."

I set my cup on the saucer and lowered my head, trying to fight the anguish that unexpectedly welled up in my throat. I sniffled and wiped my eyes with the napkin I had on my lap. Just as I thought I'd swallowed the sorrow and heartache that had plagued me the last few days, they suddenly flowed out of me in a torrent. I told her about Thea being deaf from the scarlet fever, and that my brothers, sisters, Charlie, and I knew for some months but didn't tell Mother or Popo. I told her how I'd accidentally blurted it out at Thea's birthday dinner, and how Mother had gotten upset with us, and Popo had gotten angry with Mother. I told her that Popo left, and I didn't know if he'd ever come back.

I stopped when I had nothing left to say.

She sat patiently until I regained my composure.

"I just want everything to go back to the way it was."

"Child." Her voice was gentle, yet firm. "Grief is but a temporary visitor. Sadness and despair pass eventually if you remind yourself to step into the next sunset with your eyes on the horizon. Life only moves in one direction, and that's forward. You must be brave and carry on."

"How do I do that?"

With her dancing blue eyes looking into my eyes, I heard joy in her voice. "Like everything else in life... one note at a time."

# Chapter 11

After school the next day, Charlie and I found Mother in the kitchen fixing supper, Thea at her feet stacking wooden blocks into tall towers. Mother moved gracefully around the kitchen, stepping over and around my sister in fluid steps, the obstacle in her way inspiring an intricate variation in Mother's routine. Whenever Aunt Lo showed up to help Mother in the kitchen, she always moved Thea to the parlor for safekeeping.

"Have you seen your brothers?" Mother asked when she saw us, a mother hen rounding up her chicks... that's what Popo always called it.

"Gus and Blinn are tending to Old Barney and Belva. Since it's supposed to get colder tonight, Blinn wanted to make sure there was extra bedding in the chicken coop. It's time to batten down the hatches."

Mother smiled at Charlie's description. My cousin loved words. He'd work words that were new to him into the conversation whenever he had the chance, just to try them out.

"Where's Cory?"

"He's across the street at Bernard's."

Mother wiped her hands on her apron. With her arms crossed over her chest, she looked me in the eye, her signal she needed more details. "Cory, Bernard, and Cooter were out front when Charlie and I got home. When I stopped to pet Cooter, I overheard Bernard telling Cory that the horse was lame again, and he wanted him to take another look at his hoof. Cory said they'd have to leave the cart out front to get the horse back to the shed out of the wind. He's going to get Gus and Blinn to help them push the cart around back later."

Charlie chimed in, "Cory thinks they need the farrier, but Bernard thinks his dad needs to finish paying off his bill from the last time."

"Charlie, please go across the street and tell the boys when they're finished tending to the horse, Bernard is welcome to come for supper." When Mother could spare the food, she invited Bernard for supper because she knew the boy rarely got a decent meal from his own mother. While Bernard's blessings over our table added an uncomfortable reverence to our usual mealtime commotion, I believed Mother tolerated Bernard's fervent pleas to God Almighty to make up for her own shortcomings in the prayer department.

"Gem is listening to the radio in the green room with Fred, so I expect he'll be staying for supper, too," Mother mused.

Now was my chance. "I'm going up to my room for a few minutes," I announced.

"Fine," Mother replied as she began peeling a potato, "but I'll need you back down here shortly to set the table."

"I won't be long," I promised.

After pulling off my coat and hat and adding them to the heap on the coat rack by the front door, I ran up the stairs. A moment later, I was sitting on the floor next to my bed. I lifted the edge of the blanket and spotted my beggar's sack tucked underneath where Blinn had left it. I was ready to get a good look at the Walking Liberty half-dollar Laura Beall had given me on Beggars' Night.

I undid the loose knot in the piece of cord Blinn used to secure the top of the canvas sack, climbed onto the bed and dumped out the contents of my beggar's sack, sticky stuff and all.

I picked out a few items I thought Belva might enjoy, including a couple of soft apples and another popcorn ball. Then I saw it, the shiny coin Laura Beall had flipped into my sack. Turning it over in my fingers, I inspected it... the Walking Liberty on one side, an American eagle on the other. The blue-white silver of the coin fascinated me. Of course, I'd owned plenty of pennies in my life, and a bunch of nickels, which I'd spent on candy or a film at the Clinton Theater. I'd even had the occasional dime, but this was the first half dollar I ever called my own.

A few minutes later, Mother called me to help her. I slipped the coin into a shoebox with my other prized possessions I kept hidden in my drawer, and I ran down the stairs carrying the goodies I'd picked out for Belva.

I called out the backdoor to Gus to retrieve the treats for our goat. "I hope she's not hankering for horehound drops because I'm all out."

"I think she's had enough horehound to last her a lifetime. Haven't we all?"

"Anna," Mother called. I waved to Gus and closed the backdoor and joined Mother in the kitchen. "Please set the table. Bernard, Fred, and your Aunt LoRetta are joining us, so we'll need three extra plates. Let's eat in the dining room. There's more room in there."

As I set the table, I kept one eye on the clock, as I always did on Friday afternoons. As four o'clock approached, Mother poked her head into the dining room where I was finishing up. "Tell Fred we'll be eating at half-past five o'clock, if he wants to let his mother know where he'll be."

I placed the last spoon in place and ran to the green room to deliver the message. Then I grabbed my coat from the rack, ran straight out the front door and up South Street toward the Wanatah Depot.

The 4:20 came and went without hide nor hair of my father, confirmation of what I already suspected, that my parents' most recent spat was serious. As I sat on the wooden bench on the platform, the one I'd sat on with Popo the Friday before, it occurred to me that Mother knew my father wouldn't be home for supper, although she never told me not to set a place for him at the table, or not to meet him at the Wanatah Depot.

A few moments after the 5:05 to Indianapolis pulled away from the station, my sister, Gem, appeared on the platform shadowed by Fred and Blinn.

Gem sat down next to me, took my hand, and warmed it between her woolen mittens. I thought about the brown leaf that Popo had pulled from my hair and freed to flutter along the platform last week. Where was that leaf now? Where was Popo now?

"I'll say it again, Annie. Popo will be back. I don't know when, but he will come home, eventually. I promise."

"I think he's angry with me for ruining Thea's birthday."

"You didn't ruin Thea's birthday. It was time Mother and Popo understood what happened to Thea. Now all we can do is to be patient and give Mother time to mull things over. Once she does, she'll figure out how to help Thea. As for Popo... " My sister shook her head.

"Gem, I told Popo it wasn't Mother's fault."

"I'm glad you understand that. After the fever let go of Thea, Mother still had to nurse her back to health, and Thea still has a long way to go. Popo expected Mother to do something the moment she learned about Thea's hearing loss. Mother doesn't work that way. She's a muller. Mother stays put and figures things out. That's just her way of doing things."

I couldn't stop another rush of tears.

"Annie," Gem continued, "Popo leaving has nothing to do with you. That's just his way of dealing with things. When he figures things out, he'll come back."

While Popo's weekly returns home from his travels across the state caused much excitement among my siblings and Charlie, Gem was the exception. My twelve-year-old sister seemed more an insider to my parents' troubles than the rest of us, except for maybe Gus. As a result, Gem always stood firmly behind Mother, no matter what. I think the rest of us just wanted to love both our parents, which was not always easy when Popo wasn't around to love.

Gem may be right about Popo, but I loved him anyway. I loved the Popo who wasn't too busy to talk to Oscar at the Wanatah ticket counter, or to Old Man Gregory at the Blue and White Café. I saw the interest and compassion in his eyes when he spoke to people, listened to them. I loved the Popo who bent down and picked the stones out of my knee after a fall. That was the father I knew, a man who showed kindnesses to people, no matter who they were. Mother must have known a different man. That's all I could figure.

"Popo will come back," Gem insisted again.

I wanted to believe her. Maybe Gem was right, that we could go back to the way things were. Maybe Laura Beall was wrong.

Pulling me up from the bench by the hand she still held, Gem, Fred, Blinn, and I walked home in silence.

That night when everyone was asleep, I crept out of bed, pulled the shoebox from my bureau drawer, and made my way downstairs to the green room. I turned Popo's favorite chair to face toward the window with a view of the bridge that crossed Prairie Creek. I pulled his favorite old quilt—the one MaMaw had made him when he was a child—from the back of the chair and wrapped it around my body. Then I sat, watching and waiting.

An hour later, I lifted the lid from my shoebox. The moon and the stars shining through the window gave off enough golden light to illuminate its contents.

***

Like Gus's bag of coins, and the pages of Gem's diary, my shoebox was private, a place where I kept my treasures. A lock of my hair tied with a tiny red bow from my first haircut; the cap from a bottle of Blood Orange pop I'd shared with Popo; and a Diamond matchbox containing several delphinium seeds were among my treasures. I also kept a folded scrap of paper Charlie had given me during those long weeks after I'd recovered from scarlet fever and struggled to catch up my schoolwork.

"Spell CITIZEN."

I plopped my head on the kitchen table and groaned.

Charlie was insistent. "Annie, you must know how to spell these words to get out of third grade. Spell CITIZEN."

I exhaled dramatically. "S-I-T..."

"Not S. Start again."

"C-I-T-I-Z-E-N."

"Spell RESIDENT."

"That's too hard."

"Pauline and Helen will not wait around in third grade for you if you flunk. You'll have to be best friends with Albright Flud if you don't learn how to spell these words."

"Fine. R-E-S-I-D-E-N-T."

"Spell ANTIDISESTABLISHMENTARIANISM."

I rolled my eyes at my cousin. "That's not one of my spelling words."

"I know, cousin, but it's easy. And once you learn what all the parts mean, you'll be able to figure out the meanings of other words."

"I don't want to know what that dumb word means, and I don't want to know how to spell it."

Charlie pulled his chair a little closer to mine. Then he gently turned my face toward his and leaned in. With his nose nearly touching mine, he said, "But I want you to know."

I stuck out my lip and shook my head. "Teach it to Cory."

"Oh, I learned how to spell it a while back, just to get Charlie off my back."

Without turning from the stewpot she was stirring, Mother piped up. "Me too. Same reason."

I felt my frustration rising. "Then teach it to Gem."

My sister looked up at me from the book she was reading and smiled broadly.

"Not you, too?"

Gem nodded.

"Charlie offered to buy me a roll of Necco Wafers with some of the money he earned working at the library for Aunt Lo. I took the nickel instead. I'm saving to buy a new diary."

My cousin crossed his arms. "What's it going to take? I had to buy Blinn and Gus pie at the Blue and White Café."

"What? Gus prefers Mother's pie."

Charlie shrugged his shoulders. "He thought Miss Roxy's pie was pretty tasty that day."

"I'm not learning your stupid word, Charlie."

"Fine."

The next day at school, I found a slip of paper in my spelling book. On it, my cousin had carefully lettered the longest word he'd found in the big dictionary at the library: antidisestablishmentarianism. In his precise handwriting, he wrote the definition below it: Opposition to the withdrawal of state support or recognition of the Anglican Church in nineteenth century England.

When I got home, I opened Mother's desk drawer and stuck the paper into Charlie's big stack with his other words, sure it would take him a while to discover it. That night I found the paper under my pillow. It occurred to me that Charlie expected more from me than I expected from myself. He wasn't letting me off the hook. That's when I recognized the little slip of paper for what it was, and I put it in my shoebox with my other treasures. I took it out a few days later and learned to spell the antidisestablishmentarianism for Charlie, just as he knew I would.

Now my shoebox contained the silver half dollar Laura Beall had given me on Beggars' Night. I lifted it out and turned it over and over in my hands, feeling its weight. I had told no one but Mother about the coin, and even she didn't know it was a half-dollar piece. It was something I only shared with Miss Beall, and for now, I wanted to keep it that way.

As I sat there in the moonlight, I thought about my baby sister and how her hearing loss would affect her throughout her life. Would she ever hear the clatter of forks on plates during the supper hour at the Blue and White Café or the train whistle in the distance? Would she ever hear Mother's soft humming when she was planting her beloved delphinium seeds in her spring garden?

Beyond her initial shock of finding out about Thea's hearing loss, Mother seemed to have settled into a state of indifference. Her silence frustrated me, irked me. As fear began settling into my bones, I needed Mother's reassuring words. She offered none.

I found it odd that thoughts of Laura Beall comforted me. It had only been three days since I'd met the woman my friends called Ghosty, yet she had become my port in the storm. Thoughts of the mysterious woman distracted me from the turmoil in my life. I didn't know when I'd see her again, but I knew I would.

Through the window, I watched the moon and the stars slip behind the clouds gathering in the night sky. All was dark but for one dim streetlight that flickered, then held, flickered again, then held. Finally, unable to keep my eyes open, I fell sound asleep, surrounded by my father's essence.

# Chapter 12

The first week of November passed slowly, without a word from Popo. I didn't dare ask Mother if she'd heard from him for fear of adding more grief to her troubles.

While she remained steadfast in her aloof demeanor about Popo's absence, I recognized the first crack in Mother's indifference to our financial situation one evening as she sat at her writing desk, sheer frustration enveloping her face as she shuffled a stack of bills. The sight of her there chilled me to the bone.

As I watched her silently from the doorway, I remembered overhearing Mother telling Aunt Lo that she didn't think the coal in the bin would last until Thanksgiving. I wanted to see for myself.

When Mother took Thea upstairs for a bath, Charlie and I went down to the basement. Standing on my tiptoes, I peered into the coal bin.

"That won't last until Thanksgiving," I repeated what I'd overheard to Charlie. "Mother still owes the coal man for the last load."

Concern darkened my cousin's eyes. "What should we do?"

"I don't know." Be brave and carry on? How could that help? In that moment, I felt my first flash of anger towards my father.

"So many people love us, Annie. They won't let us freeze to death."

"I hope you're right."

After I crawled into bed that night, all I thought about was my family's future without Popo. I knew people went to the poorhouse if they couldn't pay their bills. I vividly recalled seeing the poorhouse at the edge of town on our trips to Aunt Rachel and Uncle Maddy's farm. It even spooked Old Barney. Whenever we passed, Gus had to get out of the buggy and walk Old Barney past that creepy place, while Cory walked beside the horse, blocking his view. I didn't blame Old Barney... I turned my head away, too. I thought about what Gem had said... that Popo would come back... but I didn't believe her anymore.

After school the next afternoon, I found Mother in the kitchen, preparing supper.

"Where's Charlie?"

"He stopped over at Bernard's house. His mother brought home a bushel of old apples from the Little Palmer House. She said they weren't much good, but Cooter and Old Barney would like them. Charlie was helping Bernard feed some to Cooter. They'll be here soon."

"And that hungry goat of ours... I'm sure she'll get her share. She'll eat everything, including the basket, if they let her. Be sure to thank Mrs. Thompson the next time you see her."

I hadn't laid eyes on Mrs. Thompson in months, and I didn't recall her ever stopping by to thank Mother for feeding Bernard.

"Okay." I knew I wouldn't bother.

"Is Gem home?" Mother asked. "I didn't hear her come in."

"I saw her walking with Fred a while ago. They were walking slow-ly."

Enjoying my rare one-on-one time with Mother, I climbed up on a stool to watch her work. The kitchen was Mother's natural domain. Without a misstep or an unnecessary movement, she glided along that well-worn path between her stove, the cupboards, and the table, pulling out whatever she needed as she prepared the food.

I spotted two jars of spinach on the counter. "Are we having a spinach ring tonight?" I asked. Mother made a spinach ring by piling buttery mashed potatoes into the center of a platter and placing spinach all around the potatoes. Popo loved Mother's spinach rings, but I didn't dare say that.

"Yes, I couldn't face another pot of beans tonight." I spied a bowl covered with a cheesecloth on top of the Frigidaire, the place she set beans to soak overnight. We'd eat bean soup for supper tomorrow night.

"I've got biscuits ready to go in the oven. The boys will have to fill up on those."

"I don't think they'll mind."

"What do you think? Should I serve grape jam or apple butter with the biscuits?"

"Both."

She nodded. "Both it is."

After dropping the last potato into her pot and placing it on the stove to boil, she turned to me. "Anna, I almost forgot. There's a letter for you on my desk."

"Who's it from?" I asked.

"I believe it's from Laura Beall. You'll have to go see for yourself."

I jumped down from my perch and ran into the parlor. I found an envelope with my name written across it in fancy script lettering. The flap of the envelope bore a red wax seal with the image of a train engine pressed into it.

I hadn't seen Laura Beall since our tea party, that day I'd sat as a guest at her table and told her my troubles and cried my eyes out. With each passing day, I felt my cloak of indifference regarding my father gathering around me as I allowed my curiosity about the mysterious Laura Beall to distract me from the reality of his continued absence.

I slipped a finger under the wax seal, opened the envelope, and removed a sheet of Miss Beall's engraved stationery. It read:

***

*Dear Miss Ghere,*

*I enjoyed our visit over tea the other afternoon. The cookies your mother baked were delicious, just as you said they would be. Thank you again for your kindness and please thank your mother for me.*

*Would you be willing to run an errand for me? I don't want to impose on your time, but it would certainly help me a great deal. I will be out-of-town tomorrow and Friday, as I have urgent business in Delphi that I must tend to. If you are available, please come to my house at nine o'clock on Saturday for instructions? I hope to see you then.*

*Sincerely,*

*Laura Beall*

*P.S. I also wish to return your mother's plate.*

***

I re-read the letter. Saturday was three whole days away. I could hardly wait.

"Is the letter from Miss Beall?" Mother was standing in the doorway, wiping her wet hands on her apron.

I nodded. Then I read it to her, unable to hide my excitement at having another opportunity to see the woman who lived in the big Victorian house on the corner.

Our Saturday meeting marked the beginning of a business relationship between Miss Beall and me. Once or twice a week, I helped her by picking up groceries from the market or paying one of her utility bills in the public square. I loved picking up items she'd ordered from Thrasher's Department Store. The sheet music that came regularly fascinated me.

I did all the errands for her alone. No Charlie, no Gem, and no Pauline or Helen to distract me. I walked alone with my thoughts. I grew to love the time I spent in the brisk autumn air, often thinking about absolutely nothing.

Laura Beall paid me a nickel or dime for each errand I ran for her. Before long, I had a handful of coins I kept hidden away in the shoebox in my bureau drawer with my silver half-dollar.

One Saturday after I returned from Miss Beall's, I saw Gus sitting on his bed, counting the coins from his canvas sack. I stood in his bedroom doorway a few moments, watching.

"Hello, little sister." A broad smile crossed his face.

"What are you doing, Gus?"

"Can you keep a secret?" I assured him I could, thinking about Gem's secret about Fred that I'd vowed never to tell.

"I'm paying for our last load of coal so Mother can get another one."

"But Gus, what about your big adventure?"

Gus patted his bed, inviting me to come sit next to him. "There's nothing more important than helping this family. I can't bear the thought of baby Thea shivering from the cold this winter, especially if I can do something about it. I'm going downtown now to pay the bill and order another load of coal. If Mother knows what I'm up to, she'll try to stop me, so don't say a word to her, or anyone else. Do you promise?"

I nodded. "I promise."

My brother gave me a little squeeze. "Can I see a smile, little sister?"

I furrowed my brow. "If Popo doesn't come back soon, will we have to go to the poorhouse?" The thought if it sent a shiver up my spine.

"Not if I can help it," insisted Gus. "Besides, there are too many people who love us to let that happen."

I ran into my room, pulled the coins I'd earned running errands for Miss Beall from my shoebox, and returned to Gus's side. "It's not much, but I want to help the family, too."

My big brother put his arms around me and hugged me tightly.

After he left, I pulled out the half-dollar Miss Beall had given me on Beggars' Night. I turned it over and over in my hands before returning it to its safe place in the box. I knew Gus needed that coin to buy coal, and I should have given it to him. That half-dollar symbolized my new friendship with Laura Beall, and I wasn't willing to give it up. Not yet.

***

As November wore on, my life fell into a new rhythm. Between school and running errands for Laura Beall, I had little time to think about Popo. Charlie continued to help Aunt Lo at the library, and I promised I'd help again once the Christmas pageant was over.

On Wednesday morning before Thanksgiving Day, snow began falling. My classmates and I watched the snow accumulating on the ground from the second floor of Old Stoney. We talked about the white Christmases in north-central Indiana we remembered, but none of us remembered a white Thanksgiving.

By noon, three to four inches of snow had already accumulated on the sidewalk, prompting the principal to call off classes until Monday. Thrilled by our extended break, we clambered into our coats and boots and raced for the door.

As Charlie, Bernard, and I pushed through the falling snow, Bernard called out as he pointed toward our house. 'Well now, take a gander yonder!" I saw the A&P's delivery truck parked out front and a man carrying a large box to our door.

"I knocked, but nobody answered," he huffed, as he trudged back to his truck through the snow. "I got a second box for you."

"Gus could have brought the groceries home with him."

"Nah." The delivery man rubbed his hands together, then blew on them. "They're way too heavy to carry. Besides, there was a rush put on them."

The man hauled the second box to the porch. As the truck pulled away, Charlie opened one box. "Look at all the food." I peeked over his shoulder, my eyes wide with excitement.

I opened the door while Charlie and Bernard tugged the boxes inside. Blinn came down the stairs in time to help carry them into the kitchen and place them on the table.

"What's that?" Mother asked.

"It's food for tomorrow." Blinn looked through the boxes. "Everything we need for a real Thanksgiving feast."

We all helped pull the items out of the two boxes... milk, eggs, lard, butter, flour, sugar, potatoes, sweet potatoes, several cans of pumpkin, even a jar of maraschino cherries and a tin of marshmallows.

"Why, just behold the mighty size o' that bird!" Bernard's eyes widened as Blinn lifted the turkey out of the second box. "I ain't never laid eyes on a bird so grand!"

Mother frowned. "Where did this food come from?"

"The delivery man from the A&P brought it."

Blinn pulled off the bill that was taped to a box. "It's signed by Mr. Ghere."

"Well, it's about time that cheapskate brother of mine ponied up for Thanksgiving dinner." Aunt Lo stood in the doorway holding Thea. "Karl and I had it out a couple of days ago. I told him I couldn't remember him ever contributing to any of the holiday meals he's eaten here over the years. He growled something about being an invited guest and not wanting to insult his host and hostess by paying for anything. Karl claimed Iris contributed plenty, but I emphatically disagreed... horehound drops from Woolworth's do not count as plenty. He huffed and slammed the door on his way out, but apparently my brother had a change-of-heart."

"Karl had a change-of-heart?" Mother shook her head. "I doubt that."

"Maggie, I may have coerced Karl's kind gesture, but he came through, albeit at the last possible moment, with everything we need for a grand Thanksgiving dinner. It's been such a hard year for us, so let's try to be thankful and enjoy a happy day together."

"Fine."

Mother called out instructions to us. "Blinn, get the roasting pan off the back porch. You'll have to use the step stool... it's on the top shelf."

Turning to me, Mother pointed to items on the table. "Anna, put the eggs and butter in the Frigidaire, and count how many eggs we have left from our chickens."

When it got cold outside, any eggs my brothers collected from our chickens went directly into the Frigidaire because Mother feared they'd freeze on our back porch.

"Charlie, go down to the cellar. Make a list of everything that's down there. Can you do that for me?"

"Okay, Aunt Maggie. I'll get a scrap of paper and a pencil from your desk and write it all down." Off he ran. Charlie loved anything involving paper and pencils.

"It looks like there's ample sugar and flour in this box," Mother noted. "I think Karl wants his favorite sugar-cream pie."

"He loves your sugar-cream pie, Maggie. Truth be told, I might enjoy a wee taste of it myself."

"I'd better get busy. Thanksgiving is tomorrow. Let's get the rest of this moved off the table. I need it to roll out my pie crusts."

We all pitched in, excited that we weren't having chicken pie for Thanksgiving. Mother had Blinn put the turkey back into the box and set it on the back porch. "Cover the box with a towel," she instructed. "I don't want that turkey to freeze before it's time to dress it."

Mother spent the rest of the day making pies, two pumpkin, two mincemeat, and two special sugar-cream pies for Uncle Karl. As the pies awaited their turns in the oven, she completed the next day's menu as Gem and I checked off the ingredients she needed.

My sister frowned. "With all the pies you made, we may be short on sugar."

"Rachel is bringing honey when she comes tomorrow. We'll make do, in the meantime."

At five minutes until five o'clock, we heard a knock.

"Gus, who's at the door, son?"

"It's the coal man, Mother. He's here to deliver a load."

Mother walked out of the kitchen.

"I didn't order coal."

The man looked down at his pad. "It says right here you did, madam. Sorry I'm so late getting here. The snow slowed me down."

The man scribbled a note on his pad with his pencil stub. "If the shoot's clear, I'll get the load dumped right away. I'd just as soon get on home and out of this cold."

When Mother turned her back on us, Gus looked at me and winked.

# Chapter 13

I awoke to the aroma of a savory hodgepodge of holiday fare wafting up the staircase from the kitchen. The smell of roasted turkey tickled my semiconsciousness first, but hints of oyster dressing, spicy mincemeat, and apple-rhubarb compote followed, one at a time, sparking memories of Thanksgivings past.

Through the worsening economic conditions, Mother feared her children going to bed cold and hungry. That fear had grown into a real possibility since the disappearance of my father. However, the unexpected gift of food from Uncle Karl soothed Mother's troubled soul, shifting her attention (if only for a day) from her daughter's hearing loss, her absentee husband, and the growing stack of bills to an outcome she could control. Today, the Ghere family would eat like royalty. I didn't know about tomorrow. No one, including Mother, knew our future.

Gem stirred next to me, then settled back into a morning dream. Before going downstairs, I pulled the blanket Thea had kicked off in the night back over her, tucking it gently under her chin. She slept peacefully, an innocent captive of her noiseless world.

Aunt Rachel and Aunt Lo sipped coffee at the kitchen table while Mother fed cranberries and oranges into her old cast iron grinder she'd clamped to the countertop. Mother never served turkey without cranberry salad. The three women chatted as if nothing outside our tiny world touched them, not the snowstorm, nor the uncertainty, nor the despair of those (mostly women and children) forced to live in the poorhouse. I wondered what the poor people would eat today.

"Annie, come give your favorite aunt a hug."

Aunt Lo grunted at the comment, so I gave her a reassuring smile as I fell into Aunt Rachel's arms.

My aunt's face looked much like Mother's, but that's where the resemblance ended. Two shades darker than Mother's, my aunt's hair hung to her waist. Although she'd wear it up when she worked alongside her husband on the farm, she often wore it down. Today, she'd tied it into a ponytail with a band and pulled it forward over her left shoulder, the perfect accent to her wholesome, freckled face. While Mother epitomized all things traditional, Aunt Rachel constantly redefined the unconventional. She was a rebel, and proud of it. Family lore included several stories about how Rachel's rebellion nearly put Mother and Father Blinn in early graves. Then Madison Caldwell came along.

Aunt Rachel adored her husband, everything about him. Her adoration was obvious in her words and actions. I know she loved her son, Charlie, but I doubted she could take another breath without Madison. I wished Mother loved Popo the same way. My aunt squeezed the breath out of me before I wriggled free. "When did you get here?"

"We arrived about an hour ago. Your Uncle Madison was none too happy getting out of a nice warm bed earlier than usual, but we had chores to do before we could leave."

"Did you have a hard time getting through the snow?"

"It wasn't easy, but Rosie was up to the task."

I saw a jug of honey on the counter, along with several other items Aunt Rachel and Uncle Maddy brought in from farm country.

"Is Charlie still asleep?"

"He's out in the barn with his father tending to Rosie. Madison wants her well-fed and well-rested before we head for home in the morning. We may be in for more snow."

I sat at the table with my aunts as they chatted with Mother. They knew to stay out of her way. She'd ask for help when she needed it.

"Is Augie coming for dinner?" Leave it to Aunt Rachel to question Mother about Popo.

Mother turned and glared at her sister. "Anna, go upstairs and get dressed. Gem was up late helping me get a jump on some of the preparation and dress the turkey, but it's time she got up. Our other guests will arrive soon."

Upstairs, Gem had taken Thea into the bathroom, so I crawled back into bed. All the Thanksgivings I'd ever known had been a blend of Mother's delicious cooking and Popo's exuberance for life. I'd coped with his absence for nearly a month, but today my longing to see him, to hold his hand, to be his angel, rolled over me like a wave. Would he come for Thanksgiving dinner? Would he walk through the front door as if nothing had happened between him and Mother and take his rightful place at the head of our table?

By noon, family and a few friends filled our house to the brim. With the coal bin full, Mother splurged and opened the doors to the green room to allow warmth to flow in. The children gathered around the

Zenith radio, listening to music while playing cards on the floor. Aunt Rachel brought us a jigsaw puzzle... a picture of children ice skating on a pond... but she told us to wait until after dinner to put it together.

As the snow began falling again, Uncle Karl, Aunt Iris and MaMaw Ghere tramped over the bridge across Prairie Creek. At the door, Aunt Iris presented Gem with her usual contribution to the feast, a small candy dish of horehound drops. Bernard and Fred Moore came in the back door so as not to track more snow into Mother's entryway.

Gem retrieved Mother's best linens from the china cupboard and placed them on the dining room table. Eager to sit with her special guest, she left arranging the dishes, glasses, and silverware precisely at each place setting to me. Popo always carved the turkey, so I placed the big carving knife at the head of the table next to his plate. When I finished, I went upstairs to my parents' room and sat in Mother's chair by the window, looking for any sign of my father coming down the street from town.

"Are you okay?"

"Charlie, you startled me."

"I didn't know what happened to you. You were setting the table one minute, then you disappeared the next. What are you doing up here?"

"Thinking."

"About Popo? Do you think he'll come for dinner?"

"No, but I was hoping..."

"Hoping what, Annie?"

"I was hoping Popo hasn't forgotten about me, about us. He's been away a long time."

"Popo would never forget us. He loves us, especially you."

The *tink-a-link* of Mother's bell called us to dinner. Charlie lifted my hand from my lap and pulled me up. "Come on. Let's eat."

At Aunt Lo's insistence, everyone gathered around the dining room table while Bernard said the blessing. It was shorter than usual. Then Charlie, Thea, Cory, Blinn, Bernard, and I retreated to the kitchen. The twins had given up their places at the adult table for Gem and Fred.

When the children finished eating, Charlie suggested we go to the green room and work on the jigsaw puzzle while we waited for Mother to serve dessert. I remained in the kitchen to help clear the table. After I carried the dishes to the sink, I stepped into the dining room next to Mother to tell her that Thea had eaten almost everything on her plate. I knew that would make Mother happy. Just as I turned to leave, I noticed Uncle Karl sitting at the opposite end of the table in Popo's chair.

"The gravy was delicious, if I say so myself," quipped Aunt Lo, to the delight of the others. It was the only thing on the table Mother hadn't prepared. I kept my eyes glued to my uncle.

"A perfect meal, as always, Maggie." Uncle Maddy, the gentleman farmer, never failed to offer a compliment when one was due. "I hope I saved enough room for one of your delicious desserts."

"Sister Maggie, I believe the stuffing was a bit too salty this year." My eyes widened as I glared at my Uncle Karl, trying to image how he and my father grew up to be such different men.

Aunt Iris lacked the sense to keep quiet. "Actually, Maggie is always heavy-handed with the salt. You don't mind a bit of criticism, do you, dear? That's how we learn."

Mother said nothing, but I could feel her anger rising. I took a step closer to her side.

"I hope you haven't ruined the sugar-cream pie, as you did the stuffing."

Mother tensed. I snapped. "What is he doing in Popo's chair?" The words spewed out of mouth before I realized I had yelled them.

"Anna." I felt Mother's hand touch my arm.

"Popo sits at the head of the table, nobody else. What are you doing there?" I glared at my uncle.

"Maggie, that insulant child of yours needs to apologize to me this instant or I'll turn her over my knee myself," shouted my uncle. "No dessert for you, young lady, until you learn to respect your elders."

Mother was on her feet. "I think you've said quite enough, Karl. While I appreciate you providing the food for this Thanksgiving dinner, I will not... "

"I didn't provide this food."

"Is that right?" Mother's words hung in the air like a foul odor.

"That was another one of my sister's cock and bull ideas, suggesting such a thing. I am a guest in your house, so why should I pay for the food? If I want to give to charity, I'll give to the poorhouse."

I glanced around the table at all the astonished faces. My eyes met Gus's. He shook his head once, enough to let me know he didn't have the food delivered from the grocer.

Popo. Popo was the Mr. Ghere who signed the bill. He hadn't forgotten us after all.

"Karl, as a guest in this house, you will not speak to me or my daughter in that tone of voice ever again."

Uncle Karl rose to his feet. "I am certain," he spat, "that my brother would have something to say about the way you've treated me in his house. *If he were here.*"

"For your information, my name is the only one that appears on the deed to this house, not Augie's. I inherited this house from my father. It belongs to me. If memory serves, the house on the other side of the creek that you live in belongs to MaMaw. That makes you a guest in both houses, and an awful one, at that."

"Can I hear an amen to that?" MaMaw seemed to enjoy the unexpected turn in dinner table conversation. The other children gathered in the doorway as Mother continued her rant.

"My daughter wants you to get out of her father's chair and I want you to get out of *my* house. Take that insufferable wife of yours with you."

"Fine." My uncle stood and threw his linen napkin onto his dinner plate. "Iris, MaMaw, LoRetta, get your coats. We're leaving."

"I'm not going anywhere." MaMaw crossed her arms and looked her son in the face. "I've been looking forward to Maggie's sugar-cream pie all day."

"LoRetta?"

"I'm staying right here with my family."

"Well, I never."

Calm but emphatic, Mother took full control of the situation. "Gus, see your aunt and uncle out, please."

I slipped closer to my sister and whispered in her ear. "Is this going in your diary?"

"You know it, little sister. You know it."

After we heard the front door close, MaMaw opened her arms and shrugged. "I wonder what got into him."

"I've tolerated those two for years. If they want to insult my cooking, Iris can prepare Thanksgiving dinner next year."

MaMaw said what everyone else was thinking. "Oh, dear Lord, not that." Then she burst out laughing. The rest of us did, too.

All the children moved into the dining room to have dessert with the adults. I enjoyed my favorite, a piece of pumpkin pie heaped with whipped cream dusted with a sprinkling of ground cinnamon.

Despite our circumstances, the absence of Popo, and the dinner table drama, it turned out to be the most joyful Thanksgiving I'd known.

After dinner, the men and boys retired to the green room while the women and girls cleaned up the kitchen. Just as we were finishing, the telephone in the hallway rang. Mother picked it up.

"What can I do for you, Iris?"

"Maybe she called to apologize."

Gem looked at me and rolled her eyes. "I wouldn't count on that."

"You're saying that Blinn went on your back porch and stole your broom?"

I looked at Gem. "Oh, no."

"When did this theft occur?" Mother listened to her raving sister-in-law. "It happened on Beggars' Night? And you're telling me about it now?"

After Aunt Iris gave her an earful, Mother turned to my sister. "Gem, would you find Blinn and ask him to come in here, please?"

A moment later, Gem returned with Blinn in tow, Cory trailing behind. "Blinn, I have Iris on the telephone, and she claims you went on her back porch on Beggar's Night and stole her broom. Is there any truth to that story?"

"No, ma'am. I never go near there, not since Aunt Iris whacked me with that broom when I was little."

"Did you hear that, Iris? Blinn doesn't know what you're talking about."

My eyes widen. Gem leaned down and whispered in my ear, "Close your mouth, Annie."

"Tell that crazy woman I used that broom just yesterday to knock the snow off the back steps," stated Aunt Lo. "She can go look for herself. It's in the corner of the back porch where it belongs."

"Would you like to apologize to Blinn now? I can put him on the line." Mother listened a moment. "I didn't think so. It's been nice talking to you, Iris, but I've got to go. We're cutting the last of the sugar-cream pies now. It's the best I've ever made... not too salty."

As my brothers left the kitchen, Mother called out. "Cory, do not touch Aunt Iris's broom again without permission. Do you understand?"

"Yes, ma'am."

As the last of the daylight faded, Mother pulled me aside. "Anna, do you know if Miss Beall had plans for Thanksgiving?"

"She didn't mention them if she did."

"I wish we'd invited her to dinner. Then again, as things went, it was probably best we didn't. I have plenty of leftovers. Do you want to take her a plate?"

"Mother, I love that idea."

"Before I get it ready, I think you should call to be sure she's there. She may have gone off to be with family or friends."

"I'll call her now and check."

After arranging Thanksgiving dinner on a plate, Mother placed a second plate upside down on top of the first, then wrapped them both in a kitchen towel to help keep the food warm.

"What kind of pie do you think she likes?" Mother asked as I put on my coat. I shrugged.

"Everyone likes pumpkin." She placed the pie on a small plate and covered it with wax paper. Then she slipped it into a paper sack along with a couple of cookies.

"Anna, you'll have to hurry so the food doesn't get cold. And don't stay long. We still have guests."

With Laura Beall's Thanksgiving dinner in hand, I dashed out the door and into the falling snow.

# Chapter 14

Just as I stepped onto the porch, the front door opened. What Laura Beall lacked in sight she made up for in hearing.

"Hurry, child. I don't want you to freeze."

I was shivering as I passed through the half-open door. After lifting the plate from my hand, she closed the door. "Would you like to stay while I enjoy my Thanksgiving dinner? Then you can take your mother's plates back to her."

I nodded, then pulled off my scarf and coat and hung them on her hall tree next to her long black wool coat.

"I've made tea." Miss Beall turned and made her way to the kitchen. "Would you care for a cup?"

"Yes, please." I had grown to love her tea. "Thank you, Miss."

"Thank you for thinking of me. Railroad business has kept me so busy all day that I haven't had a moment to stop and eat. I haven't had a traditional Thanksgiving meal since my father died. This looks delicious. Did your mother make all this?"

I nodded, overwhelmed with pride for Mother.

As she ate, I told her about Thanksgiving with my family, about how Mother had thrown Uncle Karl and Aunt Iris out of her house. Miss Beall smiled. Her face was so beautiful when she smiled, her light blue eyes sparkling behind the thick lenses of her spectacles. I wondered if she knew how beautiful she was.

Just as she was finishing her pie, I heard Miss Beall's telephone ringing in another room. "Forgive me, child. I should answer that."

I sat in the kitchen alone for a few minutes, watching the snow outside the window swirl in the fading light. Finally deciding to go home, I walked into the parlor to find Miss Beall to say my goodbyes. As I passed through the parlor, I stopped to gaze at the glowing embers in the fireplace. Popo once told me that a fire burns its hottest just before it goes out. That's the time to stoke it, to make it ready for the next day.

I followed Miss Beall's voice to the room off the parlor and pushed open the door. She was sitting behind a large desk scribbling on a pad, the telephone receiver to her ear. Unlike our old wooden wall phone, her telephone sat on her desk. Black with a dial face, it was like the one on the counter at Woolworth.

The room reminded me of the office Popo once occupied at the Ghere-Douglass Company before he took the job selling feed and seed for a company out of Indianapolis.

Popo's desk had been plain and scarred. One of the drawer fronts had fallen off, so Popo used the hole to store his hat and gloves. I remember the carved wooden name plaque that sat at the front of his desk read, "Augustus J. Ghere, President." Gem told me it had once belonged to PaPaw Ghere.

In Miss Beall's office, a burl oval partner's desk that expressed power, strength and importance dominated the room. Several neat stacks of papers covered one side, and a lamp illuminated its leather top and reflected off a magnifying glass that lay there. Her name plaque read, "Laura Beall, President" with the words, "Wanatah Railroad" inscribed below her name.

Miss Beall finally caught sight of me and motioned me in. She pointed to the chair across the desk from hers. I sat down and remained quiet while she continued her discussion. As I waited, I noticed a framed cross-stitch piece hanging on the wall next to the desk. A quote from Michelangelo, it read, "The greatest danger for most of us is not that we aim too low and miss, but that we aim too low and we reach it." I read it several times so I could recite it for Charlie when I got home.

Miss Beall's voice remained firm, never giving away any grief she may have felt. "This is such a tragedy. As soon as the weather permits, I will come over to Delphi to meet with the family. Will you make those arrangements for me as soon as possible?"

She placed the telephone receiver in its cradle and took a moment to compose herself. Before I could ask questions, she told me what I wanted to know. "It's a sad story for Thanksgiving Day. From what I understand, a man was so distraught over losing his job and not being able to support his family that he walked into the path of one of our trains just outside of Delphi. He died instantly, according to the reports I'm hearing."

I gasped. "Did he have children?"

"Yes, he had three sons, with a fourth child on the way. The police believe it was suicide. The event delayed the train about three hours, which is nothing compared to this tragic loss of life, but it's something that I must deal with."

We sat in silence for a while before returning to the kitchen. Laura Beall tended to a fresh pot of tea before washing and drying Mother's plates in her sink. Then she sat down across from me at the table.

"May I ask you something, Miss?"

"Child, you may ask me anything you wish, though I may choose not to answer."

"Who runs the Wanatah Railroad since your father passed?"

"I do. I not only run the line, I am its sole owner."

"I thought running a railroad was man's work."

"You and most everyone else." Miss Beall smiled, her eyes sparkling. "I'm not the first woman to run a railroad. Have you ever heard of Sarah Clark Kidder?"

"No."

Miss Beall told me that Sarah Clark married John Flint Kidder in 1870. A few years later, he became president of the Nevada County Narrow-Gauge Railroad, a 22-mile-long line in California. When he died in 1901, he left the company heavily in debt.

"A vast majority of the railroad's stockholders elected Sarah president and tasked her with turning the line around," Miss Beall said. "Within two years, she'd paid off the company debt and built the railroad into an economic force in California. She also oversaw the construction of a trestle over the Bear River. At 173 feet, it was the highest one in the country."

She paused, her nearly blind eyes looking upward as she searched her memories.

"My father met Mrs. Kidder in California on a trip he took there once. After their meeting, they communicated through letters. I have shoeboxes filled with her letters offering advice when my father was starting the Wanatah."

"Please, Miss, tell me how you came to run the Wanatah."

She smiled. "I'd be happy to."

Her voice was calm, almost emotionless, as she began. "My father told me this story when he was sick and dying. I haven't shared it with anyone until now. Maybe you'll appreciate it as I do. He was a fine man, a good man, and a wonderful father, but he said he was quite ashamed of how he reacted when he first laid eyes on his newborn daughter."

According to Miss Beall, as Edward Beall lay dying, his many business accomplishments throughout his successful career as a railroad executive seemed the furthest thing from his mind. With his weak hand, he reached out to his daughter, who placed her delicate white hand into his.

"When you were born, I did not know what to make of you, with your pink skin, tuft of white hair, and eyes that didn't focus," he confessed. After a violent wheezing spell brought on by the consumption ravishing his body, he continued. "There I was, a man of business, the right hand to the successor of the Pullman Car Company with a baby with needs beyond what I thought I could provide. I never felt such fear in my life, before or since."

The man took another raspy breath before continuing. "You and your mother stayed in the hospital for two weeks after you were born," he continued softly, every word causing him pain. "Oh, how I wished it could have been longer, but that difficult day, that uncertain day when I had to take you both home, came upon me like a thief in the night."

***

The cold licks of wind across Lake Michigan on that frosty day in March 1891 chilled Edward to the bone as he helped his wife into the new Flint Road-Cart he'd borrowed from his boss. The nurses at Mercy Hospital had bundled the couple's baby in layers of cotton and wool blankets and placed her in the Moses basket her mother had lovingly prepared for this special day, trimming it with embroidered lace bedding.

At home, a nurse and a housemaid Edward hired awaited the new mother and her unusual daughter. Mr. Beall planned to place his daughter in their care and await the inevitable, whatever that might be. He also planned to pour his precious few off-hours away from the office into an exciting new idea he had about creating a railroad to serve the people of his beloved home state of Indiana.

During those few weeks after bringing Laura home, that's exactly what he did, and his wife, Elizabeth, sat in the parlor of their small house, contemplative and morose, while the nurse and housemaid ran rough-shod over what had once been her exclusive domain.

On the two-month anniversary of their child's birth, Edward received a frantic telephone call at his office. "You must come home immediately, sir," pleaded the voice of the housemaid. "Poor Mrs. Beall has gone stark raving mad." Then the telephone line went dead.

Again, borrowing his boss's road-cart to cover the few blocks to his house as quickly as possible, he rushed home, climbed the few steps to their front porch, and paused there, trying to prepare himself for the worst. After turning the key in the lock, he pushed open the door and stepped in. The house was silent. He stepped forward and made his way down the narrow hallway. As he stood in the parlor's archway, he heard the faint cooing of his infant daughter. The relief he felt knowing she was safe surprised and overwhelmed him. Following the pleasant sound of his baby girl, he made his way to the kitchen.

"Darling, you startled me." Elizabeth turned from the pot of soup she was stirring on the stove to look into her husband's face. "What brings you home this time of day?"

"I received a frantic call from Melba... something about you... " He paused, weighing his words carefully. "She said something about you not feeling well."

"Poppycock."

Edward looked around the small kitchen and noticed the Moses basket on the breakfast table, his daughter's legs kicking about inside it.

"Elizabeth, where are Melba and Esme?"

"I fired those two old biddies," Elizabeth reported. "I'm back in charge of this household and that's final."

Edward edged closer to the table and peered into the basket at his daughter. Blinking back tears, he asked what had been pressing on his heart since her birth. "Elizabeth, how will we manage..." He paused again to search for the words. "How will we manage with this unusual child of ours?"

Elizabeth joined her husband at the table, placing her arm around his waist. "After a lot of prayer, I think I've figured it out. We're going to treat her the way we would treat any child we brought into this world. We'll accommodate her unusual needs without dwelling on them. And we'll love her just as she is because she's perfect, just as she is."

"What if she can't see?" Edward questioned his wife, still skeptical.

"Then we'll teach her to see with her heart. I promise you, my darling, our Laura will see many things in her life we've never dreamt of."

Edward nodded as he pulled his wife into his arms.

Elizabeth leaned up and whisper into her husband's ear. "We'll figure it out together."

"Together."

"Let's get on with it."

"Get on with what, Elizabeth?"

"Let's build a railroad."

Edward smiled. "The three of us will do it together."

And that's exactly what they did.

***

I heard Laura Beall's telephone ring again. She rose from the table. "I apologize, child. That call may be an update on our situation in Delphi. Please excuse me."

She soon returned to the kitchen table. "That was your mother. She is sending your brother, Gus, to take you home, as she doesn't want you out alone in the dark."

"But I still don't know the story about... "

"We'll save the rest of the story for another time."

# Chapter 15

The days following Thanksgiving proved as cold and blustery as those more typical of the early weeks of the new year in north-central Indiana.

On the Thursday after Thanksgiving, all eyes looked upward, where dark gray clouds blanketed the early afternoon sky. As the school day dragged on, the teachers talked of nothing but the forecast for another late autumn snowstorm.

In my classroom, we lined up early. Miss Baxter paced as she inspected her bundled students, buttoning coats, tugging stocking caps over ears, locating lost mittens.

"Pauline, do you have Helen's scarf?"

The sparkle in Pauline's brown eyes gave her away. "Yes, Miss."

"I suggest you return it to her now."

As Pauline pulled Helen's scarf from her coat sleeve, Miss Baxter called out, "Marshall Manning, this is not the time or place for any of your monkeyshine. Please face the door until the bell rings."

Pauline elbowed me, making me giggle. "Pauline, would you like to wait for the bell in the principal's office?"

"Oh, no, Miss." My friend's eyes widened as big as saucers.

Before Miss Baxter made a pronouncement about Pauline's immediate future, the bell rang. Doors popped open along the hallway, and we raced for our freedom as teachers urged us to go directly home... and to hurry.

I discovered Charlie waiting for me on the school's front walk, where I said my goodbyes to Pauline and Helen. The junior high school students came out of Old Stoney on the opposite side of the building, but Charlie insisted we wait for Bernard to catch up with us before walking home.

After Charlie tugged his stocking hat over his ears, he stopped on the sidewalk and shook his head. "Aunt Lo will not be happy if we don't show up to help her at the library this afternoon."

"Lord knows ye be needin' it, fer sur!" Bernard never sugar-coated anything.

"Next week, we meet at the church fellowship hall instead of the library," Charlie replied. "We'll be rehearsing our parts on a proper stage with piano accompaniment, which will make things better. You'll see."

"I surely do appreciate yer faith, Charlie, I do."

As we walked, I clung to my cousin's arm. The moisture seeping into my shoes and socks through the cracks in the bottoms of my old rubber boots numbed my feet, making it difficult to walk. With Charlie supporting me, we hurried along the icy sidewalks as fast as I could go.

"Oh, Annie, I almost forgot. Tomorrow's your birthday!" I detected excitement in his voice. "What did you tell Aunt Maggie you wanted for supper?"

"Please say ye picked the chocolate cake, won't ye?" mumbled Bernard, panting heavily from our brisk walk in the cold. "I could sure a piece o' yer mama's cake right now, I could!"

I shrugged.

"Angel food, again?" guessed my cousin.

"I didn't tell Mother anything. She didn't ask me what I wanted."

"Aunt Maggie has a lot on her mind. Don't be sad. I'm sure if you remind her, she'll make you a special birthday supper and bake you a cake."

"Angel food? I reckon it's better 'n no cake at all, that's for sure."

"No, I'm not reminding Mother of my birthday, and neither are you."

Charlie stopped and turned to face me.

I looked at him, tears welling in my eyes. "Thea is sick again." Bernard crowded closer to us, blocking the wind. "She's slept a lot since Thanksgiving. Last night, she coughed so much that Mother took Thea into her room to sleep. This morning, I overheard Mother on the telephone with Doc Becker. She told him Thea had a fever and wasn't eating much. I think Thea has the croup."

Charlie took a deep breath. With a nod of understanding, we continued our walk home. As we made our way across the Prairie Creek bridge, Bernard sighed with relief. "Well, ain't it a blessin' ol' Cooter's not a-shiverin' out front in the bitter cold. Seein' as how folks ain't much hankerin' for ice these days, Pops ain't makin' his usual rounds. Now, I best be scurryin' off to tend to my horse. See ya'll later!"

In the kitchen, Gem lifted the teakettle from the burner and poured hot water into Mother's teapot, an old ceramic one that had seen better days. The teapot looked drab compared to Laura Beall's pretty hand-painted one.

"Doc Becker just left. Thea's been running a fever since early this morning. Mother's upstairs tending to her, so I'm making supper."

"Is it the croup?" asked Charlie.

Gem nodded. "Would one of you take this tea and toast up to Mother? She's trying to get Thea to eat something."

Charlie picked up the tray. We didn't see him again until Gem called him for supper. From the kitchen window, I watched as delicate snowflakes began to fall. "Are Blinn and Cory home?"

"They're out tending the animals. Cory said he would stoke the fire in the furnace when he comes in since Gus headed to the A&P to deliver groceries. Two of the regular delivery boys laid out, so the manager called him to help ahead of the storm. He is worried people might not have food for a few days."

As soon as Charlie finished supper, he climbed back upstairs, carrying a tray for Mother. The tray included a small dish of mashed potatoes and another of applesauce for Thea. Blinn and Cory headed back out to the barn to check on Old Barney, Belva, and Mother's chickens before the snowstorm hit. Charlie even donated some of his beloved newspapers (the ones he'd already read) for the twins to shred and use for extra bedding for the chickens.

Alone in the kitchen, my sister pushed her chair closer to mine, sat back down, and draped an arm around my shoulders.

"You need to stop pushing your food around your plate and eat. Mother doesn't need you getting sick, too."

"I'm not hungry."

"I know you're upset about Thea being sick again."

"Gem, where's Popo? Why hasn't he come home? Thea needs him. We all need him."

"I don't know where he is, little sister. I'm sorry, but I just don't know."

"Did Popo send us the food for Thanksgiving? Gus told me he didn't order it, so it must have been Popo, right?"

Gem hesitated. "Mother thinks it was Popo, too."

My sister's answer surprised me.

As the snowstorm hit, I climbed into bed early to warm my feet and to have time alone to think.

I'd tried to push Popo out of my thoughts for weeks, but my efforts came undone at dinner on Thanksgiving Day. I considered going to the train station tomorrow to meet the 4:20. Would Popo be on that train? Would it be too snowy for me to venture out?

Knowing Mother believed Popo sent us the food comforted me. But why hadn't he joined us for dinner? Why hadn't he taken his place at the head of our table, the jovial host entertaining his guests with the latest gossip from across the state? It made little sense to me. Nothing made sense to me anymore.

Since Gem didn't know where Popo was, maybe Gus did. If he did, he'd tell me, I was sure of it. I climbed out of the warmth of my bed to look for my big brother.

As I passed through the hallway, I noticed things were quiet in Mother's room. I hoped Thea and Mother had fallen asleep since it had been another long day for both of them.

I pushed open the boys' bedroom door and saw Charlie sitting on his bed with a book open on his lap. He looked up and nodded at me. The twins were playing checkers on Blinn's bed.

As I crept down the stairs, rustling in the kitchen caught my attention. Gus? A single lit bulb on our back porch cast a dim light through the door pane into the kitchen. Instead of Gus, Mother stood in the kitchen in her nightclothes.

"Anna, what are you doing up? Are you feeling sick?"

"No, Mother, I'm fine. I thought you were Gus. Is he home?"

Mother smiled. "He planned to take groceries to Vivien's house before he came home. I'm sure he'll be here any minute. I'm making cocoa. Do you want me to make you some?"

I nodded.

After Mother placed a cup of hot cocoa in front of me, she sat down across the table from me. Behind the drifting steam off her cup, Mother seemed an illusion, an unfamiliar soul masquerading as my mother. A moment later, she blew the steam away, and I saw her as clear as day, her beautiful face haloed in the dim light of that single bulb. I saw the woman who had given birth to me, who'd held me to ground when the grim reaper came calling last winter.

"Is Thea feeling better, Mother?" I asked.

"Her fever is down and she's resting now. I think she's out of the woods. We'll have to wait and see what the morning brings."

We sat in silence for a while.

"I'll wait up for Gus if you want to go back to bed."

"When Thea and I had scarlet fever, you sang to us. During the day, you sang us the latest songs from the Hoosier Hot Shots you'd heard on the radio."

Mother took a deep breath and nodded. "Yes, I remember. But at night, when I felt so alone, when the thought of you or Thea leaving haunted me, I sang a lullaby."

"Do you remember the lullaby you sang to us?"

"Yes, it was a song my mother sang to Rachel and me." Almost imperceptibly, she began singing:

> *"Sleep my child and peace attend thee,*
> *All through the night.*
> *Guardian angels God will send thee,*
> *All through the night.*
> *Soft the drowsy hours are creeping,*

*Hill and dale in slumber sleeping*
*I my loved ones' watch am keeping,*
*All through the night."*

"Was that your prayer for us?" I asked.

She paused before answering. "I suppose it was."

"I hung onto your song, Mother. I heard you singing, and I hung on tight."

A single tear slipped from Mother's eye and rolled down her cheek.

"Mother, I'm frightened that Thea hasn't heard your voice for months. She hasn't heard you singing. Please, Mother, speak into her ear so she has something of you to hang on to. Please."

"Oh, Anna, my dear girl. I am struggling to come to terms with Thea's... " Mother paused, searching for a word that avoided mentioning my sister's hearing loss. "With Thea's condition," she continued. "I just don't know what to do to help my sweet baby girl."

"That's easy, Mother. Love her the way she is. She's perfect the way she is."

Mother smiled. "I think you're as smart as your cousin."

"No one is as smart as Charlie. I'll go back to bed now. I'll talk to Gus in the morning."

"Is there something you want to discuss with him?"

I hesitated. "I want to ask him if he knows where Popo is. If he knows, he'll tell me. Gus won't lie to me."

"Anna, please understand things between your father and me... well, they're complicated."

I looked at my mother's sad face. "But things between Popo and me are simple."

"I know you miss him, but I don't want you to get your hopes up that he'll come back."

Hope was all I had left.

# Chapter 16

Laura Beall never asked me to take over for her regular errand boy who had moved to Terre Haute with his family. I learned about him from the clerk at the power company when I stopped one day to pay her bill. It occurred to me that Gus would have been a better choice, but Miss Beall had chosen me for the job, which I did without complaint. Even on those days that my feet hurt and nearly froze from the walk, I always did the job alone because I didn't want to share her. I wanted the mystery of Laura Beall all to myself.

When Miss Beall needed me, she'd call and leave a message with Mother for me to come after school. Usually, she'd meet me at the door with the envelope she wanted delivered or opened the door just far enough to receive whatever I'd picked up for her. But on special days, she invited me in. I loved those days, sitting across from her over a pretty china teacup, chatting about the weather or something that happened at school. I loved it most when she'd talk about the Wanatah Railroad.

On one of those special days when Miss Beall had time to talk, I asked her to finish her story.

"Which story is that?"

"The story about how you came to run the Wanatah Railroad."

She gathered her thoughts while she stirred her tea. "Now, where were we?" Then she picked up her story, where she'd left off on Thanksgiving Day.

***

Edward Beall conceived of building a railroad years before Laura was born, but it was in those first few months after she arrived, colorless and nearly blind, that the idea blossomed. He came home from work every evening eager to spend his spare time studying the existing lines and making plans for his own. In a matter of months, he memorized every inch of railroad track across the state. On a map of Indiana, he sketched his new line from Chicago to Louisville, delighting in every little town he planned to serve.

Edward often held Laura up to the table where he'd spread out his map. As she leaned in, he'd talk about his dream to his young daughter.

"This is the third section of the northern half of the freight line." Edward traced the line with his finger, his daughter's hand atop his.

"Do you remember the names of the towns in the next section?"

"Guernsey, Monticello, Yeoman, Delphi, Radnor," Laura recited from memory. "Ockley, Rossville, Frankfort, Kirklin, Sheridan, Westfield, Carmel, Nora, Broad Ripple, and Boulevard Station."

"And then?" Edward prompted.

"Right into Union Station." Laura pumped her arm in victory.

"That's my girl."

Laura's eyes were weak, but not a single detail about building the railroad escaped her young ears or her imagination.

Elizabeth embraced her husband's vision. With Laura in her arms, she sat in the rocking chair in his study and talked with her husband about the railroad long into the night. The more they talked, the more alive it became. When Edward laid down his work for the night, Elizabeth knew exactly where to pick it back up the next morning.

After getting her husband off to work at the Pullman Car Company, she went about her household chores with little Laura in tow. Once she finished, she'd sit at her husband's desk and review the notes she'd made of ideas they'd shared the night before, always expressing her thoughts aloud to keep her daughter's attention.

Several times a week, when weather permitted, Elizabeth pushed Laura's carriage to the public library, where she culled through books and directories, and read the latest financial newspapers, making notes of anything relating to the railroads that might interest Edward. She made lists of the names and address of anyone who might be helpful along the way.

Before she fixed supper, she summarized what she had learned in a handwritten memorandum, along with any insight she had during her day's exploration and presented her paper to her beloved Edward that evening. After their day's discussion, which usually began over supper, she'd jot down Edward's insights on a pad of paper to prompt her research the next day.

One evening in late October, Edward made a big announcement to his wife. He pulled her to his side, pointing to the map.

"Look, darling, I've mapped out the last section of the line."

Then closing his eyes, he called out the towns in order with little Laura joining in: "Michigan City, Otis, Westville, Alida,

Haskell, Wanatah, South Wanatah, La Crosse, Wilders, San Pierre, Medaryville, Francesville, and Monon."

Elizabeth could hardly contain her excitement. "You've done it, Edward!"

"We're so close. We're almost ready to present our plans to our investors, but we're missing one crucial element."

"What's that, darling?"

"What shall we name our railroad?"

Throughout their years of intense planning, the couple always referred to their project as the "Hoosier Line," but the day had finally arrived to give their dream a formal name.

"That's easy, Edward. We'll call it the Wanatah Railroad." Edward loved the idea. He had grown up in La Porte but spent a great deal of time with his grandparents, Harry and Laura Mae Beall, in the tiny town of Wanatah. He often described his time with his grandparents as "the best years of my youth."

"What's next?"

"I must formally present our plans to our investors, including Mr. Pullman. If everything goes as planned, we can start leasing tracks early next year."

That's exactly what they did.

***

Laura leaned back in her chair, enjoying the recollection of the Wanatah's beginning. "My parents believed it was possible to create a railroad that would serve the people of Indiana," she continued. "Believing is the first step toward making things happen. My parents believed they could create a new railroad, when no one else thought they could. Who were they?" Miss Beall shrugged at the question. "Just two young people from modest backgrounds who shared a big dream. They knew that believing something with all your heart, mind and soul is how all great and noble ideas take root. Becoming a tiny force standing against the mighty wind of doubt may not seem like it matters, but it does. If you remain standing through the storm, then others will stand with you. When the storm suddenly subsides, you realize your idea isn't an idea anymore... it's a reality."

Laura sipped her tea before continuing. "Plant your feet and stand up for what you want, child. Act, even if you don't know if it's the right action, because you learn from actions, while you learn nothing from standing still. Most importantly, know that everything you want in life lies just beyond your fear."

I sat in silence, trying to take in all Miss Beall was telling me.

"I am not the heiress to the Wanatah Railroad. To my father, the Wanatah wasn't a gift to his daughter. The Wanatah is a legacy he left to the people of Indiana that he entrusted to me because he believed I was best suited to run it. He knew I loved the railroad as much as he and my mother did, and that I knew as much about running it as he did. My father believed in me. When he passed away five years ago, he knew I could keep the Wanatah running, despite my limitations."

"Do you run it alone?"

"Good gracious, no, child. I have many good people in Delphi who help me run the line. And there are many more up and down the line who play crucial roles in our success, especially during this economic depression. But I couldn't do my job without Michael."

"Who's Michael?"

"He's someone I've known most of my life, but that's another story altogether. Maybe we should save it for another day."

"Please, Miss, tell me about Michael."

# Chapter 17

When Laura was four years old, Elizabeth decided it was time she began her formal education. Because the family lived just south of Chicago in Englewood, Elizabeth wrote a letter to the Illinois School for the Visually Impaired asking if they knew anyone in the area who would be an appropriate tutor for Laura. The school wrote back, suggesting Mr. Stephen Ellis of Chicago.

Elizabeth wrote him immediately, but Mr. Ellis replied, saying he'd recently lost his wife and wanted to continue teaching in the school his only son attended. Because the boy was struggling with the loss of his beloved mother, Mr. Ellis didn't want to disrupt his son's life any further. Not one to accept no for an answer despite being presented with the logic and grace with which Mr. Ellis declined her generous offer, Elizabeth bided her time.

On a spectacular spring day in mid-May, Elizabeth dressed her daughter in her prettiest dress and took her to the Wanatah Depot for the short ride to downtown Chicago. After the porter gave Elizabeth directions, the mother and daughter walked to the school where Mr. Ellis taught.

"Be on your best behavior, dear girl," Elizabeth urged her daughter. "We must make a good first impression. If we are successful in our mission today, we will celebrate with ice cream before going home. Or maybe there's a bakery nearby. How does that sound?"

Elizabeth inquired at the school office as to the location of Mr. Ellis's classroom. Attracting a great deal of attention, the mother and daughter walked hand-in-hand through the hallway against the rush of children just dismissed from classes for the day. Young Laura remembered the excitement and energy of those children all around her as her mother pulled her through the crowd. "It was exhilarating," she recalled, "and I longed to be like them."

Once Elizabeth found his classroom, she walked in and introduced herself to Mr. Ellis. Before she left, she'd persuaded him to move to Englewood with his son to tutor Laura for the summer. "I'll arrange everything," she promised. "You'll have a lovely apartment near our home and a train pass to anywhere the Wanatah travels for your days off. A change of scenery will do Michael good."

The day Stephen Ellis and his ten-year-old son arrived in Englewood marked the beginning of a glorious summer for the Bealls. Elizabeth sent a driver with a horse and buggy to pick them up from the depot and greeted them when they arrived at their apartment. Sparkling clean with refurbished paint, fresh linens and stocked food cupboards, Elizabeth had seen to the last detail of the small walk-up.

With the Wanatah expanding, Elizabeth suddenly became the most sought-after socialite in the entire Chicago area, and four-year-old Laura had a tutor and a friend. Mr. Ellis was a kindly man who carried the loss of his wife on his shoulders. He spent the first week getting to know the girl, determining the best path forward for her education.

"She certainly knows about railroads," he told Elizabeth over afternoon tea one day.

"Of course she does," stated Elizabeth. "That's the native language of this household."

"She has a firm grasp of numbers, and she can recite the alphabet," he continued. "However, it's time she learned to read and write. I know she's only four, but because of her vision impairment, it is best we begin now."

"You're the expert."

"One more thing. Your daughter needs spectacles."

Elizabeth nodded. "I'll see to it immediately."

Mr. Ellis returned from his first weekend trip home with a stack of books he'd collected during his years at the Illinois School for the Visually Impaired. He read to Laura from the large print books and employed the patience of a saint as she bent over the pages to study the letters up close. It was when he put the fat pencil in the child's hand and asked her to draw the letters that she became frustrated.

One afternoon, when Elizabeth and Mr. Ellis were discussing Laura's progress in the parlor, they heard laughter in the small room off the kitchen that Elizabeth had converted into Laura's classroom.

Laura sat at her desk, pencil in hand, scribbling on a piece of paper Michael had laid out for her. "See there." The boy pointed to the paper. "That looks like an L, and there's a perfect 'C.' You can do it. I told you so." The child leaned forward and looked closely at the letters Michael picked out in her scribbling, then giggled with delight.

Mr. Ellis asked, "Michael, what's going on in here?"

"Laura just needs to get the feel of the pencil, Papa," Michael replied. The boy adjusted the position of the pencil in the girl's small hand. "Make more letters," he instructed, as she scribbled away. As she gained control of her pencil, she worked to make perfect letters, mostly to please Michael.

About mid-summer, Mr. Ellis returned from his weekend in Chicago with a book of music. Michael sat down at the Beall's old upright piano and played the simple songs in the book.

Laura soon joined him on the piano bench. After he played a song, he'd place the music book in her hands and point to the letters.

"That's a C."

Laura squinted. "It doesn't look like a C."

"Well, it is." Then he took her hand and placed it on the keys. "That's middle C, Laura. Play it with your thumb."

"But I can't see it."

"You don't have to see it. Just feel it."

From then on, when Laura's lessons were over for the day, she pulled the music book from the shelf, climbed on the piano bench next to Michael and insisted he tell her the story of the notes. He told her that music was like the map of the railroad lines her father kept on the table in his study.

"Music tells you where to start, where to go, how to get there, and how long to stay."

One day she asked, "How do you know about music?"

"My mother taught me," Michael replied.

By the end of the summer, Elizabeth had found a music teacher who came to the house two afternoons a week to give Laura piano lessons. At first, Laura resisted her new teacher, but when Elizabeth asked Michael to sit in the room during Laura's lessons, things turned around. As her teacher played simple combinations of notes, Laura quickly learned to mimic them by ear. As time passed, Elizabeth began insisting that Laura learn to read the music of the songs she played.

"But Mama, I can't see the notes on the music stand, even with my spectacles," Laura cried.

"Then memorize them before you sit down to play," Elizabeth urged.

"How do I do that?" Laura asked. Handing Laura her magnifying glass, she had replied. "One note at a time, dear child. One note at a time."

Elizabeth became a second mother to Michael, their voices often heard chatting and laughing together. Some days during that first summer, when Mr. Ellis was teaching Laura, Elizabeth enlisted Michael's help with simple chores such as posting letters, picking up groceries from the corner market, or carrying paperwork to Edward at his new office near the Englewood train depot. Elizabeth soon realized Michael's competence in everything she assigned him.

Stephen Ellis eventually learned to enjoy his newfound status at the Beall's social table. He particularly enjoyed the luncheons Elizabeth organized to introduce him to people around town. He also became particularly infatuated with Laura's new piano teacher. Stephen and Michael accompanied her and Laura to several concerts. Even Stephen became more jovial as time went on.

By the end of summer, Stephen accepted Elizabeth's offer to be Laura's year-round tutor. He sold his house in downtown Chicago and moved with Michael permanently to Englewood.

***

"Of course, it worked out just as Mother had planned. Mr. Ellis served as my tutor for the next six years."

"And Michael?" I prompted.

"Mother recognized Michael's potential early on and insisted Father hire him. He's been with the Wanatah ever since. When my father became ill, Michael stepped up. Anything Michael didn't already know about the railroad business, Father or I taught him. He became Father's point man with the company, bringing us contracts and other paperwork almost daily. For those long months before Father's death, the company ran as usual."

Now Michael serves as Laura's point-man. "He's my eyes and ears inside the Wanatah. He comes by early in the morning, a couple of days a week, to review contracts and other paperwork with me. Then he returns to headquarters in Delphi and carries out my orders. Most importantly, he takes me to meetings in my office in the Pullman Car and accompanies me when I travel the line. Because of him, I can do my job as well as some with all their sight."

# Chapter 18

"Are you coming to the library with me? Aunt Lo says the library fills up every day with people who are desperate to get out of the cold. She could use our help."

"Not today, Charlie. Miss Beall asked me to pick up a package for her from Thrasher's."

"Okay, but don't forget Aunt Lo wants us at the church by eight o'clock tomorrow morning to help her pull out the stage sets she painted for the pageant. They're in the church basement."

I groaned. "Can't you and Bernard do that job? That basement gives me the creeps."

"Don't be such a grump," Charlie poked me in the rib. "See you at home later."

I walked to Thrasher's for Miss Beall a couple of days a week. Today, the department store's two front windows held nothing but toys, displayed beautifully around a Christmas tree trimmed with colorful ornaments, sparkling with silver garland, and covered in tinsel. I loved tinsel, but Mother insisted we put it on our tree one strand at a time. It was tedious work, but the result was worth it.

Amidst the vast assortment of the latest toys, I spotted a Kewpie doll like the one I'd seen in the Sears and Roebuck catalog that arrived at our house last week. The doll, wearing the cutest smocked dress, sat at a small table with a tea set. It reminded me of the tea parties I'd enjoyed with Miss Beall over the last few weeks.

After ogling the toys, I went inside to the front counter. "Good afternoon, Miss Ghere" The salesclerk always greeted me with a big smile, but she only ever wore the one dowdy dress which she doused with perfume from the sample bottles on the cosmetic counter. I'd seen her do it a dozen times. "I have Miss Beall's order right here."

She pulled out a thin paper bag from under the counter and handed it to me. "Is this everything?"

"Yes, dear. That's it for today."

"Thank you."

Outside, I opened the bag and peeked inside. As I suspected, it was more sheet music to add to the collection Miss Beall kept in an ornate cabinet in her music room. I slipped the bag under my coat to keep the wind from blowing it out of my hand on my walk back.

As I stepped onto Miss Beall's porch, the oak door swung open.

"Thank you, child." Miss Beall lifting the bag from my hand. "Would you care to come in for a few minutes?"

I nodded.

I followed the woman into the reception hall. "Come into my office, if you don't mind. I'm expecting a telephone call."

I slipped off my coat and settled into the chair across the big desk from her.

"I've been so busy these last few days, we haven't had time to talk. I wanted to tell you that Michael arranged for me to meet Mrs.

McPherson in Delphi. Poor dear, she's really struggling with the death of her husband. I'm also hoping to meet with one of my suppliers while I'm there."

I didn't know what a supplier was, but I didn't ask.

"I'm expecting a delivery on Wednesday. Are you familiar with the stationery store?"

"Yes, Miss."

"If you could go pick it up after school, I would appreciate it. I should be back by then, but if I'm not, can you keep the package at your house?"

"I can put it on Mother's desk in the parlor. It will be safe there."

Laura opened her desk drawer, took out a dime, and placed it in front of me.

"You must have a dollar or more saved up by now. Are you saving for something special?" When I didn't answer, she prompted me again. "Child, I asked you a question."

"I was saving to buy new shoes, but I gave my coins to Gus. He used them and most of his own money to buy coal. Mother owes several bills, so Gus is trying to help her. He told me he's looking for a better job. Since Popo left, Gus may have to quit school to work to support the family. Mother will be angry if he quits, but Gus says it may be the only way to keep the family going."

I stopped to take a breath.

"I see."

"Today's my birthday," I muttered. "Mother forgot my birthday."

"How old are you, child?"

"Ten."

"I remember when I was ten. It was a difficult time for me, as well."

I looked up at Laura's colorless face set against the blackness of her dress. As she sat motionless, her hands folded on the top of her desk, I saw a hint of sadness cross her face, the first tiny crack in her otherwise steadfast composure.

"I hope you understand your mother's predicament. She has her hands full, and I'm sure she didn't mean to forget your birthday."

"Mother didn't forget Thea's birthday." I closed my eye, fighting back the tears. "But she... "

"Listen to me, child. Life is too short to be angry with your mother. Times are hard, and your mother is doing the best she can under the circumstances."

"I know."

"I lost my mother when I was your age and have missed her every day since. She left this earth too soon."

We sat in silence for a good long while. Laura seemed at ease with nothing but the ticking of a clock, or the sound of the wind rattling the trees outside the window. Charlie was like that.

I finally broke the silence.

"How did your mother die?" I asked.

Laura Beal took a deep breath, exhaling slowly. "She was murdered by a madman."

***

"Let's have a cup of tea and a cookie to celebrate your birthday. I hope you like oatmeal."

Laura rose from her desk and slipped past me. I stood up and closed my eyes, following the sound of the swishing of her long black dress into the kitchen. We chatted as Laura prepared the tea and set the table.

Again, I mimicked her every move as we sipped our tea and nibbled our cookies. I told her that Thea had the croup but was better today. Then we talked about Aunt Lo's plans for the Christmas pageant.

Miss Beall dabbed the corners of her lips with a linen napkin. "Tell me, child, what do you think of the oatmeal cookie? Oatmeal is one of my favorites."

I looked up and saw her eyes dancing behind her thick lenses.

I hesitated a moment. "It's good."

"But?"

"It's not as good as Mother's oatmeal cookies."

She smiled. "You sound certain of yourself?"

"Oh, yes, I'm certain. Mother has a knack for baking cookies."

"You were certainly correct about the sugar cookies you brought me the other day. Delicious, just as you said."

Miss Beall took another sip of her tea, then settled the china cup back into its saucer.

"You haven't told me what happened to your mother."

She gave me a weak smile. "It's not a story I like to tell, so let me show you."

I followed Miss Beall into the music room. There she lifted the heavy cover from the family Bible that lay on a table near her piano. Then she held a delicate newspaper clipping out to me. My hand trembled as I read the *Chicago Tribune* headline and news item dated March 11, 1907.

***

## WOMAN FOUND MURDERED IN HER HOME

**Mrs. Elizabeth A. Beall Killed By "Mad Strangler" at Her Home Outside Chicago**

*Mrs. Elizabeth A. Beall was recently strangled to death by an unknown person designated as the "Mad Strangler" at her home in Englewood. Mrs. Beall was found dead in the bedroom of her home one day last week, and her body bore evidence that she had been choked to death. Her husband, Edward Beall, was out of town at the time of the murder. Mr. Beall is president of the Wanatah Railroad.*

*Mrs. Clair Newton of Mount Carmel, was also strangled to death in her home recently and officials of the two cities believe both murders were committed by the same person. Two women in Chicago have reported being attacked in the same manner but were able to escape with their lives. At last report, the strangler had not been captured.*

***

Miss Beall told me that when her father returned home the next morning and found his wife dead, Laura was still sound asleep in her bedroom. The police immediately suspected Edward of doing his wife in, but there were many witnesses to his whereabouts during the previous two days.

The porter from the train station, who had driven him that morning, was just stepping off the front porch from delivering his bag when he heard Edward scream. The death of Elizabeth devastated his husband and daughter, and the entire Wanatah family.

The day before her funeral, Police Detective Mills stopped by the house and asked Edward if he could have one last look around the crime scene to see if there was anything he might have missed. Laura followed the two men into the bedroom, threw her head back, and took a deep breath.

"I can still smell him," she whispered.

"What's that you say, darling?" Her father fell on his knees in front of her and put his hands on her shoulders. "Tell me. Please," he pleaded.

That's when Laura told her father and the police detective that a man had come to the house the day of her mother's murder looking for work. Her mother paid him to remove the sticks that had fallen during the winter and to till the dead leaves into her flower beds to make them ready for her spring flowers.

"I was with Mother at the door, and I was with her when she paid him. I thought he had the oddest odor. He smelled of mildew, manure, and burning wood. And yet there was a hint of spring to him. Also, he had been drinking. Whiskey, I'm sure of it, maybe a Kentucky blend, but not exactly like the one you like, Father."

Edward gently smoothed his daughter's hair.

"His smell is still in the house."

Edward stood up. "Listen to my daughter," Edward had urged the detective. As a courtesy to the grieving man, the police detective talked to several of the Bealls' neighbors. Two women gave the detective a description of the kindly man who had been in the neighborhood looking for work.

The police put together a rendering of him, had them printed and sent copies to several newspapers, along with a story, asking readers to keep a lookout for the man. Horrified that the story referenced his ten-year-old daughter's contribution to the lead, Edward refused to leave Laura's side.

A month passed with no new leads. Then Edward discovered someone had slipped a note through the Bealls' mail slot. It read simply, "You are next." Edward didn't think the killer was after him. He believed he was after his daughter.

Edward Beall insisted he and Laura leave their house immediately. The Wanatah became their temporary home. On his journeys between Chicago and Louisville, Edward conducted business in a Pullman car he had converted into an office and boardroom.

Because his wife and daughter often travelled with him, he also had a personal sleeping car just behind the office car. It was comfortable and familiar to Laura, the obvious place for Edward to hide his daughter from any threat from the "Mud City Strangler," a moniker coined by one of the *Tribune's* crime reporters. "Mud City," a reference to the fact the terrain of the city used to be a mud flat, first appeared in an article that reported muddy boot prints at the home of a third victim, who suffered grave injuries from the attack, but survived.

***

Miss Beall replaced the yellowed newspaper clipping back inside her Bible. I waited for her to continue.

"My father hired three young men to assist him," Laura recalled. "He did business at a rapid pace, so it amazed me he didn't need an army of assistants.

The assistants would get off the train at various stops to make telephone calls, post letters, arrange meetings, that kind of thing. Then the train would pick them up on our way back through. One of the young men was my former tutor's son, Michael Ellis. He was only sixteen when my father hired him, but very capable. I always felt safe when Michael was aboard the train."

Laura Beall took a deep breath, her eyes closed behind her thick lenses. "We lived on that train for six months. One day, I told my father I wanted to go home. The police caught the Mud City Strangler weeks before, although not before he killed two more innocent women. But my father was still hesitant to return to our home in Englewood. That's when he bought this Victorian and moved us here, lock, stock and barrel. He also moved the Wanatah's headquarters to Delphi. We still spent a great deal of time in the Pullman car, but at least I had a proper home again... and my piano."

Miss Beall sat down on the bench. "Music saved me. When I play, I remember her beauty, her vivaciousness, her determination that composed my mother's entire being. Sitting here allows me to push away the tragedy of her death and relish the gifts she gave me."

I walked over to the piano, stood next to her, and waited.

"My mother often told me that one day I would play a concert in front of hundreds of people. It was a silly notion, really, for a girl with my limitations. But I'm certain she believed such a concert lay in my future. To this day, I study and memorize music, and I practice for that concert my mother will never hear. I now imagine my father sitting in that chair." She pointed at the old leather chair with the shawl draped over the back, "...humming along, shouting 'Bravo' at the end of each performance. Mother wasn't here, but I prayed that the music somehow reaches her."

"Will you play for me, Miss?" I asked. She nodded, then pointed to her father's favorite chair, an invitation for me to sit down. She placed her hands on the keyboard, closed her eyes, and played the most beautiful music I'd ever heard.

When she finished, she placed her hands on her lap, her voice now almost imperceptible. "I wear this black dress to express the grief I feel over losing my mother so many years ago."

I sat in the chair, my hands in my lap, my head down. I felt the grief of losing Laura's mother, as if it happened yesterday, collide with the grief I felt about losing my father. The joy of the music did its best to overwhelm my grief, my anger, and most of all, my fear, of my father's absences. I felt as confused as I did the day I watched him walk away from me.

"Where are the angels when you need them most?" I muttered, more to myself than to my hostess.

Miss Laura stood up from her place behind her keyboard, fell to her knees in front of me, and took my hands into hers. I marveled at those hands that had played the magnificent music that had burst to life from her grief. She's played it just for me on my birthday. Just for me.

"The angels are right here, holding you up. They're guiding you along the path God has planned for you in His Book of Life. Things don't always go the way you think they should. But the angels are here to whisper the story of eternity into your ears that refuse to hear, because you want to know about something that is so insignificant when compared to the vastness of eternity."

I lifted my head and looked into her face.

"Your mother and father will love each other, or they won't. It's your job to love them both, no matter what. Promise me, child, that you'll do that."

I took a deep breath. "I promise." It's what I'd been doing all along.

As I opened the front door to leave, Laura Beall called out to me. "Remember to cherish your mother, child. Cherish your mother!"

Not a suggestion. A command.

# Chapter 19

He flowed into my awareness, one sense at a time. The creak of the door, his slow, rhythmic footsteps across the wooded floor barely entering my consciousness. Then the faint smell of his favorite pomade tickling my nose; the gentle touch of the back of his hand as it stroked my cheek, nudging me from my sleep. I felt a weight lift off my life.

"Happy birthday, Angel," he whispered.

"Popo, you remembered."

"Of course, I remembered. How could I forget my favorite girl's tenth birthday? What a glorious day when Doc Becker laid you in my arms for the first time. You seemed as happy to see me as I was to see you."

I sat up, rubbed my soft cheek against his rough one, then collapsed into his full embrace. I pulled back so I could see his face. The nightlight in the hallway cast enough light for my eyes to believe that Popo had really returned. My memories of him filled in details. His firm chin, aquiline nose, and full lips hiding a perfect line of teeth. The laugh lines that had already formed around his sparkling blue eyes. I touched the brown, wavy strand of hair that had escaped his morning application of pomade.

"I've missed you so much," I whispered. "Where have you been?"

Popo brought his index finger to his lips, then pointed to Gem, who stirred in the bed next to me. Then he picked me up and tiptoed out of the bedroom, gently pulling the door closed behind us. He slipped down the staircase, avoiding the two squeaky steps that always got Mother's attention.

Still wearing his winter coat, he sat down in his favorite chair in the green room, me in his lap, and switched on the reading lamp on the side table. Then he pulled the old quilt from the back of the chair and wrapped it around me. I noticed the folded newspaper, the one with a photograph of the local pumpkin patch, was still on the side table, his reading spectacles resting on top of it. I wondered why Mother hadn't used the old newspaper to wrap her garbage or in the chicken coop as she usually did.

With Popo's arms around me, he said, "Tell me, Angel, how is everyone?"

I started with the most important thing. "Thea has the croup. She got it a couple days after Thanksgiving, but I think she's better now. Thea hasn't seemed so frail lately and I think Mother was worried that another fever, another illness, might cause a setback."

Popo nodded for me to continue.

"Rehearsal for the Christmas pageant begins soon at the church fellowship hall," I pause to think for a moment. "I almost forgot. I've become friends with Miss Laura Beall."

"Laura Beall? Good heavens." A broad smile spread across Popo's handsome face.

"I run errands for her."

"Apparently, I've missed a lot."

"Yes, you have." Then I asked him the question I'd struggled with since he left.

"Popo, where have you been?"

"Here and there. Remember me telling you about Jerry, one of the other salesmen at the company I work for? Well, he's the boss's son-in-law. He broke his ankle after he tripped on a tree root while getting chased by a farmer's dog. I've been working part of his route, making a little extra money. I don't know how long that will last. The boss seems determined to kick Jerry out of the office and get him back to supporting his only daughter."

"Thank you for sending the food to us for Thanksgiving."

"I'm glad it arrived on time."

"You didn't come for Thanksgiving dinner, but you're back now." I fell into him again, wanting to hold on to my father forever.

"Yes, I'm here now. Tell me all how Thanksgiving Day went."

"It was good, especially when Mother threw Uncle Karl and Aunt Iris out of our house."

Popo chuckled. "She did, did she? I'll bet that was something to behold."

I giggled. "It was the best part of the day, besides the pie."

We sat in silence for a while. I counted the ticks of the big clock that sat on a shelf over the Zenith radio, each one a moment I had Popo all to myself.

After a while, Popo asked, "How did you meet Laura Beall? She's been reclusive since her father died a few years back."

I told him the story, holding back none of the details.

When I finished my story, I felt Popo shift in his chair beneath me. "Angel, it's almost midnight. If you don't get your birthday present now, I'll have to keep it until your birthday."

"No, I want it now."

"Go get my satchel. It's by the front door."

I carried it into the green room and set it by his feet. Then I watched as Popo pulled out a small bundle wrapped in white cloth tied with a piece of twine. After I crawled back into his lap, he handed it to me.

"Be careful. Don't break it."

I placed the bundle on my lap, gently pulled off the twine, and carefully unwrapped it. Inside was a beautiful ceramic angel. Miss Laura's words slipped across my mind. "The angels are right here, holding you up."

My beautiful angel had hair the color of mine, topped with a halo of gold, and wore a flowing blue gown. The silver tray in her hands held blue flower blossoms.

"They're the color of Mother's delphiniums." I pointed to the delicate details. "Oh, Popo, I love it."

"I knew you would. It reminded me of *my* angel." I turned the ceramic figurine over and over in my hands, amazed by its perfection.

"Be sure to put your angel on top of your bureau, where it can look down on you while you sleep... and where Thea can't reach it."

"Popo, you're going to stay, aren't you? I need you. We all need you, but I need you the most."

He shook his head. "Your mother made it clear to me that..."

"When are you leaving?" I crossed my arms across my chest.

"Angel."

"That's what you do, Popo. You leave. When we need you the most, you leave."

I slide off of his lap and took a step back.

"It's not about you, Angel."

"Yes, it is. It's about all of us. We're a family."

"I'm sorry, Angel. Please forgive me."

"No!"

As tears streamed down my cheeks, he pulled me to him and held me tight. When I cried myself out, he offered me something comforting to hold on to.

"Tell you what, Angel. The next time you need me, write me a note and have Gus deliver it to Old Man Gregory at his office. He'll get the note to me. Is that a deal?"

I nodded, believing his promise with all my heart. After my father gathered up his satchel and left, I made a promise to myself...

I wasn't losing him again.

# Chapter 20

"Mother said to hurry." Gem stood in the doorway of our bedroom, a hand on her hip. "Breakfast is almost ready, and Aunt Lo is downstairs pacing like a caged tiger."

"I'll be down in a minute."

After Popo left last night, I'd re-wrapped my birthday angel in the white cloth, re-tied it with twine, and placed it in my shoebox in the bureau before climbing back into bed next to Gem. Now I lifted it out of the shoebox, excited to open my birthday gift a second time. I ran a finger around her golden halo, then along the ridge of her wings, one at a time. In the morning light coming in through the window, I realized the color of her gown was the same color as that of my favorite blue dress, the one Mother made for me last autumn to wear on my first day of fourth grade.

I re-wrapped my birthday angel and gently laid it back in my shoe-box. Then I sat down on the bed and thought about the day Mother had given me the shoebox three years ago. The story flooded back to me.

***

When Charlie spotted the faded-green farm truck sitting at the curb in front of our house, he yelled, "Mama and Papa are here." He took off running, me at his heels. As we bounded in the front door, Gem collared us.

"Where's Mama?" Charlie asked, wriggled out of his cousin's grasp. "She's upstairs with Mother, but we have to stay down here." She put an arm around each of us and guided us into the kitchen.

"What's going on?" I asked.

With tears in her eyes, Gem said softly, "Mother's in labor."

"The baby isn't due until early January," said Charlie, worry creasing his brow. By the look on my cousin's face, I knew something was terribly wrong.

Gem told us Mother had summoned Aunt Lo from the library soon after we left for school. When she arrived at our house, Doc Becker was already at Mother's bedside. Aunt Lo telephoned Rachel, who made it into town in record time in that old truck that rarely left the farm.

"Where's Popo?" I asked. "Does he know?"

Gem shrugged. "I don't know."

My brothers, Charlie, Gem, and I passed the evening in the green room, listening to the Zenith while playing Rook without our usual enthusiasm. Gus and the twins went out to the barn to tend the chickens and Old Barney. After Charlie fell asleep reading in the window seat, Gem and I curled up on the sofa. I stared into space until I fell asleep.

Just after midnight, Aunt Lo appeared in the doorway. "You have a baby sister." The exhaustion in her voice was palpable. "Your Mother wants you to come upstairs to meet her."

We scrambled to our feet and pounded up the stairs. Popo was pacing in the hallway. I didn't know when he arrived home, but I was happy to see him. I ran to him and wrapped my arms around his leg.

He leaned down and kissed the top of my head. "Your mother wants to see you, so go on now," he said. "Don't keep her waiting. She's had a rough day."

Crowding into the doorway, we saw Mother sitting up in bed, holding a tiny white bundle. Aunt Rachel laid on the bed next to Mother, sound asleep. Charlie crawled up next to his mother, and put his arms around her.

"She's so tiny," I said. She wasn't the least bit cute, but everyone could see that for themselves.

"I've named her Dorothea," Mother said. "The name means 'miracle.' After everything we've gone through tonight, I know this child is a miracle."

We agreed it was the perfect name.

"I think we'll call her Thea." Mother lifted the tiny bundle to her lips and kissed her gently.

Looking as if he'd been through a war, Doc Becker paced the area around the bed. The worst was over, but it seemed the news hadn't caught up with his body yet.

"This child arrived too early," he said, wringing his hands. "I'd say she only weighs two pounds, so we must all prepare ourselves that she may not make it."

"Nonsense," Mother interrupted.

"Everyone out now," Aunt Lo instructed, pointing toward the hall-way. "Go off to bed, the lot of you. Your mother needs her rest. And let's not forget you have school in the morning."

We groaned.

"Can't we play hooky just one day?"

"No, Cory, you may not play hooky, tomorrow or any day." Nothing gets past Mother in this house.

Just as Gem and I climbed into bed, I heard Aunt Lo's voice in the hallway. Gem put a finger to her lips, her sign for me to be quiet so she could hear what was being said.

"Gus, where's your father?" Her voice was soft but stern. "He hasn't seen his new daughter yet."

"He left. You said Mother needed her rest, so I think he went to your house to sleep. Do you want me to go find him?"

"No, you need to go to bed. I'll track that brother of mine down. And when I do..."

Over the next few days, Aunt Lo, Aunt Rachel, and MaMaw Ghere took turns tending to Mother and baby Thea. Popo had disappeared, but no one, not even Mother, mentioned his absence.

A week after the surprise birth, Mother walked into the kitchen while we were eating breakfast, carrying her newborn infant in a shoe-box she'd lined with blankets. She set the shoebox in the center of the table before joining Aunt Lo at the sink, where she was washing the breakfast dishes. As we bounded out the door for school, Mother called out to my big brother.

"Gus, after school, please go by Ghere-Douglass and ask your father to come home immediately."

School could wait. Gus bolted past us on the street, finally getting the assignment to find our wayward father. Popo returned home than evening for supper.

Mother quickly regained her strength, and Thea grew. When she was six weeks old, Mother pronounced Thea too big for her shoebox and transferred her to a cradle Mother kept by her bed at night. It wasn't until I heard Thea cry for the first time that I believed what Mother had insisted all along.

Dorothea Lucinda Ghere would survive.

***

Aunt Lo showed no mercy for Charlie and Bernard, as they wrestled the stage sets from last year's pageant out of the church basement. As the boys carried them into the fellowship hall, one by one, and leaned them against a wall, Aunt Lo asked me to take a rag and wipe the cobwebs off. I offered to trade chores with Bernard, but he made a face and followed Charlie out of the fellowship hall.

As I was cleaning off the long, sticky strands of dusty spider web, Aunt Lo paced the line of old sets randomly propped against the back-stage wall, *um-ing, huh-ing* and *hmm-ing* as she went, the pragmatic art critic of her own art, jotting notes on a pad using a lot of exclamation points. "I'll have to rework a couple of these," she mumbled.

"Maybe you should send Cory to snag your paint boxes from under Aunt Iris's bed," I offered with a smirk.

"I think not. Watercolors aren't appropriate for this project. I'll have to beg oil paints from my friend again. I believe he owes me a favor."

At 9:15, the other children began arriving. Aunt Lo sat behind a table she's set up near the entrance to the fellowship hall where she conducted brief "auditions" with each child. Half an hour later, she assigned parts. Charlie landed the part of Joseph. I was in the multitude of the heavenly host, although my part required me to flit by the manger and gaze at the baby Jesus adoringly.

Baffled by the concept, I asked my cousin. "How do you flit, Charlie?"

"Don't ask me. I just need to learn a couple of lines, that's it."

"Do not lose your scripts, children," Aunt Lo commanded. "If you do, you'll have to stay after rehearsal and copy your part from my notebook yourself."

The rest of the morning was chaotic, reading through our parts and going through the Christmas songs we'd be singing, with Aunt Lo at the piano.

After we finished our first rehearsal, the children scattered. I made plans with Pauline and Helen to come over to play cards after lunch, as Aunt Lo locked the door to the fellowship hall.

As we began our walk home, I slipped between Charlie and Bernard, placing my hand on my cousin's elbow to keep from falling on the slippery sidewalk. Aunt Lo trailed behind by a step or two. As we walked in silence, I noticed Charlie turn and look over my head at Aunt Lo.

"I think the Widower Pastor Burke is sweet on you, Aunt Lo."

I looked up into Charlie's face, his mischievous smile spread ear-to-ear.

"Yes, it would seem so," she replied.

"Are you going to marry him?" I elbowed Charlie hard in the ribs for asking Aunt Lo such a question.

"Certainly not," she huffed.

We continued walking, Aunt Lo right behind us, spurring us forward. Mother promised us a hot lunch at quarter past noon, and Aunt Lo was always prompt. As I held onto Charlie's elbow, I noticed for the first time that he was taller than me. He was more than a year older, but we had always been about the same height. Bernard was tall for a boy of thirteen, but skinny as a pipe rail.

Finally, Aunt Lo explained her answer to Charlie's question. "The Widower Pastor Burke is a good, kind, and virtuous man. I believe he is philosophically accurate in his interpretation of the Holy Scriptures, but I find his sermons... " Aunt Los hesitated to weigh her words, "...a bit rambling and on the boring side."

"You wouldn't marry him because he's boring?" inquired the Ernie Pyle wannabe.

"There is that, but there are two other reasons I could never marry the Widower Pastor Burke that have nothing to do with his frequent lapses into tedium. Their names are Clara and Cora."

"His daughters?" I asked, my eyes wide.

Aunt Lo nodded. "Since their mother's passing, the Widower Pastor Burke has coddled and spoiled those two to the point of turning them both into insufferable brats."

"But Aunt Lo, they lost their mother." I thought about Miss Beall's command for me to cherish mine.

Aunt Lo placed a hand on my shoulder as we walked. "Yes, it's difficult to lose a mother. They were perfectly lovely girls before she passed. I think it dishonors her to behave contrary to the lessons she taught them, and I think it's worse that their father allows it. Those two flitted around during today's rehearsal as if they owned the place, not paying one iota of attention to a word I said."

Charlie elbowed me in the ribs. If I knew my Aunt Lo, the Widower Pastor Burke was in for an earful before our next rehearsal.

As we walked along the sidewalk, still wet from the melting snow, I thought about Mr. McPherson, who stepped in front of a train on Thanksgiving Day, leaving his wife and family to fend for themselves. I thought about Edward and Elizabeth Beall when their daughter was born different from other children. The McPherson children may go hungry. The Bealls' daughter now runs a railroad.

Then I thought about Mother and Popo when they learned Thea was partially deaf. Mother seemed to ignore Thea's hearing problem. Popo fled. I believed neither did right by Thea. I told Aunt Lo that.

"Annie, your mother ponders things. She turns them over and over in her head before she gets too far down the wrong road. Eventually, she'll figure out how to help Thea. I promise you that. Your mother is a wonderful woman."

"What about Popo?"

Aunt Lo paused before answering. "We don't know for sure why Popo left. What I know for certain is that my beloved brother always comes around, even if it requires someone taking a broom to his backside."

"Aunt Lo, Aunt Iris has a broom you could borrow."

"She does, indeed."

Charlie shoved his hands into his pants pockets and leaned into the wind as it whipped along the street. "Do Aunt Maggie and Popo's problems have anything to do with her never leaving the house or yard?"

Both Aunt Lo and I gasped.

"What are you talking about, Charlie?" Aunt Lo took his arm and turned him around.

"She stopped going out a while back. Doesn't anyone notice what goes on around them?"

Aunt Lo ignored Charlie's question. "When did she stop?"

"I'm not exactly sure, but it was before Thea turned a year old. She always has an excuse not to leave the house. She always sends one of us to do her errands, the ones she used to love to do herself to get out of the house."

Speechless, I thought about how Mother and Popo didn't realize for many months that Thea couldn't hear. I now understood how you can miss something that's right in front of your face.

We continued walking, the wind pushing us toward home.

"My ma and pops, they had a right smart tiff a while back," said Bernard. "Cain't recall what caused it. They ain't said hide nor hair to t'other since then. An' sometimes I jest reckon I'm the growned-up, you might say, a-raisin' up them young'uns in our house and I ain't a-doin' much of a job, far as I kin see."

"Do you think your parents are bad people?" I asked.

Bernard shook his head. "They done got stuck in a mighty deep hole. 'Stead o' climbin' out, they just kept on a-diggin'. Now they's so far down, they can't see the light. An' they's plumb tuckered out from all that there diggin'."

Aunt Lo stepped up next to Bernard and put her arm around him. "You're a good man, Bernard Thompson. I'd be proud to have you as my son."

We walked in silence for a block, enjoying the slight break in the inclement weather.

"I'll tell you what, Bernard. If you'd like, you're welcomed to join our family, as long as you understand that we've got just as many problems as the next one."

"Thankee, Aunt Lo, fer yer mighty kind offer. I'd be right honored!"

"Who's going to tell Mother she's got another mouth to feed?" I just knew it wasn't going to be me.

"Bernard eats with us half the time anyway, so I don't think she'll notice," said Charlie.

We walked in silence for a couple of blocks before Charlie continued. "Bernard, have you thought about what you'll to say to close the pageant?"

Aunt Lo assigned Bernard the closing prayer, a natural choice for a boy who had conducted so many bird funerals and meal blessings.

"Naw, I'll jest hearken to the Lord when I git up there, same as I always do."

"So, you're going to improvise?" The mischief was back in Charlie's voice.

"What does 'improvise' mean?" I whispered to my cousin.

"It means to make it up as you go along," Charlie whispered back.

"No, no, no!" insisted my aunt. "There will be no improvising during my pageant. Bernard and I will sit down next week and write out the closing prayer, so he has plenty of time to memorize it before Christmas Eve. Won't we, Bernard?"

"Jes' as ye say, Aunt Lo, sure as shootin'."

"No improvising," repeated Aunt Lo. "Perhaps an elocution lesson or two might be in order, as well."

I looked at Charlie, who knew exactly what I wanted to ask him. "I'll tell you later," he whispered.

"I talks jist fine. Larnt from ma's folks."

Aunt Lo promptly changed the subject. "I still haven't come up with a closing act."

"What's that?"

"The closing act, dear girl, is the grand finale. A gifted young woman sang for us last year, but her husband took a job in Chicago and left her behind. She ended up in the poorhouse. Fortunately, her parents got wind of their daughter's predicament and rushed over from Bloomington, paid off her debts, and took her home. I heard she cried so much in the poorhouse that she lost her singing voice."

"What about Pauline?" I suggested. "She has a beautiful voice."

"That's a thought."

Charlie laughed. "There's no chance of improvisation there. If Pauline sang solo in front of a crowd of people, you might need a big hook to pull her off the stage."

I was about to defend my friend when Bernard shouted.

"Look!" He was pointing to a motor car parked in front of our house. Charlie, Bernard, and I took off running, leaving Aunt Lo to complete her journey home alone.

# Chapter 21

"What are you doing here?" My words sounded harsh and angry. Seeing Miss Beall sitting on the sofa in our parlor next to Gem talking to my mother shocked me. My family knew of my friendship with Miss Beall, but I held back talking about it because I wanted to keep her all to myself. She was *my* friend.

Mother's teapot was on the coffee table in front of the sofa. I couldn't help but think how shabby it looked compared to Miss Beall's ornate china teapot. Mother sat in a side chair at one end of the coffee table. She was holding Thea in her lap.

With her back to the door where I stood, Miss Beall held out her arm without turning around. "Child, come here so I can see you."

I felt Charlie give me a little nudge in the back. "Go on," he urged.

I walk over to Miss Beall and took her hand. It was the first time I'd ever touched her delicate white skin. A few of the mysteries about my friend fluttered away with this intimate connection, but new ones rushed in to fill the void.

"Goodness, child, your hand feels as cold as ice. Where are your gloves?"

"In Mother's mending basket," I replied. Mother promised to mend the holes in the fingers weeks ago, but never got around to it. She offered nothing in her own defense.

"Sit down next to your sister and me. I've been waiting for you. In the meantime, it has been a pleasure to get reacquainted with your mother."

"But what are you doing here, Miss?"

"Truth be told, child," she replied, "I've been trying to get the courage up to ask your mother for another of her delicious cookies."

Her answer made me smile. This close to Christmas, Mother always kept fresh-baked cookies and homemade divinity on hand to serve guests.

"You see, Mrs. Ghere..."

"Please call me Maggie."

"You see, Maggie, your daughter told me you baked the best cookies..."

"In the world," I offered.

"Precisely. The best cookies in the world. Those were your daughter's exact words."

"Pies, too. And cake and fudge."

"Anna, please." My Mother appeared uncomfortable with my praise.

Miss Beall nodded her head. "After tasting the cookies she brought me, I realized she was correct. As your daughter can attest, I have a particular fondness—or perhaps weakness is a better description—for cookies. I'm afraid it's a trait I inherited from my mother. When Michael came by today..."

"Michael?" I think my eyes were as big as saucers.

"Annie, please stop interrupting Miss Beall."

"I'll introduce you to him in a moment, child. When Michael came by today, I insisted he bring me here to beg." Turning to me, she continued, "Your mother says you were at pageant rehearsal, so I have lingered until your return, keeping your mother from enjoying her day."

Mother smiled. "Believe me, there's nothing I would have enjoyed more than your visit. Gem, please go into the kitchen and bring out a plate of cookies for our guests."

"I'll take care of that," piped up Aunt Lo, who was now standing in the doorway with Charlie and Bernard.

"Before your aunt goes, I think it would be polite if you introduced her to Miss Beall." Mother's words didn't sound like a suggestion.

"Miss Beall, this is my Aunt LoRetta Ghere. She's my father's sister who lives on the other side of Prairie Creek. And that's my cousin Charlie." I pointed.

Charlie stepped forward with his hand extended. "Nice to meet you, Miss Beall."

"And this is Bernard Thompson. He lives across the street."

He, too, stepped forward to shake Miss Beall's hand. "Ah, the purveyor of bird funerals and blessings."

Bernard smiled broadly, knowing I included him in my talks with Miss Beall. "Yessum, I'll be a-goin' to help Aunt Lo with the cookies, an' is there anythin' else I can fetch fer you, Aunt Maggie?"

My mother looked at me with raised eyebrows. I shrugged. "Aunt Lo has something to tell you, Mother."

"Ahh... thank you, Bernard. I think that's all for now."

For the first time, I noticed a tall man standing with my brothers in the corner of the parlor. He held one of Mother's teacups with both hands.

Michael.

Finally... Michael. Distinctive with a broad face and sculpted chin, his golden-brown eyes never shifting for long from his charge.

After Miss Beall introduced him to me, I whispered to her, "He's very handsome." Looking at my sister, I added, "Right Gem?" My sister nodded once in agreement.

"Is he now?"

"Gem agrees," I added. "Gem knows these things."

Aunt Lo soon returned with enough cookies for everyone, and two for our guest of honor. After Mother and Miss Beall ate their cookies and chatted for a few minutes, our unexpected guest rose.

"Maggie, before I go, might I have a private word with you?"

Mother hesitated before replying. "Certainly." She handed Thea to Gem.

Miss Beall turned to me and held out her hand. "Child, will you guide me? I am unfamiliar with my surroundings and afraid I'll trip and break something."

I stood up, and Miss Beall placed her hand on my shoulder. I followed Mother into the kitchen with Laura Beall close at my heels. It was there I learned why she really came to visit my mother.

***

Miss Beall sat across from Mother and me at our kitchen table. I was eager to hear why she'd come, but I knew her habit of settling into her thoughts before she spoke. She would get to her reason for coming here in her own time. As we waited, my eyes traced the lines of her perfect oval face. But for her tortoiseshell spectacles, her face seemed a delicate pencil rendering awaiting the artist's brush and palette. The woman's white hair and pale skin contradicted her youth.

I wriggled in my chair. Mother placed a gentle hand on mine, her silent appeal for patience.

Finally, our guest spoke. "If you will indulge me, please."

"Yes, of course." Mother folded her hands and place them on the table in front of her.

"My father became infatuated with railroads from the time they first dominated American commerce at the turn of the century," Miss Beall began.

***

Edward Beall grew up hearing stories from his grandfather about the rail industry. Sitting on the front porch of the elder's clapboard house in Wanatah, Indiana, the old blacksmith often pulled his grandson into his lap to tell tales of the dawning of the American Railroad Age. He often bragged about making his own appearance into the world on July 4, 1828, the very day construction began on the mighty Baltimore and Ohio Railroad.

"My first boyhood memory," he told Edward, "was laying my eyes upon Tom Thumb, the B&O's first American-built steam locomotive. It was truly a sight to behold."

As a young man, Edward longed to follow in the footsteps of the greatest names in American railroad expansion and innovation. Men like Cornelius Vanderbilt, Edward Harriman, Jay Gould, James Hill, and Collis Potter Huntington fascinated young Edward, who studied their rises to success in the railroad industry.

Eventually, Edward moved from his hometown of La Porte, Indiana, to Chicago to take a position with Pullman Car Company's operation there. The young man's vast knowledge of the industry mightily impressed George Pullman, the company's founder. Edward began his meteoric rise in the company under his new boss's tutelage. After Pullman's death in 1897, Edward served as the right-hand man of the company's successor, Robert Todd Lincoln.

Located at the intersection of lake, river and railroad routes, Chicago was a natural hub of commerce in the country, with the rail industry at its heart. Trains carried coal to Chicago's steel mills, and cattle and hogs to the city's stockyards, as well as wheat, corn, and mail. But most importantly to Edward and the company that employed him, they carried passengers.

George Pullman didn't invent the sleeper car (though he never dissuaded those who thought otherwise), but he certainly added a measure of comfort and elegance to the sleeper car experience.

As hundreds of small railroad lines cropped up across the nation, Edward, too, dreamed of owning his own line. He certainly possessed the business acumen and knowledge of the industry that rivaled the captains of the industry, but after he launched the Wanatah Railroad, he refused to use exploitation, and the other unscrupulous tactics required to grow a small line into a personal fortune. Elizabeth saw to that. She dubbed the employees of their railroad the "Wanatah family," and treated them as such.

The limited freight service that stretched from Michigan City to Indianapolis was the first Wanatah line to go live. While freight service became the new venture's bread and butter, Edward's passion for passenger travel, fueled by his years with the Pullman Car Company, became his obsession... and ultimately his reality. Edward awoke every morning striving to make his passenger service fast, dependable, and comfortable. With the introduction of his impeccable dining car service, the Wanatah soon became the line of choice for passengers traveling between Chicago and Louisville, Kentucky.

Once the passenger service became fully operational, Laura's parents redefined their roles in the company. While Edward took care of business—track leases, freight contracts, labor negotiations, and so on—Elizabeth took care of the Wanatah family. Edward often said that anyone who believed his role was more important than his wife's was sadly mistaken.

Elizabeth paved the way to friendly negotiations between adversaries with civilized private dinners; and meticulously planned advisory board meetings down to the seating arrangements. She could put employee names to faces at every stop along the line, nurturing an enduring loyalty that flowed both ways. Elizabeth loved the workers who made the Wanatah possible, and they loved her.

Elizabeth never stopped doing Edward's research, which she skillfully summarized and fed to her busy husband. She kept a finger on the pulse of the Wanatah, as a mother keeps a hand on the back of her sleeping infant.

The year the passenger line became fully operational marked the culmination of all the years of planning and building that the Bealls put in. Elizabeth wanted to celebrate.

As Christmastime approached, she began searching for a way to thank all the employees along every section of the line. With many challenges still ahead for the fledgling Wanatah, Edward implored her not to spend a fortune. Elizabeth was quick to reassure him by saying, "Not to worry, darling. I promise to only spend a small one."

After days of contemplation, Elizabeth settled upon the perfect gift for the Wanatah's employees: cookies. Other than the Wanatah and her family, cookies were her one indulgence, and she wanted to share that indulgence with her Wanatah family.

Elizabeth set out to deliver a box of cookies tied with a red bow to every member of the Wanatah family. In a matter of days, she established her supply chain. She hired six bakers, one for each of the six sections of the line, and devised a rigorous delivery schedule.

With young Laura in tow, Elizabeth rode the various sections of the line, getting off just long enough to drop off the boxes of cookies to the stationmaster for delivery, and to greet as many employees and passengers as possible before climbing back aboard the train for the short trip to the next station. Edward made it clear to his wife that her cookie escapade was not to delay any scheduled departures. Had he realized how much Elizabeth's warm personal gesture meant to the Wanatah family, he would have agreed to allow his beloved wife to take all the time she needed.

***

Miss Beall dabbed a single tear from her cheek.

"After Mother's death, Father and I were determined to continue the Christmas tradition she'd started. The first year after her death was difficult, but Father put everything aside to coordinate the cookie deliveries. He was the stand-in for my mother, riding the line from Chicago to Louisville to wish the Wanatah family a merry Christmas, with me at his side.

Michael helped, too, reminding Father of employee's names, and carrying the day when Father's grief overtook him. Our three days delivering cookies provided me with the only joyful memories of that

Christmas season. Despite her death, she was there with us. I'm certain of that."

Miss Beall paused, the wave of memories flooding her thoughts.

"The year I turned fifteen, Father turned Mother's cookie escapade over to me. In my mind, he'd handed me the most important task of the Wanatah line's entire year. With Michael's help, I visited the various bakers along the line in October and reviewed the cookie selection and re-sourced our packaging. Then I wrote a Christmas message on my mother's personal notecards, which I attached to each box with Mother's favorite red ribbon. I've done it every year since."

Miss Beall shifted in her chair and brushed a stray strand of white hair from her forehead with the back of her hand. "Which brings me to why I am here today."

Mother's face was placid as she waited for our guest to continue.

"I am determined to carry on the tradition. Unfortunately, my baker in Section 2 of the line, this section, suffered a heart attack last week. I learned from his wife this morning that he passed away yesterday. While I am deeply saddened by the tragic loss of this good man, I don't want to disappoint the families along this section of the line. With Christmas almost upon us, I need to replace him as quickly as possible. That's when I thought of you, Maggie."

"Me?" Mother gasped.

"Are you going to be friends with Mother now?" I asked Miss Beall.

She looked at me wryly. "I certainly hope so. But you know, child, you are my best friend, if you don't count Michael."

# Chapter 22

After the excitement of Laura Beall's visit, conversation over supper remained unusually low-key. As we cleared the dishes, Mother asked, "Girls, would you mind finishing up in here?"

"No, we don't mind," replied Gem. "It won't take more than a few minutes."

"Check on Thea when you're done. She's with Charlie and Bernard in the parlor. I'll be upstairs, if you need me."

Gem and I finished our kitchen chores in silence. I wanted to ask my sister what she thought of Miss Beall, and if Mother had mentioned anything about what they talked about in private—that Miss Beall wanted Mother to bake Christmas cookies for the Wanatah family. But Gem seemed deep in thought, so I didn't ask. When we finished cleaning the kitchen, I went upstairs.

I looked in my parents' bedroom and saw Mother sitting in her chair by the window, the last of the day's autumn light fading to darkness.

"Mother?" She looked over at me standing in the doorway.

"Anna." I walked in uninvited and sat on the edge of her bed. "What did you think of Miss Beall? Is she how you remembered her?"

"Her look is distinctive... unusual. The last time I saw her, she was still young—we both were. She was a year or two older than Gem is now. All these years later, she's so poised and confident that after a few moments I forgot she is nearly blind."

"Miss Beall owns the Wanatah. She runs the railroad, too."

"Anna, you must be mistaken. Did she tell you she ran the railroad?"

"Yes, Mother, she told me herself. Laura Beall runs the railroad."

"Women don't run railroads. Running a company like that is a man's job."

"Have you heard of Sarah Clark Kidder? She ran a railroad out in California after her husband died. She made a grand success of it, too."

"Who told you that?"

"Laura Beall told me, and Charlie and I found a story about her in a book in the library. Miss Beall said her father met Mrs. Kidder once, and that she knew as much about running a railroad as anyone. Now so does Miss Beall."

Mother's eyes shifted back to the street as she pondered what I'd told her. That's when I asked, "Are you going to bake cookies for Miss Beall and the Wanatah family?"

"I promised Miss Beall I would think about it. She needs nearly a thousand cookies. Anna, I can't imagine a thousand cookies, let alone know where to start."

"You know as much about baking cookies as anyone."

"I can bake them in small batches, but that many cookies coming out of my small kitchen in three or four days' time seems impossible. Besides, I know nothing about business."

"Miss Beall knows all about business. She will help you. I know she will keep her word. You'll have everything you need, just like she promised."

"That's just it. I don't know what I need. She said I could use my own recipes, but I'd have to figure how much sugar, flour, butter, and all the other ingredients I'd need. What if I figure wrong, and don't have what I need to finish the job?" Mother took a breath and sighed. "And you know how I feel about accepting charity."

"Charity?" I stared at Mother in disbelief. "She didn't offer you charity. I run errands for Miss Beall, and she gives me coins. Is that charity?"

"I suppose not."

"She pays all her bakers. Why wouldn't she pay you? Giving cookies to the Wanatah family at Christmas is a way she honors her mother. Please think about it. We'll all help you... I promise."

"I wouldn't want to let her down."

"When Thea and I were sick with scarlet fever, you didn't let us down. You won't let her down. I know you won't."

We sat in silence for a good long while. She looked up at me and smiled. "I know I don't tell you often enough, but I'm proud that you're my daughter. You're so wise for a nine-year-old girl."

"Ten."

"What?" The expression on Mother's face told me it just dawned on her that she'd missed my birthday.

"I'm ten now."

"Oh, Anna, I am so sorry I missed your birthday. I'll make it up to you. I'll make you a special birthday supper for you tomorrow."

"Don't worry, Mother. I got everything I wanted for my birthday. I got Popo for my birthday."

Mother gasped. "What! He was here? Are you sure you didn't dream it?"

"Popo was here." Gem stood in the hallway, holding Thea. I patted the bed next to me and she came in and sat down. "I saw him, too. After they went downstairs, I got up and wrote it down in my diary. Annie, show Mother the gift he brought you."

"How did you know about that?"

"Your big sister knows everything. Now go on and get it. Mother wants to see it."

I ran into my bedroom, retrieved the shoebox from the bureau, and ran straight back to Mother's side. After placing the shoebox in her lap, I removed the lid and lifted the ceramic angel out. The edge of the coin Miss Beall had given me peaked out from under the slips of paper and other treasures I kept there. I wondered if Gem knew about my Walking Liberty half-dollar piece, too. I gently unwrapped my ceramic birthday angel and placed it in Mother's hands.

"It's lovely, Anna. Your father always picks the perfect gifts."

I nodded. Then I told her about his visit, and everything we talked about, holding nothing back. I thanked him for sending us the food for Thanksgiving and how he'd worked extra to afford so much. I told her how much Popo laughed when he heard the story about Mother throwing Uncle Karl and Aunt Iris out of our house and then feeding the horehound drops to Belva. When I told Popo about Aunt Lo saying the gravy was delicious, that made Mother and Gem laugh. Then we all agreed Aunt Lo is a pistil. Everyone says so.

We talked and giggled for the better part of an hour. Three sisters and their mother, hidden away from the harsh outside world, enjoying each other's company.

Gem even told us about Fred Moore, although she didn't tell Mother he was fourteen. I kept my promise not to tell anyone. I wondered if Miss Beall was lonely this evening, or if her music kept her company.

"I think little Miss Sleepy Head needs to go to bed." On cue, Thea yawned.

"I'll put her pajamas on her."

"Thank you, Gem."

After Gem and Thea left the room, I lingered. "Mr. and Mrs. Beall loved Laura the way she was. I love Thea the way she is, don't you?"

Mother smiled at me and nodded.

"You used to love Popo the way he is," I continued. "Why can't you love him again?"

"Oh, my sweet Anna, so much has happened between your father and me over the years that's not for a daughter to know, let alone understand.

"I know," I muttered. "It's complicated."

Mother nodded. "Very much so. You know he vanishes when I need him most... when *we* need him most. He tried to stay when we learned Thea had lost most of her hearing, but he couldn't. You love your father so much. I loved him that way once, and I used to pray that I'd love him that way again. When I didn't, I quit praying."

Mother shivered. Then in a mumble not meant for me, "There's just something about humiliation that hardens the heart."

Ashes.

Tears didn't flow down my cheeks. Disappointment didn't cause me to stomp my feet, but Mother's resolve won't stop me. I was determined that Popo was coming home. I believed that with all my heart.

"At least let us love him the way he is. We're better off when he's here. We need him. You need him. Mother, Popo will come home if you ask him. I know he will."

"Even if that's true, I don't know where to find him." Her head fell into her hands.

I waited. I stood my ground.

Finally, she raised her head and looked me straight in my eyes. There was no anger in her voice. Maybe she knew what I said was true.

"Where is he, Anna?"

"I don't know, but if you ever need him, send a note to Old Man Gregory's office, and Popo will get it."

I'd left our future in Mother's hands... for now.

# Chapter 23

A house makes its own music. Its innate murmurs—creak of a step, squeak of a hinge, crackle of a fire, hum of the Frigidaire, rattle of a windowpane—harmonizing with the collective beat and breath of its occupants create a unique opus, a musical masterpiece of the lives held within its walls.

After Popo left Ghere-Douglass to sell feed and seed out of Indianapolis, our house fell into a monotonous refrain during the week. Upon his return on Friday afternoon, bringing with him the resurgence of his own brand of joy, charm, and raw exuberance, the symphony naturally resumed in all its majesty.

Now weeks without Popo (but for his brief visit on my birthday), the Ghere house on South Street felt perpetually off key, out of rhythm.

"Did you hear that?" As soon as Charlie and I arrived home from school, I knew something had changed.

"Hear what?" asked my cousin.

Strangers' voices drew me to the parlor, with Charlie at my heels.

"Hello, MaMaw." My grandmother sat on the sofa bouncing Thea on her lap. A nun sat on the sofa next to her, near Thea's better ear. Another sat in a side chair, taking notes.

"Oh, hello, dear. Come in, I want to introduce you to Sister Rosemarie," my grandmother gestured to the nun sitting next to her on the sofa, "and Sister Catherine. Sisters, this is Anna, Thea's sister, and Charlie, her favorite cousin."

"Nice to meet you." After the nuns greeted us, I asked my grandmother where Mother was.

"I last saw her in the kitchen," replied MaMaw.

Charlie and I raced to the kitchen, where we found Mother sitting at the table. Behind her, stacks of items she'd pulled from the storage room cluttered the counter and floor.

"Aunt Maggie, what's going on?"

"I was just resting a moment." Then, looking at the mess in her kitchen, she continued, "I'm turning the storage room into a dayroom for Thea. She'll be close to me but out of my way when I'm working. There's plenty of light coming in through the window in there." Barely audible, Mother added, "Thea needs the sunlight." Mother lingered in the chair a moment longer, deep in thought. Then she rose to her feet. "I could use some help."

Charlie and I immediately pitched in, carrying items to the basement and helping her re-organize the shelves on the back porch. When the twins arrived home, they helped, too.

As I swept out the empty storage room, I remembered Mother telling me that when her Uncle Frank built the house, the room with the "nice window with plenty of sunlight" was for the maid he planned to hire once he and Nina had their first child. Frank and Nina intended to fill their house with children.

After her widowed and childless uncle moved to Chicago, Mother moved into his house with Popo and their three young sons. Because a maid was out of the question, she designated the room for storage. Mother took care of her own.

As I mopped the floor of the new dayroom, the twins carried Father Blinn's old standup desk from the basement and placed it at the entrance to the hallway near the telephone. Mother sent the boys to the attic to retrieve a rug and daybed.

"What are you doing?" Gem stood in the kitchen doorway.

"Mother is turning the storage room into a dayroom for Thea so she can bake cookies for Miss Beall," I blurted out. I turned and looked at Mother. "Are you baking cookies for Miss Beall?"

She nodded. "But I'm going to need everyone's help."

I jumped up and down. Charlie joined me in my merriment. "We're in the cookie business," I proclaimed.

"Only for a few days," Mother sighed. "A few long days." Then Mother turned to my sister. "Gem, I want you to take down the curtain in there. It's worn and dusty. Would you take it outside and shake it, then wash and iron it, please?"

One look, and Gem decided the room needed a new curtain. As she removed the old one, she said she knew the perfect fabric for the replacement. "I just hope we have enough of it." With that, she ran upstairs.

"I think I found a piece of wood that will work." Gus entered the kitchen from the back porch holding an old board, smooth from age. Mother had asked him to build a gate for the dayroom's doorway. Using our mother's yardstick, Gus took a few measurements, then went back out to the barn.

A few minutes later, he returned with the gate, cut to the exact width to fill the doorway and the perfect height for Thea to see over but not climb over.

"The gate needs hinges and a deadbolt. I'll run down to the hardware store to see what I can find."

"I'll ask LoRetta to do that when she gets back. She's already planning to go to the hardware store to pick up a few items she needs for the pageant. I have something else I need you to do for me, Gus."

Mother pulled an envelope from her apron pocket and handed it to her oldest son. "Take this to Old Man Gregory at his office, please."

"I want to go! Gus, can I go with you? Please," I pleaded. Was it a note for Popo? Was Mother asking my father to come home? Did Old Man Gregory know where he was?

"Anna, I need you to do something else for me. It's important."

***

With winter only a few days away, the unexpected break in the cold weather made my short walk to Laura Beall's house easy. Over the last few weeks, I'd walked miles doing errands for my new friend, often trudging through the hard snow that accumulated on the sidewalks faster than our neighbors could shovel it. Today, the above-freezing temperatures caused a slow melting that resulted in a narrow snow-free path to form in the center of the sidewalk.

As I turned on Laura Beall's front walk, I took in the glorious sound of her playing the piano. My mind sang along, "'Hark, the herald angels sing, Glory to the newborn king!'" When the carol ended, I knocked lightly on the door. A moment later, she opened it.

"Good afternoon, Miss."

"Please come in, child." Laura stepped back from the doorway. "I've been expecting you." I handed Miss Beall the envelope Mother had given me to deliver. She raised the flap and pulled out the note. "Would you read this to me, please?" Miss Beall asked.

I took the note from her hand and unfolded it. Mother's familiar handwriting seemed foreign in its rigid formality. She'd written it in pencil, as Mother's inkwell had run dry long ago.

It read:

***

*Dear Miss Beall,*

*This is to inform you I accept your generous offer to bake cookies for your special holiday gift for your employees. Per our conversation, I understand I will provide you eighty-eight dozen cookies, ready for pickup, on the morning of December 22, 1933. I have included a list of all ingredients I will need for the various cookies you asked me to bake. As soon as I have the ingredients in hand, I will begin. I trust you will provide the packaging.*

*I look forward to discussing this with you soon.*

*Kindest regards,*

*Margaret Ghere*

***

"This is wonderful news, child. Michael and I are going to Delphi tomorrow to make the arrangements. Tell your mother to expect delivery of the ingredients and packaging the day after tomorrow. Tell her

I'll pay her in full when the cookies are picked-up. Will you remember my reply, or should I write a note?"

"I'll remember."

"Now, if you'll excuse me, I must decide what to play for your Christmas pageant."

"Anything you play will be fine. It's mostly children and parents that will be there."

"You must always give your best, child." Miss Beall's stern words shocked me. "It doesn't matter if I'm playing for the King of England or one child, I would give the same effort, and that's my best. Giving your best in everything you do is the greatest gift you can give to others and to the world. My mother taught me that."

I nodded.

As I was leaving, I turned to Miss Beall and asked her if she could play Pauline's favorite Christmas carol. "It would mean a lot to her."

"I know that one. I'll see what I can do."

When I returned home, I found Aunt Lo bent over the gate of the dayroom. "I agree with Gus. Thea might push this over if it's not attached to the doorframe. I'll see what the clerk at the hardware store recommends."

"Mother, Miss Beall said you'd receive everything you need the day after tomorrow, and that she'll pay you on the twenty-second when she has the boxes of cookies picked up."

"That means I have a lot to accomplish between now and then."

"Mother, can I go to the hardware store with Aunt Lo?" I asked. "I can help her carry things back."

"That's up to your aunt," Mother replied.

Aunt Lo agreed.

***

"Why didn't we have pageant rehearsal today, Aunt Lo?" God knows we needed it.

"I closed the library early and took the afternoon to handle several details for the pageant," she replied. "I picked up the oil paints from my friend and worked on the stage sets. I have a lot to do before Christmas."

I wondered if Aunt Lo had gone to have a word with Old Man Gregory about Popo. Yesterday, after pageant practice, I told Aunt Lo she could reach Popo through him. If talking to Old Man Gregory was one of her errands, she didn't mention it to me.

As we passed the Thompson house, Aunt Lo expressed her frustration about Bernard. "I tried again today to go over the closing prayer with him, but he's being politely defiant."

I smiled.

"I haven't spoken to your Miss Beall about the grand finale," Aunt Lo continued. "Annie, I wish you had spoken to me before asking her to play. I don't understand how a nearly blind woman can learn the music for such a performance."

"That's easy, Aunt Lo. She learns it one note at a time." I took Aunt Lo's hand and turned her around. "Come with me."

"Where are we going?" I didn't answer. I just pulled her along until we stood in front of Laura Beall's Victorian house. "Listen."

Aunt Lo stood motionless, taking in the magnificent arrangement of "Joy to the World" emanating from the house. At first, Aunt Lo was speechless. Then she muttered, "Oh, sweet Jesus." That's when I knew she understood that her grand finale would be every bit as grand as she hoped.

"Miss Beall won't let you down. You can trust her."

"Yes, maybe I can."

"You can trust Bernard, too."

Aunt Lo huffed. "I don't know about that."

"Come on, Aunt Lo. We need to go before the hardware store closes."

As we walked along, Aunt Lo put an arm around me and hugged me.

"You know you're my favorite child in the entire world, right?"

I looked up at her. "I thought Charlie was your favorite."

"Let's call it a tie, if that's okay with you. And don't tell Gem."

***

The smell of fresh baked brownies greeted us as we rounded the corner from Washington Street onto Main. We'd rushed through the public square to get to the hardware store before it closed, but now that Aunt Lo had the supplies she needed for the pageant, we slowed to enjoy our walk home.

Now brightly lit, the square twinkled from the strands of lights reflecting off the silver and gold decorations in the store windows. They reminded me of the silver and gold of Mother's hair. The sound of a faint radio playing carols somewhere added a festive tone to our town's Christmas celebration.

"Look at the tree in the Little Palmer House." I pointed toward the window. "It's the most beautiful Christmas tree I've ever seen." As I gazed into the window, Aunt Lo checked the clock on the bank building. "It's getting late, Annie. You'll miss supper if we don't get moving."

"Look, Aunt Lo, I think that's Mrs. Thompson there by the tree." Aunt Lo leaned close to the glass to get a better view.

"I think you're correct. She's sweeping up around the tree." Suddenly, Aunt Lo handed me her package from the hardware store, turned, and sashayed through the door of the Little Palmer House.

Inside, a string quartet was setting up in the lobby, and several young men dressed in starched white shirts and black bow ties bustled about, preparing the lobby for an event.

"What are we doing here, Aunt Lo?" I whispered.

Ignoring my question, she reached out and caught the arm of one worker. "Excuse me, sir. Please inform the hotel manager that LoRetta Ghere is in the lobby and would like a word with him."

"Yes, ma'am."

A moment later, the door behind the check-in desk burst open and a tall, gray-haired man dressed in a tailored tuxedo rushed through it.

"Do my eyes deceive me or has the loveliest woman in all of Indiana graced me with her presence?"

"Good afternoon, Arnold." Aunt Lo offered the man her gloved hand.

"LoRetta Ghere, you are a sight for sore eyes." He raised her hand to his lips and gently kissed it. "To what do I owe this most unexpected pleasure?"

"My niece and I were passing by, and I had to stop to compliment you on your beautiful lobby. You have done an exquisite job with your décor this season. I don't know how you'll top it next year."

"That's high praise from you, my dear."

"Well, I won't keep you. It appears you're preparing for an event."

"Yes, we're hosting the executives of the Nickel Plate Road for their annual Christmas party this evening." Mr. Grayson checked his pocket watch, but lingered.

Aunt Lo slowly turned, as if she were taking in the Christmas decorations one last time before leaving. "Arnold, is that Mrs. Thompson over there?"

"Yes, I believe it is. She's tidying up before our guests arrive."

"Did you know I am directing the Christmas pageant at Holy Cross Church again this year?" Aunt Lo continued before he could reply. "The Thompsons' son plays an important role in our production, a pivotal role, in fact. Bernard Thompson is without a doubt my favorite child in the entire production."

My aunt glanced at me, a twinkle in her eye.

"No, I'm afraid she hasn't mentioned it," he replied. He held up his hand and called, "Mrs. Thompson, may I have a word?"

"Yas, suh?" Shy and embarrassed, Mrs. Thompson cowered next to my aunt in the presence of her boss.

"Miss Ghere tells me your son, Bernard, has a major role in this year's Christmas pageant at Holy Cross. Congratulations, I'm sure you're very proud."

"I, I, I..."

"I expect this year's pageant will have the town talking for weeks, as I have a big surprise in store for our grand finale. I do hope you'll join us on Christmas Eve as my special guest, Arnold."

"I'll say yes on one condition... that you'll have supper with me here afterward."

"As long as brownies are on the menu, I'd be delighted. The pageant begins promptly at six o'clock. I suggest you come early to get a good seat."

Before Aunt Lo turned to leave, she paused. "One more thing, Arnold. Would you be so kind as to allow Mrs. Thompson to leave a bit early that evening? She and Mr. Thompson don't want to miss a moment of their son's performance."

Mrs. Thompson's eyes were as big as saucers.

"Yes, of course," agreed Mr. Grayson. "I'm looking forward to seeing you on Christmas Eve, LoRetta."

As we hurried home for supper, my aunt chuckled. "That went well, but not a word to anyone, especially Bernard, about our visit here this evening."

I smiled. Aunt Lo was a pistil. Everyone said so.

# Chapter 24

Two days after Mother accepted the baking job, I woke up to a racket in the kitchen. I dashed downstairs to discover Laura Beall calmly giving orders to three exasperated-looking workers, Michael directing traffic through the kitchen, and Mother looking horrified.

"Mother, what's going on?"

"Your Miss Beall is having a second stove installed on our back porch." Mother's face couldn't hide her astonishment.

I looked at Michael, who grinned ear-to-ear. "Don't worry, everything's fine."

Miss Beall joined Mother and me.

"Good morning, child. Did your mother tell you about my marvelous idea? When I visited the baker's widow in Delphi yesterday, she told me she planned to sell off everything and move to Indianapolis to be with her son and his family. She offered to sell me her Magic Chef stove. I bought it on the spot, along with a box of baking sheets and other utensils. Michael made the arrangements to have it picked up and loaded yesterday. It arrived on the first train this morning."

"Oh, dear." Mother's voice was barely audible.

I went to the back porch where two of the workers were re-arranging things to make room for the Magic Chef. The stove was a modern wonder, with two ovens, bread warmer and six burners.

"Michael, when will the workers hook up the gas?"

"We're waiting for supplies to be delivered from the hardware store," he reported. "As soon as they arrive, the men will get on it. In the meantime, I'll get them started unloading the flour, sugar, and other dry ingredients we brought in from Delphi. Where do you want us to put these supplies?"

Miss Beall turned to my mother. "Did you order the eggs, milk, butter, and other perishables?"

"Yes. The Ghere-Douglass Company is delivering those items in thirds starting tomorrow. I'll get a fresh delivery the next two mornings." (Mother's sizable order, which Miss Beall paid for in advance, proved to be the salve that soothed Uncle Karl's Thanksgiving Day humiliation.)

"You should store the perishables in your cellar. Once your new stove gets hot, the porch won't be suitable. Plus, I doubt they will all fit.

I tugged on Mother's sleeve. "We could store everything in the green room until you need it." I suggested. "It's cool in there, and if it needs to be cooler, we can crack the windows."

"That's an excellent idea, child."

***

With the deadline for delivery of eighty-eight dozen cookies a few days away, a shadow of uncertainty enveloped the entire Ghere household. Mother countered any doubt she felt with a flurry of activity, conscripting her family in the herculean task ahead.

The same day the workers installed the Magic Chef stove, Gus announced he'd taken a part-time job after school at Hank's Fix-It Shop over on West Washington Street. People can't afford to buy new things for their homes, so they depended on Hank to keep their old one in good repair. Besides fixing lamps and radios, Hank repaired everything from clocks to furniture to wagon wheels.

Unfortunately, he couldn't keep up with the needs of the town. Stacked floor to ceiling, the shop overflowed with unfinished work. When Gus stopped at Hank's looking for work, my brother convinced the shop owner he could earn his salary by finishing some of the smaller jobs, reorganizing the shop, and handling the customers who came in. Hank agreed to give the arrangement a try. Gus started his new job the same day Mother began baking. With school out for the Christmas holiday, Gus decided he'd get a head start on reorganizing the shop by working full time until school resumed in January.

Mother put Cory in charge of the barn and the animals and assigned Blinn the job of keeping the baking supplies stocked in the kitchen. My brother toted the bags of sugar, flour and other ingredients from the green room to the kitchen and helped by sifting and measuring to prepare for the next batch.

Gem was Mother's obvious choice for her baking assistant. For as long as I could remember, my older sister absorbed Mother's skills—sewing, gardening, and especially cooking—as most people absorb sunlight on a summer day. She knew Mother's cookie recipes by heart because she had baked them herself dozens of times. I know Gem missed spending time with Fred, but otherwise accepted her temporary confinement knowing how much it would help Mother and the family.

To everyone's amazement, MaMaw Ghere insisted on being part of the massive undertaking. "I'm about to die of boredom in that house," she pronounced that first day of baking, as she hung her overcoat and hat on the rack by the door and presented herself to her daughter-in-law. "Put me to work."

MaMaw became indispensable to Mother during those hectic three days. My grandmother took charge of Thea, feeding and otherwise tending to her in the dayroom. She found the small stack of books Charlie left by the bedside and read them into her right ear until Thea's attention waned. When Thea stood behind the gate watching the activity in the kitchen, MaMaw washed and dried the baking sheets and utensils, readying them for the next batch. She also wrapped the finished cookies in tissue paper and placed them in the bakery boxes supplied by Miss Beall.

In Blinn's free moments, he carried the boxes of cookies to the dining room table where Mother planned to tie them with ribbon and attach Miss Beall's personalized notecards once she completed the baking.

Aunt Lo's pageant prevented Charlie and me from helping Mother make cookies. With Christmas Eve a few days away, Aunt Lo summoned us to the library in the mornings to cut angel wings out of butcher paper and decorate them with glue and glitter. Bernard helped, too. After we finished, Charlie took charge of the front desk to allow Aunt Lo time to paint a sandwich board sign for the front of the church to remind passers-by of the date and time of the event.

That day a reporter from the *Morning Times* stopped by the library asking about the pageant. With paint on her hands and apron, and smelling of turpentine, Aunt Lo conducted herself as if she were

Queen Victoria, passing along details of the pageant with a flourish. Except one detail. She never mentioned Laura Beall's role in the grand finale.

"Be sure to mention that following the pageant, we'll be serving Maggie's Cookies." Aunt Lo couldn't help bragging about her sister-in-law.

"Maggie's Cookies?"

"That is correct. Margaret Ghere started a cookie business, and all attendees will be among the first to sample her wares. I assure you that Maggie's Cookies are the best you'll ever taste. They are melt-in-your-mouth delicious."

"Count me in." The reporter wrote a note on his pad and stuck his pencil behind his ear. "I'll be there." Just before the reporter left, a photographer from the *Morning Times* rushed in, set up his big camera, and took a photograph of Aunt Lo, paint and all, with Charlie and me, along with several library patrons looking on, star-struck to the last man, woman, and child.

After the hubbub calmed down in the library, I turned to my aunt. "Mother is going to kill you."

"Let's hope she does it sooner rather than later." Then Aunt Lo rushed back to the basement to finish her work.

From then on, Aunt Lo imposed a higher level of seriousness into the rehearsals, introducing of her yardstick, which she used to tap on wayward calves and hurry along the owners of said calves to their correct places on the stage. For the sisters Burke, Clara and Cora, Aunt Lo's new method of stage-directing switched from "tap and point" to "whack and *ouch*!" The girls quickly fell into line.

I think the pageant took a major turn for the better that afternoon after rehearsal when Aunt Lo marched to the piano where the church's regular pianist, Mrs. Roper, sat on the piano bench picking her nails.

Towering over the women, Aunt Lo tapped the end of her yardstick on the floor three times. "Learn the music, woman, or I'll report your woeful lack of talent to the Widower Pastor Burke tomorrow."

Mrs. Roper never hit another sour note. Of course, she professed she'd never speak to Aunt Lo again. My aunt called that a "win-win."

***

"Mother, are you okay?" I found her sitting on the bed in the dayroom, staring at the wall.

"Mother, what are you doing in here?"

"I'm thinking, is all. Why aren't you in bed asleep? Tomorrow's a big day."

"And you have more cookies to bake."

"Thanks to your Aunt LoRetta's big mouth. The idea of me being in business is absurd."

"I don't think so."

"At least baking twelve dozen isn't as daunting after baking eighty-eight dozen in three days. I'm sending ten dozen to the church for the pageant, and two dozen to the Blue and White Café. After reading that ridiculous article in the *Morning Times*—there on the front page was your aunt, bigger than life—Roxy Lockwood called and asked for a couple dozen of iced sugar cookies to sell out of her candy counter. I told her I'd also send over fudge and caramels if I have enough wax paper to wrap them in. Fortunately, your Miss Beall sent me extra sugar."

"You decided not to kill Aunt Lo?"

"Who said I decided that?" Mother's smile lit up her eyes.

"I'm proud of what you did for our family. I know it was hard and I wish I had been here to help you."

Mother pulled me down next to her and hugged me. "If it hadn't been for you and your thoughtfulness, none of this would have happened. I keep thinking about what your act of kindness put into motion."

"Christmas Eve is tomorrow. Do you know if Popo will be here?"

Mother hesitated. "Anna, I sent a note to your father through Old Man Gregory, but I haven't heard a word back from him."

"Did you ask him to come home?"

"I did. I told him that his family needed him. You are too young to understand..."

"To understand what, Mother?" Mother pulled away. Staring at the wall, she muttered, "There's nothing colder than the ashes of love."

I thought about the night those words came to me and how many times I'd thought of them since. In that moment, I knew they had drifted up the cold air return and found me in my bed. I never wanted to feel the bitter cold my mother felt in her relationship with Popo.

I ran up to my room, where Gem and Thea slept soundly. I pulled open my bureau drawer and pulled my birthday angel from the shoebox.

I recalled my father's words. "When you hold this angel and think of me, know that I'm thinking of you, too."

"I'm thinking of you now, Popo. Please come home."

I didn't cry; instead, I held onto the hope that if Popo came home for my birthday, he'd come home for Christmas. I vowed that if he didn't, I'd find him and bring him home, no matter how long it took me.

***

I awoke on Christmas Eve morning to the aroma of cookies baking wafting up the stairway from Mother's Magic Chef's two ovens.
Downstairs, I found Mother sorting through two boxes of food, both
bigger than the ones we'd received from Popo for Thanksgiving.

"Look what your Uncle Karl sent us," said Mother, waving a note
in the air. "I think he's attempting to make amends for his behavior on
Thanksgiving."

"He just doesn't want to eat Aunt Iris's cooking."

"Exactly. I was so wrapped up in baking cookies for your Miss Beall
that I completely forgot to order food for our Christmas dinner. It's
a good thing your uncle has chosen this time to grovel. I suppose I'll
have to invite him and Aunt Iris to join us tomorrow."

"Aunt Lo wants Charlie and me at the fellowship hall by nine
o'clock. We have to pin the wings to the choir robes for our last dress
rehearsal. Afterward, Bernard is going to hitch up Cooter to the ice
wagon, and he and Charlie are going to pick up Aunt Lo's pageant
supplies from the library and move them to the fellowship hall."

"How will Miss Beall get to the pageant this evening?"

"Michael is driving her in her motor car. She told me she's going
early and plans to wait in the Widower Pastor Burke's parish house
until the children's part of the pageant is over. She needs to keep her
hands warm so she can play."

"After rehearsal, please hurry home. I could use your help with the
preparations for Christmas dinner. I hate to ask Gem. She worked so
hard baking all those cookies. Fred is joining us for our mid-day meal,
and he'll likely stay a while afterwards."

"I don't know how long Aunt Lo will keep us today, but I'll get here
as fast as I can."

"I didn't know what to think when your Miss Beall showed up this
week with the baker's Magic Chef. Having two more ovens and extra

burners made my work a lot easier. I'll have to return the stove to Miss Beall after Christmas, but I don't think she'll mind if I use it one last time."

"Mother, are you coming to the pageant this evening?"

"I promise to try, Anna. I still have a lot to get done, so I'll see how it goes."

After a shorter than usual rehearsal, Aunt Lo sent us home, reminding us to arrive at the fellowship hall no later than five-thirty that afternoon. As I hurried home, I noticed the clouds, already heavy with snow, made late morning appear more like late afternoon. Light snow flurries began falling as I crossed Prairie Creek.

As I tossed my coat and hat onto the rack, Gem came down the stairs. "Go see the Christmas tree in the parlor," she instructed. "I've carried the decorations down from the attic so we can decorate it after the pageant. Mother said that after supper, we'll string popcorn and make fudge, just like we always do."

In the parlor, I admired the tree standing in the middle of the room. Gem had draped three strands of silver garland over one of our side chairs. Mother's box of delicate hand-painted tree ornaments sat open on the chair's seat. The ornaments held memories of past Christmases for every generation of our American ancestors. The ornaments were so fragile that only Mother, Aunt Rachel, and Aunt Lo touched them.

"What do you think?" Startled, I turned to see my father standing in the doorway, his worn felt fedora in his hand. I ran to him and tumbled into his arms, sobbing. "Oh, Popo, you're home."

"I'm home. It wouldn't be the holidays without my Christmas angel."

# Chapter 25

After the applause died down, Aunt Lo gestured for the children to move offstage. Charlie took the lead as we exited single file down the steps and onto a front row bench my aunt had reserved for us. When the bench filled up, the remaining children sat on the floor in front of it.

Being first in line, Charlie sat on the center aisle, followed by me, Pauline, Helen, and a gaggle of others. While the children's portion of the production went off better than anyone expected, Pauline's solo rendition of "O Little Town of Bethlehem," accompanied by the suddenly competent Mrs. Roper, brought down the house. Any flubs (Marshall Manning tripping over his own shoestring and falling with a bang) made in the production prior to Pauline's solo were long forgotten by the time she curtsied for the fifth time (I was glad I was nowhere near Charlie's elbow) and stepped back into her place among the heavenly host.

Albright Flud's violin solo followed Pauline on Aunt Lo's meticulously thought-out program. Bright-faced and gregarious, the seven-year-old charmed everyone he encountered, including the pageant patrons. Aunt Lo often described Albright as having an "old soul." To her point, he and his old soul had arrived early to scout out the fellowship hall's "acoustical sweet spot," while other members of the cast, including Charlie and me, flitted about outside catching snowflakes on our tongues.

After determining the sweet spot to be near the curve of the grand piano, Albright dragged an old wooden chair from Pastor Burke's office and positioned it there, where he had watched the audience until it was his turn to perform. Cued by Mrs. Roper's opening stanza, Albright stood and stepped into his pre-determined sweet spot and played "The First Noel." Arranged for a second-year violin student (which he was), Albright made quite the production of his playing. After taking a dramatic bow, which made the crowd applaud even louder, Albright and his violin left.

"Have you seen Bernard?"

My cousin stretched his neck, peering over and around the heads behind us. "Not since this afternoon when we dropped off the supplies for Aunt Lo. He went home after that. He wanted to get Cooter settled in the barn. Don't worry, Annie. He's here somewhere. He wouldn't let down his Aunt Lo."

I looked over my shoulder and spotted Popo sitting on the aisle three rows back, Thea wriggling in his arms. Gem sat next to Popo, with a rather stiff-looking Fred Moore next to her. Gus, Vivien Wentworth, Blinn, Cory, Aunt Rachel, and Uncle Madison filled the row. I didn't see Mother.

I tugged on my cousin's robe. "Charlie, is that Barbara Jean squeezed between Blinn and Cory?"

Charlie looked back. "It sure looks like her."

"That girl is strange."

Charlie put a finger to his lips, then pointed to where the Widower Pastor Burke wrestled a small podium to center stage just behind where the grand piano sat on the floor. Glued to the piano bench, Mrs. Roper picked away at her nails.

Pastor Burke rapped a knuckle on the podium to gain the audience's attention. "Well, folks, trudging out in the snow on this Christmas Eve was well worth your effort. You have just witnessed the finest Christmas pageant this stage has ever seen."

Everyone applauded loudly.

More jovial than usual, the pastor encouraged the crowd's spontaneous applause by holding his arms up as if he were welcoming Jesus himself to the gathering.

"I know my beautiful and talented daughters, Clara and Cora, stole the show with their stellar performances." A wry grin crept across his lips. I wondered if stellar meant off-key, but I'd ask my cousin later since Cora Burke currently sat on my foot.

"We have one more surprise for you before we close with a prayer and a sweet treat. You'll want to stick around for that... the cookies, I mean." He laughed at his own joke. "Here to introduce our special guest is none other than the writer and director of tonight's production. Put your hands together for Miss LoRetta Ghere."

I heard the applause crescendo as Aunt Lo glided onto the stage. Abandoning her signature sashay, she seemed a different person. Rather than her staid librarian attire, she wore an emerald-colored Raileen dress trimmed in ivory lace that Gem had made for her, perfect for a Christmas event. The fitted bodice hugged her like a glove. My sister had altered the Simplicity pattern, changing its lace-trimmed short sleeves to three-quarter length sleeves, more suitable for winter.

The pastor stepped aside as Aunt Lo slipped behind the podium. Her dress's flared skirt that hung to mid-calf offered a friendly wave before disappearing with her legs. Watching with rapt attention to her every movement, I suddenly saw my aunt differently. I understood why so many single men in town wanted her on their arm.

As she stood behind the podium nodding her head this way and that, thanking the audience, MaMaw's giant silver cross bobbed on a chain around her neck.

Soon after arriving at the fellowship hall, Charlie had asked Aunt Lo about her unusual jewelry selection. "Why are you wearing MaMaw's funeral necklace?"

Charlie had scrunched up his nose as if it had a peculiar odor.

"To ward off Arnold Grayson."

Then Charlie peered at my aunt, again scrutinizing her selection. "That should work."

"Thank you, Pastor Burke." Aunt Lo's dignified smile seemed just right for the occasion. "Thank you for being part of our annual pageant and sharing your Christmas Eve with us. It means so much to the children and me. Without further ado, I am pleased to welcome a great musical talent to our pageant, who graciously agreed to entertain you this evening. Please give a warm Holy Cross welcome to our piano soloist, Miss Laura Beall."

Rather than applaud, the crowd gasped as my Miss Beall made her way down the center aisle on Michael's arm. Instead of her usual mourning-black dress, she wore a magnificent blue and white gown, its skirt held in place by a crinoline petticoat. The crowd stood as they would for a bride and groom. The only sound I heard besides my heart beating was the rustling of her crinoline.

As Laura and Michael approached the piano bench, Mrs. Roper suddenly looked up from her fingernails. She seemed mesmerized by the imposing figures moving toward her. She didn't move.

"Madam." Michael held out his free arm to her. "If you will."

Mrs. Roper rose and took Michael's arm. After Laura sat down, Michael turned toward the crowd. "A round of applause for tonight's accompanist, please."

After clapping for Mrs. Roper, to her obvious delight, the audience members settled back into their places as Michael walked the accompanist up the aisle to the back of the fellowship hall.

The audience fell silent. I watched as Miss Beall pulled her spectacles from her face and placed them on the bench next to her. She tipped her head back slightly and closed her eyes before running her hands over the keyboard. An eternity passed before she struck middle C. The sound of that one lone note reverberating in the silence was jarring, nerve-racking. After the sound faded, she struck it again. My eyes shifted to Aunt Lo standing next to the stage, her hand to her throat, open-mouthed as she waited, breathless.

For nearly fifteen minutes, the audience sat in awe as the nearly blind Laura Beall played "Moonlight Sonata" in the concert she'd prepared for most of her life. When she'd finished Beethoven's masterpiece, she hesitated only a moment before beginning a set of traditional Christmas carols. As she built to the final stanza of "Hark! The Herald Angels Sing," I spotted my sister, Thea, toddling up the aisle toward the piano. I reached out to grab her, but Charlie stopped me. Thea climbed onto the wooden chair Albright had left and placed her right ear and hands against the curved black frame of the piano. As Miss Beall played, my sister remained motionless, captivated by the strains of music that had found their way into her soul.

"She hears the music. Your Miss Beall's music has reached Thea," Charlie whispered.

I looked again at Aunt Lo. She gave me an approving nod. I left my sister where she was, the sweet spot where she could hear the music.

After a few other carols, Miss Beall struck the opening bars of a carol familiar to my friend Pauline. I leaned into her and took her hand. "She's playing this for you, Pauline. Merry Christmas."

I didn't mean to prompt Pauline to sing along, but that's what my friend did. She stood, turned to the audience and sang the song that began:

> *"O come, O come, Emmanuel,*
> *And ransom captive Israel*
> *That mourns in lonely exile here*
> *Until the Son of God appears.*
> *Rejoice! Rejoice!*
> *Emmanuel Shall come to thee, O Israel."*

Haunting and beautiful, the impromptu duet left the audience breathless, the music calling forth the spirit of Christmas in every person in the hall. When they finished, Laura rose, placed her spectacles over her eyes, and bowed slightly to the cheers and bravos that lasted almost as long as Laura's entire concert. At one point, she held out her hand toward Pauline, who stood and curtsied for her new fans.

As my friend sat back down next to me, tears streamed down her face. "Thank you, Annie. That was the best gift anyone has ever given me. You're my best friend forever."

"You're my best friend, too." I didn't add, "If you don't count Charlie and Miss Beall."

As demand for an encore grew, Laura sat back down on the piano bench and played a magnificent arrangement of "Silent Night," which lasted another five minutes. Then she closed with, "We Wish You a Merry Christmas." The audience stood, joyfully singing along.

As soon as she played her last note, Michael was at her side. He placed Miss Beall's hand on his arm, then picked up Thea with his free arm and escorted them both up the aisle as the crowd cheered and applauded. Michael paused next to our father, offering him his little daughter.

As my baby sister reached out for him, she squealed with joy. "I love you, Popo."

"I love you, too, little darling."

I turned to see Aunt Lo beaming with pride. I knew for sure I'd secured my place as her favorite child—maybe her favorite person—in the world forever.

Now all that stood between the crowd and Mother's special Christmas cookies was Bernard Thompson.

***

"If you'll remain at your seats for the closing prayer," the Widower Pastor Burke called out from the floor next to the stage. Everyone settled down again and waited.

Bernard slipped out of the shadows of the stage and appeared behind the podium.

"For God so loved the world, that he gave his only begotten Son, that whosoever believeth in him should not perish, but have everlasting life." His voice sounded crisp and commanding as he bowed his head. I looked at Charlie, my eyes as big as saucers. My cousin shrugged, just as baffled by Bernard's elocution as I was.

"Aunt Lo?" I whispered. Charlie shook his head slowly

"Thank you, heavenly Father, for bringing us together on this Christmas Eve to contemplate the birth of your only son, Jesus Christ, our Lord and Savior, Your greatest gift to us, the gift that transformed our fleeting souls to souls that will live in Your light forever."

Bernard raised his head and looked out across the crowd. As he stepped from behind the podium, the paper upon which Aunt Lo written his minute-long closing prayer fluttered to the floor in his wake.

Now flanked by the Widower Pastor Burke and Arnold Grayson, Aunt Lo stood next to the stage holding an arm of both men, a look of horror on her face. Certainly, they will keep her from falling if her perfect pageant takes a sudden, unexpected turn for the worse.

My cousin stirred next to me. "Uh, oh, I think Bernard is about to improvise."

Standing front and center on the edge of the stage of Holy Cross Church's fellowship hall, Bernard Thompson found his heavenly muse.

"The other day, I crossed the schoolyard to get to my class before the bell rang. As I neared the door, I heard a boy call out to me. 'Hey Thompson, why do you carry that Bible around everywhere you go? Haven't you heard? God is dead.' His friend piped up to agree. 'You're damn right He's dead.'"

Aunt Lo gasped at the use of the curse word on her pageant stage.

Bernard didn't seem interested in what Aunt Lo or anyone else thought at that moment. He was listening to God.

"I told those boys that I had not heard of the demise of my Creator."

Bernard paused, giving the crowd a moment to contemplate the concept of a dead Creator.

"The boy got within inches of my face. 'Where are the miracles?' Then his friend added in the most defiant tone, 'I don't see any miracles. Do you see any miracles, Thompson?'"

Looking at the floor, Bernard shook his head back and forth. "I couldn't help but admit to myself that people are crying out in need and in pain. Where is God? Where are His miracles? I've been praying for God's miracles for so long my knees hurt."

I saw the sadness on my friend's face.

"For the rest of the day, I could think of nothing but what those boys told me in the schoolyard. When I got home, I told my horse, Cooter, what had happened, then looked into his soulful eyes and asked him straight out the question that had burdened my soul all day. Is God dead? My horse reared his head and said, 'Nay, nay.'"

The audience chuckled at Bernard's tale, but I knew he told it exactly how it happened.

"I have trusted that horse with my very life many times, but standing outside under the stars on that cold night, Cooter nudging my shoulder to get him out of the cold, I had my doubts. I led Cooter into the barn, gave him a good brushing, and fed him some apples. They were old, but he didn't seem to mind. He was full and happy and grateful. After settling him in for the night, I went outside, leaned against the barn and looked up into the sky. God, are you there? I asked. I waited for His answer, but it never came."

Bernard pace back and forth, back and forth, amping up the audience's growing discomfort. When the boy's sadness enveloped the fellowship hall, Bernard suddenly stopped and raised his hand above his head, his finger pointing toward heaven. "Where is the God of Abraham, Isaac, and Jacob? The God of miracles? The God who created the heavens and the earth? Where is the God who parted the Red Sea, the God who picked up his servant Elijah and carried him up to heaven? Where is the God who felled the walls of Jericho and made the sun stand still?"

A small voice from the third row interrupted. "God made Balaam's ass speak, just like He made Cooter talk." Laughter swept across the audience.

"Thank you for reminding us of that, Barbara Jean. 'Am not I thine ass, upon which thou hast ridden ever since I was thine unto this day? Was I ever wont to do so unto thee?' I'm sure that makes those of you who doubted Cooter's ability feel a little silly."

Bernard began pacing the stage again, rebuilding the tension. Then he stopped and looked out over the audience. In that moment, Bernard's face looked like that of an old man.

"If God lives, where is He when we need Him most? I had to consider that maybe the boys on the playground were right. Maybe God is dead. But where am I without my Creator? Where am I without my Bible? As I stood there, the wind suddenly felt colder on my face, nudging me toward my godless existence. I went into my house, climbed the stairs to the attic, threw off my boots and climbed into my cold bed, tired, hungry, and all alone. For hours, I tried to surrender myself to a life without a living God. I finally fell asleep, exhausted from praying for miracles I never received."

I heard a gut-wrenching sob from behind us. Bernard's mother?

I fell against Charlie, crying into his shoulder, Pauline falling against me, Helen against Pauline. Charlie bore the weight of us all, stretching an arm around us as far as it would reach to comfort us.

"Bernard is family now. Aunt Lo said so. We can never let Bernard feel hungry and alone again. Promise me, Charlie. Promise me."

Choking back his own tears, my cousin leaned over and kissed my head. "Never again." That vow echoed down the row. "Never again. Never again. Never again."

Now Bernard's voice was almost imperceptible. "Where is the God who sent us His only begotten Son to save us so that we might live in His light forever and ever? Where, oh where, are the miracles when we need them the most?"

In a few brief moments, Bernard had picked our emotions raw, then thrust us into a vast wasteland without our shepherd. Then Bernard did what we should have known he'd do all along: He guided us back to the beginning, where we could sit together on Christmas Eve to contemplate the birth of God's son.

"'For God so loved the world, that he gave his only begotten Son, that whosoever believeth in him should not perish, but have everlasting life.' The birth of Jesus is imminent. Mary labors to bring forth the miracle we need, the miracle we prayed for. As I sat over there..." Bernard turned and pointed to the corner of the stage where he'd watched from the shadows. "...God opened my eyes to the miracles happening all around me. I watched as twenty children performed without missing a mark on stage or a word of their script. Just two days ago, this production was a disaster after many rehearsals. God heard the prayers of LoRetta Ghere and guided the performers' every move and word. Miracle given by God; miracle received by us.

"We heard the voice of an angel calling out to the King of Kings and the Lord of Lords to save His people; and we felt the vibration of violin strings reminding us of why we celebrate Jesus's birth. Miracles given, miracles received.

"Miss Laura Beall honored us with a concert befitting Carnegie Hall... music so beautiful that it lifted us all up to the gates of Heaven to celebrate with the angels the coming of our Lord. During her performance, we witnessed a child who lost much of her hearing to scarlet fever find music again. Miracles given; miracles received. Today, I witness the miracle of a family healed... I pray for the miracle of another family healing this Christmas Eve."

Again, standing center stage, a sense of peace having fallen over him, Bernard straightened himself to his fullest height.

"God Almighty is very much alive."

The fellowship hall filled with the sound of a collective sigh of relief.

"Please bow your heads. Dear heavenly father, Creator of all, thank you for sending your only begotten Son so that we can live with You forever. I ask that You open the eyes of everyone here to Your daily miracles. As we go out into the world with kindness, thoughtfulness, selflessness, and love toward each other foremost in our hearts and actions, You will look upon us as You look upon the face of your son, Jesus, with whom You are well pleased, and say yes to our requests for miracles. In Jesus's name we pray. Amen."

Charlie put his lips near my ear. "I think Bernard is out of the bird funeral business." Through my tears, I smiled and laid my head on his shoulder.

"Yes, I believe you're right."

# Epilogue

After the laughter died down, the tears ended, and Bernard delivered his captive audience into a state of unbounded joy, everyone lingered for a time. Rather than return home to their Christmas Eve traditions, the people in attendance at Aunt Lo's pageant moseyed about the freshly invigorated fellowship hall, greeting friends and neighbors in the genuine spirit of the season.

As Bernard so sagely pointed out later, the aura of miracles is the perfect spawning ground for more miracles. I wasn't sure if God began performing more miracles in my life, or if I just learned to recognize His ceaseless handiwork when I saw it.

No doubt, the one hundred and seven people in attendance that Christmas Eve took heed of a teenage boy's urging to be the miracle for which their fellow citizens prayed. Kindness, thoughtfulness, selflessness, and especially love multiplied across our little town in the weeks, months, and years to come. Before long, much of the community viewed the world through the same pair of rose-colored glasses. A few holdouts and holders-on clung to their fear, anger, and selfish ways, but we loved those people all the more.

For another half-decade, talk of God's miracles on that one Christmas replaced talk of the economic depression. How could we live in poverty when we had so much? We couldn't! As I grew older, I thanked God for His miracle of perception more than any other. On that one Christmas, even when Mother's cookie plates held nothing but crumbs, and the giant coffee urn held nothing but sludge, the people lingered, even as fresh snow fell and the north wind blew. Two circles formed at the back of the fellowship hall, one around Laura Beall and the other around Bernard Thompson. While Bernard's circle was smaller than Miss Beall's, it included the two people he needed most: his parents. Bridging the chasm between them certainly ranked among the miracles God sent our little town that Christmas, but it would take time to undo what years of silence did to their marriage. Bernard once told us he'd considered the rocky road ahead but took it anyway. In the meantime, he wasn't taking any chances.

"I'm still an honorary member o' yer fambly, ain't I, Aunt Lo?"

"Forever, dear boy. Forever."

After pulling off my choir robe and hanging it in the cupboard, I slipped through the crowd and took my place between Miss Beall and Aunt Lo. I stood on my tiptoes and whisper into Miss Beall's ear. "Your mother would be so proud if she were here."

Miss Beall put a hand to her heart. "She was right here with me, child. I played for her."

"Did you play 'Moonlight Sonata' because it was your mother's favorite?"

"Dear sweet child, 'Moonlight Sonata' is everyone's favorite."

Both Miss Beall and Aunt Lo graciously greeted people who waited their turns to thank the two for the wonderful evening. When Popo stepped forward with Thea in his arm, I reintroduced him to Miss Beall. To my delight, Popo invited my best friend (besides Charlie) to Christmas dinner at our house, though he was quick to point out that the curmudgeons of the Ghere family would certainly have dibs on the sugar-cream pie. (Loving Uncle Karl and Aunt Iris proved challenging, through the years.) Despite Popo's warning, Miss Beall accepted his invitation.

I introduced Pauline to Miss Beall, the accidental duo who awed the audience with an impromptu rendition of a classic carol. Miss Beall lavishly praised my friend's singing and offered to accompany her again. Taking Miss Beall at her word, Aunt Lo would bring the two together again several more times in front of larger audiences, changing both of their lives.

As the crowd made their demands on Miss Beall's attention, Pauline drifted to Bernard's circle to be close to the boy who said she had the voice of an angel. Pauline developed a crush on Bernard. That crush developed into an abiding friendship that, years later, became a lifeline to my talented friend.

Albright Flud, accompanied by his neighbor the Widow Winslow, stepped up to introduce himself to Miss Beall. The old widow looked at me and sneered sweetly, "Little Anna Ghere, now go mind your business."

I didn't budge, but in the spirit of love, I resisted sticking my tongue out at her.

Albright told Miss Beall he'd considered giving up music to go into politics, but after hearing her magnificent performance, he thought he'd stay with the violin a while longer. "I may have to give it up when I become mayor," he told her. Albright practiced his violin every day until he went off to fight in World War II.

When the circle around Miss Beall broke apart and people began fading into the night, Gem pushed Emerson into the woman's presence, egged on by Marshall Manning and two other boys from the pageant. I introduced him to Miss Beall as the boy who had thrown the egg that hit her door. With his hands folded and his head down (not to mention the sharp poke in the back of my sister), Emerson apologized. Miss Beall accepted his apology but pointed out that, if he hadn't thrown that egg on Beggars' Night, she wouldn't be standing among so many new friends on Christmas Eve.

Miss Beall told Emerson that once he graduated from high school, she'd find him a job on the railroad... if he wanted it. Gem later told me the only way Emerson was getting out of elementary school was to out-grow it, but Emerson proved her wrong. Under Charlie's after-school tutorage, Emerson's grades soared to passing, and on his sixteenth birthday, he quit school and went straight to work for the Wanatah Railroad as a baggage boy. He spent the rest of his days serving that railroad.

As Emerson turned to walk away that Christmas Eve, Miss Beall offered him a piece of advice, delivered as a command. "Master Keller, you owe Mrs. Ghere an apology for stealing her egg. I suggest you get that burden off your chest promptly."

"Yes, ma'am."

Roxy and Paul Lockwood finished cleaning up the cookie and coffee table before offering their warm wishes to Miss Beall and Aunt Lo. Roxy told Miss Beall that after she heard Maggie had baked cookies for the Wanatah's employees, she ordered a couple dozen for the Blue and White Café.

"I sold every one of them!" she declared. Roxy also told Miss Beall that Mother sent over a batch of fudge and a batch of caramels to put in the café's candy case. After suggesting to a customer that they'd make great additions to Christmas stockings, the fudge and caramels sold out in less than an hour.

In the coming weeks and months, news of the miracles that unfolded at the Holy Cross Church spread like wildfire at the Blue and White Café. Being an eyewitness to the events of that evening, Miss Roxy answered questions while serving her customers.

"Can Ghosty really play the piano, her being blind and all?"

"Her name is Laura Beall, and she's a maestro worthy of the stage at Carnegie Hall. Call her Ghosty again in my establishment, and I'll ask Paul to pitch you out on your ear."

"Gee, Miss Roxy, what happened to being kind to your neighbor?"

"I'll *kindly* ask Paul to *kindly* pitch you out on your ear."

And so it went.

Two more miracles happened that Christmas, in one of which I played a minor role. After Arnold Grayson helped Aunt Lo into her coat, she hugged Miss Beall. "Thank you for making the pageant, and Christmas Eve, special for so many people. I owe the success of this evening to you and to my niece."

"I'm her favorite now," I said, eyeing my cousin.

Miss Beall squeezed my hand. "It was my honor to be part of your pageant. In the short time I've known her, Annie has changed my life."

My aunt put her arm around me. "How are you getting home, dear?"

"Gus took Popo, Thea, and some others home in the carriage. He's coming back for Charlie, Bernard, and me. After he puts up Old Barney, he's going to walk Vivien home in the snow. Gus loves Vivien, you know."

"Does he, now? Did your brother tell you that?" asked Aunt Lo.

"He didn't have to, Aunt Lo. Love is easy to spot when you know what it looks like. Gus loves Vivien, Paul Lockwood loves Roxy Lockwood, Gem loves Fred Moore, and Michael loves Miss Beall."

"Now you're being silly, child."

"No, I'm not. You don't see well, Miss Beall, but I see it in his eyes every time he looks at you. Michael loves you, I'm sure of it."

Aunt Lo took Miss Beall's hands in hers. "Let me tell you what I know about love. Love needs tending. If you ignore it, or take it for granted, it eventually burns out, leaving you alone and shivering in the night. Take hold of it and breathe life into it while you can."

I knew Aunt Lo spoke from experience. As my aunt took Mr. Grayson's arm and walked toward the door, she called over her shoulder. "Listen to my niece."

Miss Beall stood in silence for a few moments. "Child, it is always best to allow people to speak for themselves."

"She's right, Annie. I can speak for myself." Michael stood a few feet away, Miss Beall's black wool coat over his arm. "I should have told Laura I loved her a long time ago. She stole my heart when we were young, and my love for her has grown every day since. She is the most amazing woman I have ever known."

What Miss Beall couldn't see, her heart felt. Michael's eyes had found the woman he loved. I stepped forward and took Michael's hand, pulling him closer to Miss Beall. After taking her hand, I placed it on the side of his face.

"Miss Beall, see what everyone else sees... the man who loves you." I saw her index finger gently stoke the underside of his eye, catching his tears as they fell.

"By the way, Michael, you're invited to Christmas dinner at my house. Be there with our Miss Beall by two o'clock."

"Thank you, Annie. We wouldn't miss it for the world."

"Oh, and Miss Beall, did I tell you I love your blue and white dress? You look like an angel."

She never wore her black mourning clothes again, not even for funerals. Gus called to me from across the fellowship hall. "Let's go, little sister, or you'll be walking home."

"Michael, one more thing."

"What's that?"

"She loves you, too."

I ran to my brother, who picked me up in his arms, swung me around, then carried me outside to the carriage.

As Old Barney stopped in front of our house, Charlie poked me and pointed. I looked up just in time to see Fred Moore kiss my sister, Gem, on our front porch. She told me later that the kiss was more glorious than she'd ever imagined. It became the first link in an unbreakable bond between her and her first love, the first chapter in a love story that spanned decades.

"Someday a boy will kiss you right on the lips. Will you tell me when it happens, since I'm your best friend?"

Bernard opened the carriage door and jumped to the ground. Then he offered me his hand. "I recon Marshall Manning'll be Annie's fust kiss, don't ye, Charlie?"

I kicked snow at Bernard. "Yuck."

"Nah, I think the first boy she kisses will be Albright Flud."

I shoved my cousin into the foot of new snow that had accumulated in our front yard. He laughed and rolled over. As he made a perfect snow angel, he chanted prophetic words. "Annie loves Albright. Annie loves Albright. Annie loves Albright."

Bernard and I fell into the snow on either side of Charlie and made our own angels. Soon chilled to the bone, we rushed inside for a cup of

Mother's hot cocoa and our traditional Christmas Eve festivities with our family.

***

Despite what she told me, Mother didn't attend the pageant. Many years passed before I fully understood why my once outgoing and sociable mother became reclusive. The only consolation was that Mother thrived in her self-imposed prison. With Miss Beall's help and encouragement, she made a success of her cookie and candy business. Miss Beall called upon Mother to bake cookies and other goodies for the Wanatah's dining cars, and to provide cookies for her employees at Christmas time, but it was Popo who kept a steady stream of local customers coming in.

Mother earned her pay a dollar or two at a time. Through careful planning, she always seemed to have enough money left over to buy supplies for her next orders. That Christmas, my respect and admiration for my mother grew by leaps and bounds as I watched her indifference to life develop into courage, resolve, and ultimately, confidence in what she did to provide for her family.

I wish I could say my parents never had another disagreement. In the coming months and years, I learned what it meant to occupy that common ground between my parents, that place Gus filled before me. I soothed the tensions that erupted between them by keeping them focused on what they both loved the most. I knew Popo would leave again, but he never stayed away for long.

That Christmas, and every Christmas for as long as they both lived, I prayed that my mother would love my father again.

She never did.

<h1 style="text-align:center">Postscript</h1>

"**A**unt Lo, do you believe in miracles?"

"That's an odd question after all the miracles we experienced over the Christmas season."

"Bernard told me all about God's miracles. He said God could do *anything*. He parted the Red Sea. He raised the widow's son from the dead. He sent manna from heaven to feed the people. Bernard said God even made the sun stand still!"

"Bernard knows the Word."

"But our miracles seem so small in comparison to God's big miracles."

"He brought Popo home for Christmas, didn't He?"

"I thought that was you, Aunt Lo."

"Annie, think about the snowflakes that fell on Christmas Eve... all different, all perfect. When I think of all those millions of snowflakes that fell that night, I can only see a huge miracle.

"Well, I still don't know."

"Dear girl, if you don't believe in miracles, perhaps you've forgotten that you are one."

# Also by Patra Ann Taylor

"Edge of Summer," the first novel in Patra Ann Taylor's Anna Ghere Mysteries series is now available. The series is based on the lovable characters in "Christmas. Angels." Enjoy the following sample of "Edge of Summer."

# Prologue

To hear Aunt LoRetta tell it, Pauline and I almost drowned when we fell through the ice on Prairie Creek last winter. My aunt's version of the incident didn't quite match up with Pauline's or my first-hand recollections, but facts seemed irrelevant in the shadow of an epic tale.

"What happened out there today, Annie?" Popo sat on a wooden stool he'd pulled next to the feather bed I shared with my sister, Gem. Mother had tucked me and my friend into the bed after she'd dried us off and slipped us into flannel nightgowns. Pauline and I sat draped in blankets playing with a deck of cards Gem had slipped us while we waited until Doc Becker came by to pronounce us still among the living.

Unlike Mother's outburst of hysteria, which helped fuel Aunt Lo's already-vivid imagination, Popo's calm questioning put me at ease.

"Well," I began slowly, not wanting to stir up a frenzy all over again, "Pauline and I walked Helen home after school. Her mother wasn't there, so Helen said we couldn't stay, not even long enough to warm up." I pursed my lips and shook my head.

"That explains why Helen wasn't part of your shenanigans today."

"When Helen got home, she didn't want to come here with Pauline and me to play Rook. Helen doesn't like cold weather. When it's cold outside, she stays in her house all weekend, until her mother drags her out to go to church on Sunday." I wriggled and rolled my eyes to make Popo smile.

He nodded as if he was taking it all in. "I can't say I blame her, but let's talk about what happened with you and Pauline."

"Popo, Helen stays in bed all day and *reads*," I added. "She even reads schoolbooks!" I couldn't hide my astonishment.

"You like Charlie to read to you."

"That's different."

"You and Pauline could learn a thing or two from Helen."

"Why do people always say that?"

"Because it's true." Popo drummed his fingers on the headboard. "Can we get back to how you ended up in Prairie Creek this afternoon?"

"Popo, it was so cold outside today! Since we were freezing to death, we ran up the alley on this side of Washington Street, then ran through the trees along the creek. Instead of going up to South Street and crossing over the bridge by our house, we took a shortcut." I paused, hoping the story made sense to my father. "That's when we fell through the ice," I added under my breath.

I gave Popo my best "end of story" face. He wasn't buying it.

"You know your mother doesn't want you wandering through the woods on the other side of the creek. With good reason!"

We were running, not wandering, but I didn't think pointing that out would help me end this conversation any faster. "Mother doesn't want us on the other side of the creek because she'll get a telephone call from Aunt Iris about us being in her yard," I stated matter-of-factly.

"Your mother is not concerned about your Aunt Iris. She's concerned about your safety."

"We go through those woods all the time with Blinn and Cory. The trees aren't even thick there near our house. When they're bare, we can see across the creek to Aunt Lo's painting shed from the windows in the green room."

Popo shook his head. "That is beside the point, young lady. Do what your mother tells you. If you'd listened to her, you wouldn't be in the situation you're in now."

I wondered what situation my father was referring to, but didn't dare ask.

The sternness had slipped from his voice when Popo continued. "Besides, the twins are older, and I hope they have a little more sense than two seven-year-olds. Where did you get the idea that the ice was solid enough to hold you? Did one of your brothers tell you that?"

I sat looking at my hands.

"Did Blinn or Cory or Gus tell you the ice was safe to cross?"

"No."

"Angel?"

"No one told us it was safe, but last week when Pauline and I went out to the barn to tell Gus that Mother needed him, the twins were out there sharpening those old ice blades... you know, the ones that hang on the wall next to Old Barney's Christmas bells."

"Go on."

"Cory told Blinn he heard the ice might freeze solid in the next few days. Blinn got real excited. He said that if it did, they could skate all the way to the Barner's Woods on those ice blades. That was a whole week ago, Popo."

"Those old blades belonged to Karl and me when we were young." Popo paused a moment, his eyes cast upward, searching his childhood memories of that bygone era when he and his only brother were still close. In a soft voice, he told us that during their youths, he and Karl loved to ice skate up Prairie Creek during winter. "We'd skate all the way to the edge of town," he recalled, contentment on his face. "The thick stand of trees along both sides of the creek was bare that time of year, yet beautiful against a translucent azure sky. We used to bet who could spot the first cardinal perched on a limb high above the icy creek. I always let my younger brother win."

Lost in his memories, Popo sat for a moment longer before continuing. "I hope you know the temperature needs to stay below freezing for several days before the creek is solid enough for ice skating... or cutting across on foot. Haven't you noticed the snow melting off the last couple of days? When the snow is melting, doesn't it make sense that the ice on the creek is melting too?"

"I suppose. We're sorry."

"I don't want you to be sorry, Angel." Popo tapped my forehead with his index finger. "I want you to use your head before you do impulsive things that could cause tragic consequences. That goes for you, too, Pauline."

"Yes, sir."

Despite his gentleness, Popo's scolding hurt my feelings. I looked up into his face. He placed his palm on my cheek and used his thumb to wipe away a tear that had slipped from my eye.

Popo continued his questioning in a gentler tone. "What happened after you two silly girls ran onto the ice and it gave way?"

"Pauline was ahead of me..."

"Why am I not surprised?"

I rolled my eyes over to my friend, who was staying quiet. I felt Popo's hand on my knee, which prompted me to continue.

"Pauline was ahead of me when the ice broke. She went down into the water up to her chin and started screaming. I was only in waist-deep, so I reached out to pull her up. I had just gotten her back on her feet when a man stepped into the creek, grabbed me under one arm and Pauline under his other, lifted us out of the water, and set us back on the bank.

Popo jumped to his feet, his eyes wide with surprise. "What? A man pulled you out of the creek? Are you sure about that?"

My father's reaction confused me. I nudged Pauline with my elbow. "Right?" I prompted her.

My friend nodded.

Concern spread over Popo's face. "Did you tell your mother this?"

I thought about it for a moment. "I don't think so. She already had us dead from drowning.

"And exposure," Pauline whispered.

"And exposure, so we were busy trying to convince her we were still alive."

"Then what happened, Annie?" Popo's voice had dropped an octave, and taken on a cool, controlled tone.

"The man set us on the bank, like I said, and then shouted, 'Run, Annie, run! Don't stop until you're home.'"

Popo stepped back, a hand clutching his chest. "The man called you by name?"

I looked at Pauline. She nodded once.

"Yes," I confirmed. "He called me Annie."

"But you didn't know who he was? Did you get a good look at him?" Popo's agitation took over as he paced back and forth in the small room.

"No, he didn't look familiar. When we got up on the bridge, I looked back through the woods, but there was no sign of him anywhere."

Popo thought for a moment. "Maybe he was under the bridge or down the street by that time."

I shrugged. "Maybe."

Popo stood in my bedroom doorway, deep in thought. "The worst part is," I said, invading his thoughts. "I lost my boots."

"Your boots?" My father looked puzzled.

"My red rubber boots," I reminded him. "The ones Aunt Lo found at the rummage sale a couple of years ago. They fit Gem when she brought them home, but this year, Gem had out-grown them and passed them on to me. They were a little too big, so when the man pulled me out of the creek, he lifted me out of them." I sighed. "I loved those boots. No one in my class has red boots except me."

"I'll walk over to the other side of the creek and see if I can find them, Angel. Since they're red, I might be able to spot them and fish them out of the water before the ice freezes again. I want to go look around, anyway."

Popo stepped back into the room and kissed me on the head. "Your sister will be up soon with some chicken soup. You girls stay put."

As he turned to leave, I said the obvious. "He was an angel. We're certain of it.

The gentleness disappeared from my father's voice.

"He damn well better have been."

# Chapter 1

Aunt LoRetta referred to the illusive interlude between late August and late September as "the edge of summer." To linger too long in summer, or rush too eagerly into autumn, was to miss the many delights that defined this special time of year. Aunt Lo often reminded me that God's plan for summer's beginning and end was His alone, that He delighted in challenging our made-up notions about His perfect timetable.

"Be vigilant, Annie," my aunt urged me. "Pay attention or you'll miss the moment of its coming."

"But how will I know, Aunt Lo?"

"You'll just know," she assured me. "When you sense the first wisp of a breeze kissing the fringe of autumn, you'll know our beloved season within a season is upon us."

Oh, the many wonderful pleasures that arrived at the edge of summer: picking the last of Mother's green beans for supper, the singing of the cicada choir in the evening, catching lightning bugs in Mason jars past dark, the rising white mist off Prairie Creek at dawn, and sleeping late into the cool of the morning.

It's the time of year when the pace at the Ghere-Douglass Company, the wholesale dairy business owned by my father and his brother, returned to its normal rhythm after a hectic summer, and when Mother's attention turned from growing and canning to sewing and mending to prepare her children for the new school year.

I loved being tucked under Aunt Lo's arm as she whispered to me about the stealth approach of our favorite time of year. "Just another day or two, a week at most, before the music begins," she whispered, her sweet breath tickling my ear.

I nodded, hopeful that my ears would not fail me.

I watched when she pointed skyward at the undulating ribbons of grackles or starlings or red-winged blackbirds, making their way south. She always watched intently until each flock was out of sight.

"There's only one thing more glorious than the edge of summer."

I awaited her answer, knowing Aunt Lo would tell me in her own time. Finally she sighed and closed her eyes again, imagining. "Heaven," she breathed.

I giggled. "How do you know, Aunt Lo? You've never been to heaven."

"Not yet, but I believe it's wondrous... so beautiful that we can't describe it with mere words."

I stood at her side as I imagined such a place.

"We're on its doorstep." Aunt Lo's face shined. "If you listen closely, you might hear summer preparing its encore, even as autumn rehearses its sonata."

My aunt paused, looking upward. I slipped her arm around me, my eyes following her gaze, hoping it would help me see what she saw. She continued in a whisper, "To witness the moment those two full symphonies commingle is to wait breathlessly for the moment they collided in a jarring cacophony of past and future. In the meantime, we stand in the breach, living in the tension, that incredible place where the present stalls, if but for a moment, our attention fully on what was and what will be, before it all disappears into the mundane rut of autumn, while the dreaded winter closes in at its heels."

We waited patiently for our beloved season within a season to be upon us. It seemed we lived our best lives... at the edge of summer.

***

On the first Saturday of August 1931, I stood on the platform of the Wanatah Railroad Depot, holding my father's hand. Gem fidgeted beside me, a finger twirling her wavy blond hair as she shifted from one foot to the other, watching Aunt Lo as she prepared to take her leave, her hand on the arm of the conductor as if he were her date to the prom. Aunt Lo turned with a swish of her skirt, pulling Oscar to a stop before delivering her instructions to the porter, who straggled along behind them.

"Would you look at that," my father whispered to Gem and me. "Your aunt's new skirt gives her usual sashay a bit of added flair."

My sister and I laughed. Popo enjoyed poking fun at his sister.

I admired my aunt, dazzled by the elegance in her new traveling clothes. Her gored, calf-length skirt with a deep yoke fit her trim body like a glove. The colorful summer print skirt paired perfectly with her simple creamed-colored blouse of silk *crepe de chine*.

Several months ago, Aunt Lo saw a similar ensemble in the spring issue of *Gazette du Bon Ton* she'd received secondhand from her cousin Louisa Rousseau, whom she was off to visit for two weeks.

Aunt Lo couldn't read the articles written in French, but enjoyed the photographs immensely. The moment she discovered *"les dernières nouvelles de France,"* the only French phrase her cousin had taught her, my aunt insisted she must have the outfit. With some cajoling, she convinced my mother to make it for her.

The crowning glory of the skirt were four gold and royal blue metal buttons she'd asked Mother to stitch vertically in a row onto the front of the yoke.

"Where in the world did you get these?" questioned Mother after Aunt Lo had placed them in her hand. Mother pushed away from her sewing machine to give her sister-in-law's reply her full attention.

"Genuine Lalafina," Aunt Lo answered. "I'd swear to it. I took them off of one of PaPaw's old blazers."

"One of PaPaw's old blazers?" Mother asked. "I'm surprised you didn't take them off of Karl's blazer while he was wearing it."

"Of course not, Maggie. My brother hasn't an ounce of fashion sense, or any sense at all, for that matter."

Mother and I chuckled.

Aunt Lo continued, "I found PaPaw's old blazer in a dusty box in the attic. Aren't the button's divine?"

"Are they real gold?" I asked as I peered into Mother's hand at the Aunt Lo's prized buttons.

Aunt Lo knelt in front of me and leaned her nose within an inch of mine. "I believe they're brass," she whispered. "But if people mistaken them for gold, who are we to argue?" Then she placed a finger on my lips. "Mum's the word, Annie."

I frowned. "Is it a secret, Aunt Lo?"

Aunt Lo pulled me into a hug. "Oh, no, dear child. Secrets are burdens far too heavy for seven-year-olds to bear."

I looked up at Mother, but her eyes wouldn't meet mine. I thought about the two cards of beautiful buttons she had shown me in early spring. She'd called them enameled openwork floral buttons before hiding them away in her bureau drawer. I wondered if they were still there, but I hadn't gotten up the nerve to peek.

*** 

As we watched her on the Wanatah platform, I thought Aunt Lo was every bit the fashion plate as the models she'd shown me in her French magazines, especially compared to the wholesomeness of the young farm women who lived around our town.

"Be careful, Jacob," Aunt Lo's sweetness disguised her emphatic orders. "Nothing damaged, nothing lost between here and Chicago, if you please. I need every article in pristine condition for my stay."

"Yes, ma'am."

Gem snickered at the sight of poor Jacob struggling under the load as he made his way along the tracks to the baggage car.

"Be careful with my hat boxes, dear," she called to the porter's back.

He nodded once, his black bobbin cap now askew on his head. "Yes, ma'am."

"Come along, now, Miss Ghere." Oscar patted her hand that still clung to his arm. "It's time to get you settled aboard the train. It's scheduled to depart soon."

"Of course, Oscar. A moment, please. It's a long sit between here and Chicago."

"It is that, Miss Ghere."

I took Gem's hand with my free one and pulled her close to me. We looked at each other, holding our words for our carriage ride home.

My eyes followed hers to the single strip of sunlight that had fought its way onto the platform where Aunt Lo now stood.

As she turned her head for a look around, I glimpsed Aunt Lo's soft gray eyes, the gentle slope of her up-turned nose, and her rosy lips, extraordinary features that had somehow come together on an ordinary face. Yet my father's only sister personified elegance. Poised and confident, witty and charming, my aunt was like no one else I knew except maybe my father.

As we waited, I replayed the words Aunt Lo had whispered to Gem and me during our brief carriage ride to the Wanatah Depot. "Expect the mysteries we solve during the heat of summer to yield a harvest of truth at its edge." I couldn't wait to ask Gem what Aunt Lo meant.

"Are there mysteries to solve awaiting you in Chicago, Aunt Lo?" Gem asked her.

She sounded sad and serious. "I hope so."

"Oh, tell us, Aunt Lo. Please tell us," my sister urged.

"Let's hope there's nothing to tell." Then she turned to the conductor. "It's time, Oscar." She kissed Gem's cheek and then mine. Popo returned his sister's hug, then kissed her on the forehead.

"Have a wonderful trip, Sister. Say hello to Louisa and Jean-Claude for me."

"I will, Brother." Then she winked at me and Gem. "Stay here, girls. I'll wave to you from the passenger car."

That was Oscar's cue to help her aboard the train.

I turned and glimpsed at the place where Aunt Lo had stood in the single beam of sunlight. It had faded. Even the sunlight shone brighter when she stood in it.

When the train whistle signaled its departure, we spied our beloved aunt leaning from a passenger car window, waving her hankie with a white-gloved hand. "Toodle-oo," she called, as the steel wheels of the train screeched against the rails. "I'll be back before the cicadas sing."

# Chapter 2

After breakfast, I ran upstairs to collect a stack of old blankets while Gem wrestled our old baby carried from the porch. With the blankets in carriage, Gem placed Thea on top of them and pulled the canopy into place. Then I followed my older sister down the front walk, and took a left turn onto the sidewalk that ran along South Street, the first leg of our usual summer morning strolls. When we reached the corner, we crossed over and started back on the other side of the street.

"How many more days?" I asked my sister.

"How many did I tell you yesterday?" Gem's voice was calm and breathy as she pushed the carriage up the slight incline onto the bridge over Prairie Creek.

"Eight."

Gem's head bobbed up and down. "That means Charlie will be back in seven days. That's next Saturday... one week from today. Gus, Blinn and Cory will be back, too. You can wait that long."

"I suppose."

The first autumn he came to live with us for the school year, Charlie preferred playing with my brothers, especially Blinn and Cory. I tagged along whenever they'd let me, which wasn't that often. When school started, I'd watch at the window every afternoon for the boys to come home, yearning to start school myself so I could walk back and forth with them. Charlie loved to read, something the twins viewed as a chore. I loved to sit in the window seat next to Charlie, engrossed in whatever book demanded his attention. By the time I started first grade, I could read, thanks to Charlie.

When we walked Thea, Gem and I liked to pause atop the bridge to have a look around. Looking south down the creek, we often saw the Interurban rattling its way along the shoreline for a short distance before crossing over the bridge that bears its special tracks. Mother forbade us from setting foot on that bridge, but I knew my brothers sometimes crossed over it. I'd seen them do it with my own eyes.

Today, it was quiet on the south creek, so we continued our journey another two blocks before crossing back to our side of the street at the corner next to Mrs. Parlett's house, and then heading for home. I wanted to be there to kiss Popo goodbye before he left for work.

"When will Aunt Lo be back from Chicago, Gem?"

"She'll be back a week from Friday, six days after the boys' return. Gus will be back in time to pick up Aunt Lo from the Wanatah Depot when she arrives on the afternoon train." Gem took a deep breath as she bounced the baby carriage along. "Maybe we can go with him!

I wrinkled my nose. "It was crowded in the carriage when we took her to the Wanatah Depot. Aunt Lo takes a lot of baggage when she travels to Chicago." I recalled how Popo had struggled to get it all into the carriage for the trip to the train depot. He'd suggested that Gem and I stay home, but Aunt Lo wouldn't hear of it.

"I think she takes everything she owns for a two-week visit." Gem chuckled. Aunt Lo's ways tickled Gem.

"Tell me again who she visits in Chicago?"

"She stays with her cousin, Louisa Rousseau, in a little town outside of Chicago called Wheaton. There's a college there."

"Is Louisa our cousin, too?"

"I suppose she is." Gem lifted the canopy of the carriage to check on Thea, who seemed content sucking on the edge of her rag doll.

"Louisa is married to Jean-Claude," added Gem. "Aunt Lo told me he's French and very handsome."

We strolled along in silence for a bit, both of us deep in thought. Finally, Gem continued her story about our aunt's trip. "Louisa also invites two other friends to visit in during the first week Aunt Lo is there. They're librarians, too. They also stay with Louisa and Jean-Claude, to catch up, whatever that means. Popo said he doesn't know how Jean-Claude survives the week." Gem shrugged and rolled her eyes.

As we approached the bridge, I ran ahead. I stepped up on the bottom rung of the wooden railing to get a better view north toward Barner's Woods. Popo told me that where we live used to be part of Barner's Woods, a vast expanse of thick woods in all directions. He said the trees along this stretch of Prairie Creek are all that's left of those woods this far down the creek, but a couple miles up creek a portion of the woods remains on Barner land, with the massive Barner Farm beyond that. Popo and Uncle Karl's company does business with Barner Farm so Popo often travels there to visit Joshua Barner, the farm's current proprietor.

The view from the bridge differs completely from any seen from the windows of our green room that extended along the entire west side of our house. During the summer, the sound of meandering water over stones and the patches of blue sky filtering through the branches overhead are the only assurances that the creek still exists beyond the dirt path that runs between our house and the thicket of trees and bushes that hug the creek bank.

Up the north creek, the people who live there have cleared most of the trees on either side, carving a sculpted view from the wilderness for as far as the eye can see. (In all seasons, I loved leaning over the railing and breathing in the beauty.) Even with my eyes completely engaged, I caught a whiff of the last of the musk melons still in the rich soil around our town, awaiting the light touch of the field hands to separate them from their vines. The aroma of tomatoes from earlier in the summer now gone—Mother put up the last from her garden weeks ago—its absence giving way to that delicious musky aroma that made my taste buds tingle. Though faint, I knew that as the sun climbed in the sky, the smell would grow in intensity and drift for miles. The musk melons in their final stage of ripening are a sign that the edge of summer will soon be upon us.

I also knew that Mrs. Barner's abandoned cottage was tucked into the woods at a place where the creek widens next to a clearing in the native woods. Popo says there's been talk for years that Joshua Barner planned to tear it down, but the nostalgia of his carefree days growing up there always stops him.

-to be continued